Also by Sarah Rodi

Rise of the Ivarssons miniseries

The Viking's Stolen Princess
Escaping with Her Saxon Enemy

Look out for more books from Sarah Rodi
coming soon!

Discover more at millsandboon.co.uk.

ONE NIGHT WITH HER VIKING WARRIOR

Sarah Rodi

MILLS & BOON

First published in Great Britain 2022
by Mills & Boon, an imprint of HarperCollins*Publishers* Ltd,
1 London Bridge Street, London, SE1 9GF

www.harpercollins.co.uk

HarperCollins*Publishers*
1st Floor, Watermarque Building,
Ringsend Road, Dublin 4, Ireland

One Night with Her Viking Warrior © 2022 Sarah Rodi

ISBN: 978-0-263-30208-0

12/22

This book is produced from independently certified FSC™ paper
to ensure responsible forest management.
For more information visit: www.harpercollins.co.uk/green.

Printed and Bound in Spain using 100% Renewable Electricity
at CPI Black Print, Barcelona

For my mum-in-law, Jane,
for your support, understanding and fun-loving ways.

Chapter One

Ryestone Keep—ninth-century England

The Northmen were coming.

Rooted to the spot, Lady Rebekah was unable to take her eyes off the fleet of dragon ships with their raven banners snaking their way up the river towards her, like an unstoppable dark wave. The church bells were pealing out throughout the fortress of Ryestone Keep, warning the already frantic men, women and children that they were under attack.

The people of the Saxon burgh had been preparing for this day as best they could for some time, having heard stories of barbaric raids by these pirates from the north and knowing it wouldn't be long before they found their way from the sea inland. Now it seemed that day of reckoning was upon them.

Lady Rebekah knew all too well what the Northmen were capable of, she had witnessed it first-hand when she was a child—a dark memory she could neither forget nor forgive. It was their fault she had grown up an orphan. These heathens were more monsters than men—they cared nothing for Saxon homes or monasteries, burning everything in their sights, causing all that they touched to wither and die.

The late afternoon clouds darkened with the threat of an almighty storm and Rebekah sensed the moment the longships and their warriors hit Saxon soil—she felt it in the trembling of her legs, the tremors coming from the ground. She saw the forking flames of the raiders' torches burst into life, assisting their ascent through the scatter of farmsteads on the outskirts of the fortress walls, drawing closer and closer, and she propelled herself from her viewpoint on the ramparts.

Racing down the steps to the courtyard, she called for any women and children to enter the great hall, to seek shelter inside. Lord Atol of Ryestone had sent every able man who could fight to the battlements, and she couldn't just sit idly by and do nothing—she would do her best to protect their subjects from harm.

Ryestone Keep had never felt like home to Rebekah, not since she'd been a young girl and her parents had died, when she'd been brought to live here as the ward of her powerful Uncle Cynerik. Although she had always been treated well, at least until her uncle's death a few years back, this place hadn't even come close to replicating the warm family home she'd been born into. Yet right now she would do anything to protect it—the people—against this pagan enemy.

After ushering the last of the villagers through the heavy oak door, she pulled it towards her on the outside and she rested against the wood, taking a moment to gather her strength. She knew how to use a sword and shield. If she could help the men to fortify the battlements, she should fight. The Northmen couldn't be allowed to breach the walls. If they did, then what? What would that mean for the brave Saxon soldiers and the women and children inside?

Her own daughter...

Dashing back up to the bridge, through the now driving rain, she watched as the gates slowly opened and Lord Atol led out a cavalry to meet the heathen force of ninety or so men. The soldiers on the barricades took aim and released their fire arrows, but the barbarian warriors continued to advance, like savage, wild boars charging, meeting the Saxon army head on.

Rebekah had never witnessed fighting like it—the chilling clashing of metal, grunts coming from the mouths of the men with every heave of their lethal weapons and unforgettable groans of pain. The pagans seemed half-mad, so driven and ferocious. It was bloody and brutal and raw. And to her horror, she saw boorish, beastly-looking men were beginning to scale the crenels at the top of the towering walls. The guards tried to cut them down, three against one, just about holding their own, but for how long? Flames were beginning to lick at the wooden fort, just as fear was engulfing her, as she surveyed the sickening scene before her. Because with terror thundering through her heavy heart, she knew the Saxons of Ryestone Keep would soon be at the mercy of the Danes.

Her eyes sought out the leader of the heathen army. Easy to spot in the fray, he was the most muscular man she had ever seen and he carried a large sword and shield. An iron helmet covered his head and shielded his eyes, and rope-like strands of dark hair descended from beneath. His body screamed danger, his actions ruthless and deadly. He fought with such skill and power, and she watched in morbid fascination as he bore down on Lord Atol, skilfully knocking the weapon out of his hand, sending her Saxon leader cowering backwards.

The battering ram came crashing against the gate, as a deafening crack of thunder reverberated through the fortress, echoing the pounding of her pulse, and just for a moment, she wondered if she could let Lord Atol die... She and the people of Ryestone deserved a better leader and Gytha a better father. They would finally be rid of him, free. And yet seeing the formidable warrior's boot pin her Lord's body to the ground, she knew she had to intervene— to try to end this, to stop the heathen running his blade through their ruler and taking control of the fortress. She reached for the white flag of defeat, furiously waving it back and forth along the top of the battlements, hoping in vain that they would see her desperate plea and be merciful.

'*Stǫðva! Enda!*' Rædan roared.

He gripped the hilt of his sword tighter, his

big body freezing in shock. He hadn't counted on her being right there, on the battlements.

Rebekah.

Glancing up and seeing her frantically waving that ridiculous flag, for a heart-stopping moment he was rendered breathless. It was as if he'd been struck by Thor's hammer itself, a thunderbolt hitting him hard in the chest.

He had sent a silent word up to the gods that if he saw her again he would feel just a flicker of disdain, a mere memory of a happy youth, but of course, the gods were never that kind.

Rebekah's dark auburn hair was still as vibrant as fire, but no longer loose and flowing free. It was tamed and bound in a braid down the side of her long neck, signifying she was spoken for, and she wore an exquisitely embroidered gown that matched the evergreen of her eyes. Eyes that were focused on the man beneath his boot—her precious Lord in danger, causing her to wave the flag faster, harder. He should have expected her response, that she would try to stop him from killing her lover, for she had shown where her loyalties lay, yet he wasn't prepared for his chest to burn with such bitterness. He pressed down harder with his foot in anger.

'Halt your attack,' he fiercely commanded his men.

Usually, nothing would stop him from storming a Saxon fortress. They didn't care for the rules of battle. He'd put himself in the heart of the fight many times, driven by his dark memories and the desire to make a name for himself, to make history. And taking down Ryestone Keep meant more to him than anything. He had imagined a great battle, with the fighting going on long into the night, a meeting of strength and skill, but seeing Rebekah again had stopped him in his blood-soaked tracks, and all around them the Saxon soldiers were dropping their weapons in defeat.

When Rædan met the eyes of the man lying on the ground beneath him, he expected to see fear and recognition in Lord Atol's gaze—perhaps the dawning realisation that the heinous crimes of his past had finally caught up with him—but there was nothing. It was as if not even one memory had been stirred. And instead of begging for forgiveness, the man began begging for his life.

Rædan felt raw anger and disdain rear up inside him. How could his enemy not remember him, when he had often woken in the years since, covered in sweat and reliving the worst evening of his life—the night he'd been parted from all that he knew and cared for in the world?

He wanted to crush the Saxon Lord like the vermin that he was, but the sour taste of dissatisfaction filled his mouth. While this man had destroyed his life and Rædan wanted revenge, an honourable death in battle now seemed too good for him.

Aware of everyone's eyes on him, especially Rebekah's, Rædan roughly bundled the Saxon Lord to his feet. He took pleasure in tightly binding the man's hands with rope and gagging his mouth. He wanted this mighty Lord to be humiliated, to lose all he held dear, to suffer as he had suffered. And a plan began to form in his mind. His men had been tasked with bringing riches back to Nedergaard and Rædan had unearthed a particular prize of his own.

First, he would take Lord Atol's freedom, next, his wife…

He placed his sword across his hostage's chest and jostled him forward. 'Signal to your guards to open the gates,' he barked. And the Saxon did as he commanded. Rædan turned to his best men, Erik and Arne, and beckoned them to follow, while instructing the rest of his warriors to wait, to maintain their positions over their captives.

His lips twisted at the irony of the familiar large wooden gates of Ryestone Keep slowly opening, welcoming him back inside. And as he crossed the courtyard towards the old stone keep, a cascade of memories crashed over him, for this place had once been his home—another lifetime ago, when he'd been a different person. It was a place where he'd found happiness for a time, before it had been cruelly ripped from him. This fortress represented his past—was it so wrong he wanted to tear it down, eradicate it and all that it stood for?

His strides were long and purposeful as he headed towards the great hall, where the women and children huddled together, comforting each other amid the chaos of the conflict. As a boy, he'd been in awe of the size of this place. It hadn't changed, but as all eyes turned towards him and his hostage, and muffled gasps rippled around the hall, he realised many of the faces had. He felt a pang of remorse at having in-flicted this discomfort upon them, for forcing his way into their home—after all, he had once been one of them—but he instantly crushed it, as he'd learned to suppress all emotions.

A path cleared for him and he shoved the Saxon forward. Rædan allowed himself a moment to bask in his victory, to have their lives in his control, for he had thought of this day of retribution often.

At the top of the hall, he had been expecting to find Lord Cynerik, but instead Rebekah stood in front of a grand wooden chair, waiting for him to draw near. He was impressed by her courage and he wondered, having taken Atol as a hostage, was he responsible for putting her in charge? Where was her uncle?

'That is close enough,' she commanded, her eyes flashing as she held up her hand to halt his advance.

She was even more beautiful than he remembered, despite her rain-washed hair and damp clothes. Born into nobility, she had always had power over him—and right now, she looked as if she was ready to fight, wearing leather bracers and boots, holding a sword of her own in her right hand. Did she know how to wield it? Would she consider using it against him? The thought sent a throb of unexpected desire to his groin.

But despite her highborn blood, there was nothing honourable about this woman. He must keep that in mind, despite her beguiling looks. How soon had it been after he'd left that Rebekah had fallen into Atol's bed? He'd always wondered if the Saxon Lord's status and wealth would turn her head and the treachery cut deep, wounding his heart and his pride, even now.

He stopped before her and the tension in the air was so thick, he thought he could slice it with his blade, her nearness causing a tightness in his chest. *Damn him,* he didn't want to still be attracted to her—he hated himself for being so—for her betrayal had been the worst of all.

'I am the Lady of Ryestone Keep,' Rebekah said evenly, willing her knees to stop trembling and her voice to sound bolder than she felt.

'You need no introduction, I know who you are, Lady—your legendary beauty precedes you.'

She gripped the handle of her late father's sword tighter in her lap, seeking some of its strength.

'I ask that you put down your weapons and you will be rewarded. It seems you have something of ours,' she added, motioning to Lord Atol. 'And I am willing to negotiate.'

At any other time she would have been pleased to see her tyrannical Lord in bonds, restrained. But right now an even more fearsome enemy commanded her attention.

'You are in no position to bargain, Lady,' he said. 'We have won this fight. What's stopping us from simply taking what we want?'

Anger fired up inside her. How dare this heathen attack them! And how could she reason with such a savage man? Yet, she knew she must try, for the sake of her people and especially for her beloved daughter...

'I'm certain I can offer you more than what you could rob or pillage—and you won't have to fight for it.'

'Is that so?'

The Northman took another step towards her, towering over her, causing her to recoil. She had never seen a man look so intimidating, so strong—and in total control. He wore the clothing of a warrior, the skin of a wolf, and carried the weapons of a killer, and yet, regardless of the fact his face was half covered with tarnished metal, his jaw hidden by a thick dark beard, there was something familiar in the curve of his mouth, the lilt of his voice…

'No one else needs to get hurt,' she said, her chin tilting upwards.

In a sweeping gesture, his free muscled arm came up to remove his headgear, finally exposing his full face and her lips parted on a gasp. His grey gaze met hers and the overwhelming shock of realisation—*that it was him*—made her throat constrict, her heart clamour to a momentary stop. And then a jolt of awareness sent her blood racing.

Only one man had eyes like that, but that man had disappeared eight winters ago. He'd walked out of her life without even saying goodbye.

It couldn't be, could it?

Rædan, *her Rædan*, had died. Lord Atol had told her so himself.

And yet, as certain as she was that the sun would rise tomorrow, she knew she was staring up at the boy she had thought she would never see again. He was alive!

She gave a little disbelieving shake of her head. He had changed—he had transformed beyond recognition from the boy she had known. His face had grown into that of a man and, although he now had a deep scar etched through his right eyebrow, splashes of mud and blood over his skin, it didn't detract from the rugged handsomeness of his features.

His body was now much more muscular and imposing and his skin on his bare forearms was covered in whorls of black ink. She marvelled at how his hair had grown longer and was tied up and tightly braided, wet from the storm, and yet, despite all this, she had still known it was him. Instantly.

The shock of the realisation made her hands tremble, her knees shake. She glanced up at Lord Atol's face, desperately searching for any signs that he recognised this man, too, for confirmation of what she was seeing, but there was nothing, not even a glimmer of awareness in his eyes. Atol was simply struggling under the warrior's grasp, no doubt fearful for his life.

'You…you must be the man they call the Ghost—the Draug, the Reborn…' she stuttered, bringing her attention back to the Northman, her voice not sounding real. Was it just wishful thinking? Was she seeing things now—because of a ridiculous longing to see a man she had once thought she'd cared for more than anyone else in the world, to put an end to the ongoing ache that thinking of him caused? 'Why is it that they call you that, I wonder?' she asked.

'I'm sure you know the stories,' he said, inclining his head. 'That I raid your kingdoms searching for my lost soul.'

Yes, she had heard the barbaric tales of devastation and destruction he caused. But rather than quelling her foolish notions that the man who stood before her was the only man she had ever loved, his distinctive voice stole into her heart. It was deeper, different to how she remembered, with a gravelly, roughened tone, but it was still a sound that took her back to a summer, years before. Alone at her uncle's fortress, grieving her parents, her only pleasure had been befriending the animals in the stables…until she'd met Rædan.

Instinctively, she turned to glance at Gytha, hiding in the crowd, and she knew she had to keep her head. She didn't know what this man wanted and she had to be strong, for her child and her people.

'I have heard the stories of your brutality… You're a man who behaves how he likes and takes what he wants without restraint.'

But how was it possible that the boy she'd

once known was this fierce warrior now standing before her? After all, her Rædan had been a stable boy. A Saxon. She hadn't known he could fight. And she'd never imagined him commanding an army, especially a Danish one.

'I hope you find what you're looking for and that all the bloodshed will have been worth it,' she spat.

The last time she'd seen him, they had just become lovers. It had been the best night of her life, but also life-altering. She knew he hadn't been able to afford the bride price to ask for her hand in marriage, but she had been willing to wait until he could. She'd been determined to convince her uncle to let her marry for love.

If this man was who she thought he was, he had made her believe he cared for her—and then vanished from her life. She'd believed he was dead. Now he was back? Her throat felt thick with tears she knew she could not shed.

But Rædan wouldn't attack Lord Atol or Ryestone. Her home. She had suffered the consequences of the Danes' attacks her whole life and she had spent the past years fearful of their return. Him being one of them didn't make any sense. She despised everything this man stood for…

She sank into the wooden chair, suddenly needing its support as her legs gave way.

'Well,' she said, clearing her throat, smoothing her hand over her skirts. 'What is it that you want here?' Apart from destruction and bloodshed. 'What will it take for you to leave these shores?' She didn't think anything could have stopped her eyes from glancing up and finding his again, causing another blow to her heart as their gazes collided.

Riveted, she saw the edges of his eyes were painted with black warrior's kohl and she found herself looking for clues of his past. His tanned, weathered skin suggested a life spent outdoors, his muscles perhaps honed through physical work… Where had he been all these years?

'I can offer you a ransom to withdraw. An agreed amount of gold and silver to leave Ryestone and never return.'

When he'd disappeared without a trace, she'd begged her uncle to search for him, telling him she was worried for her friend, knowing something was wrong, disbelieving that he would have abandoned her. But finally she'd heard he'd been caught and it was impossible not to believe what Atol told her—that he had stolen silver from Lord Cynerik and fled, that he'd been captured and killed for his crime. Rædan's father had refused to believe it and she hadn't wanted to either, yet her uncle had confirmed the silver was missing.

But if any of that had been true, he wouldn't have returned. He wouldn't be standing before her now, as a Northman, a fierce fighter, who killed for sport and relieved men of their gold, their lands—and their wives.

'I knew you would offer to buy us off, to save your kingdom—and your lover—from being torn down. I had counted on it,' he said darkly.

'Many raiding Danes before you have been paid to leave Saxon burghs alone.'

'And has that been successful?' he mocked. 'Why don't you make me an offer I can't refuse?' he said, spreading his arms, his lips curling upwards into a hard smile.

Her eyes flashed at the challenge. 'All right. I will give you five hundred pounds' worth of gold and one hundred pounds' worth of silver.' How absurd, she thought hysterically, that she was offering to pay him to leave, when eight years ago, she would have paid that and more to find him, to bring him back to her.

The Northman let out a low whistle. 'You must really want us gone.'

'Indeed,' she said. But not without getting some answers first.

'Or is it land you are after?' she asked, her gaze narrowing on him.

Rædan released a long, slow breath. Her all-too-familiar voice swept over him, like a drifting fog wrapping around him, trying to block out the past and all its abhorrent, unspeakable memories.

Was Rebekah really going to offer him land that he had lived and worked on and been exiled from years ago? His fists bunched at his sides. Sheep now grazed the fields where he and his father had once owned a small farmstead. He had heard the old man had died not long after he'd left these shores and their home had been razed to the ground. Had they buried him in that land? Even though Rædan's home was now across the ocean, there was still a part of him that wanted his old settlement and that time with his father back. He hadn't even had the chance to say goodbye. He had been denied his grief and he wanted vengeance. A fresh fury churned within him and he vowed to himself once more that he would destroy the Lord and Lady of Ryestone's lives, as they had ruined his.

That night he'd spent with Rebekah had been incredible, unforgettable, but after she'd departed his bed, he had been awoken in the early hours by armed men forcing their way into his home. He'd been blindfolded and taken by force down to the river. He'd been stripped of his clothes, beaten and put in a boat… Had some of the men who he'd fought outside been responsible for that? If so, then they deserved everything they got today. And as for Rebekah…he couldn't be sure what part she'd played in his demise, but he knew she couldn't be trusted.

'Which land is it that you speak of?' he asked.

Did she realise who he was? He had heard her sharp intake of breath when he'd removed his head armour, but she hadn't spoken out. If she had recognised him, she was hiding it well, yet she had always been a good performer, for she had fooled him before.

Even so, he sensed she was aware of him, as her pulse was fluttering fast at the base of her throat, and he was drawn to her full bottom lip and the way she kept tugging it between her teeth. He recalled how he'd done the exact same thing to her lips that night and just that one memory caused a sudden responsive throb of desire. He tried to fight it, clenching his jaw.

'There is a piece of good farmland to the other side of the river. It stretches all the way to the coast. It has fertile soil and a small harbour,' she said.

He nodded. 'I am interested in the land down by the creek as well,' he said. 'By that lone old oak tree.'

Her beautiful green eyes widened. They both knew it was where his father had buried his mother...

'It can be yours,' she said slowly. 'But you will have to agree to our terms.'

His eyes skimmed over her stoic face. Had she always been this determined—or had the years changed her, too? She was certainly a strong adversary and he found himself admiring her for it.

His eyes swept over the generous curve of her breasts, the swell of her hips. Damn, he still wanted her—and yet she belonged to another. But he could be just as determined when he wanted something... 'Which are?' he asked.

'I can give you the gold and silver now, but I will need some assurance you will retrieve your men from our fortress and that you'll relinquish any prisoners—to show willing,' she said. 'The deeds to the land will have to be drawn up. You will need to release Lord Atol as he is the only one who can arrange for the land to be given over to you.'

His brow furrowed. Of course she wanted her lover back and was prepared to negotiate for his release. His nostrils flared.

When he had heard of their engagement he hadn't been able to believe it, that she would say yes to that man—until he'd seen it with his very own eyes. When the ship he belonged to had sailed back up the river into Ryestone just two weeks after he'd been forced to leave, to stock up on supplies under cover of a large celebration taking place at the fortress, his heart had lifted in hope. He had thought he might see his father and be able to signal for help, or perhaps see Rebekah and she could explain to her uncle there had been a terrible mistake.

But then the happy couple had stepped out on to the bridge, overlooking the delighted crowd of villagers, to announce their upcoming nuptials, and suddenly it had all made sense—why he'd been sent away. And the pain he'd felt had been far greater than any he'd experienced at the hands of his captors.

That vision was now branded into his memory. Although he'd tried, he couldn't erase the image of Rebekah looking stunning in a deep purple gown. He'd watched Atol's hands roam over the pale, bare flesh of her arms, circling her waist, as he'd bent down to whisper something in her ear, and Rædan had known his life was over.

After that, he had no purpose, no reason to live. He'd worked from dawn to dusk, not even feeling the beatings any more, not caring about his empty stomach, or his aching, bruised body. He'd survived on a diet of hate and shame.

If there was one thing he'd learned during those years, it had been how to endure pain, how to shut off his feelings and keep control, to reroute his anger to make him stronger. They were all traits he prided himself in possessing now, so he was incensed with himself that he couldn't control the way his body was responding to her.

He had come here wanting the Lord and Lady of Ryestone Keep to experience how it felt to have their home threatened, their lands taken away—to have your loved ones stolen from you. He had been thinking about this for eight long years. And suddenly, he knew what he had to do.

He shook his head. 'No, I will not release the prisoner, or how can I trust you will stick to your end of the bargain? Unless...'

He wished he could have sacked the fortress, having dismantled Lord Atol's kingdom and destroyed all that he cared for, leaving this place for good. But here she was, still looking like that, pretending she didn't know him. He pressed his lips together into a thin, hard line. It made him want to take her right here, to slam into her hard and fast, making her cry out in pleasure, to fire up that shocking memory of hers and remind her of the night they'd spent together. But he told himself to be patient...

Instead, he nodded slowly. 'I will leave with my men now and hand over my prisoners, but I shall need some assurance... Let's call it a form of protection, until I know you'll be true to your word.'

Her chin tipped up, in that challenging way of hers. 'The gold is my assurance.'

'Something far more valuable than gold.'

'There is nothing more valuable than gold,'

Lord Atol spat from beside him. He had seemingly worked free the gag over his mouth.

Rædan gave his prisoner a cursory glance. 'I shall take a hostage in your place—as collateral—until the deal is complete.'

A sneer slashed across Lord Atol's face. 'Who?'

Rædan was aware of Rebekah's eyes upon him, her hands gripping tighter on to the arms of the wooden chair, her knuckles turning white, as if she knew where this was going. A long time ago she'd stared at him with passion in her eyes. Now, was it fear or hate? He didn't care. He had nothing to lose. Not any more. And yet he had the sense that she was still as drawn to him as he was to her. Was it the flush of heat in her cheeks, or the rapid rise and fall of her chest, as if she was struggling to breathe?

'Someone of importance to you.'

Lord Atol sneered. 'No one is that important.' And as if arrogantly trying to show that was the case, he nodded at a young maiden. 'I presume it is a woman you are after, to entertain you as you wait. May I suggest Lady Mildrethe? She is very beautiful and will no doubt prove satisfactory.'

'Please, Lord, no,' the girl whimpered, practically shrinking before them.

Rædan barely glanced her way. 'No.'

The man's presumptuous attempt to intervene, even while he was a captive and had no say in this, was maddening. But Lord Atol wasn't finished with his foolish attempt at a display of power. He summoned another woman towards him with the flick of his head. What was it about this man that made him think he could rule over people, treating them as if they were animals? 'Then how about Lady Aswig? A rare prize indeed.'

With long blonde hair, this one was a beauty, but Rædan felt...nothing. She wasn't the prize he had in mind. 'No.'

'Enough of this. I shall go.'

Rebekah...

There was a unified gasp from the people in the hall as she propelled herself out of her seat. And no one was more shocked than Rædan. He closed his eyes for just a moment, savouring it, taking it in.

'I shall spend the night with the Northman.'

'The hell you will!' Lord Atol roared, struggling against his bonds, and Rædan tightened his grip.

Rebekah turned to whisper something to the young women and children gathered around her, who were also protesting, trying to talk her out of it, to tug her backwards. But she disentangled herself and stood tall, stepping towards the two men, her lush green eyes flaming. 'That is, if I should be to the Northman's liking.'

Rædan gave her a cool smile, but he was all too aware of his heated blood beginning to pound through his body, the hardening of his groin. To his liking? He had seen her in his dreams, but she was even more beautiful in the flesh. She had been but a teenager when he'd seen her last—now she was a stunning woman who had grown in confidence and curves and his mouth dried.

'A noble sacrifice. You are very brave, Lady.'

'I am willing to do whatever is necessary for the safety of my people—and my Lord.' She turned to Atol. 'It's a small price to pay for your freedom, is it not?'

Atol gave a last struggle and then nodded, decisive. 'Damn it, so be it,' he snarled. 'She will make this sacrifice for me and for the people. She will be yours for one night, but she will belong to me for the rest of her life. Now release me.'

Rædan's eyes narrowed on him. He really was a snake, to allow this to happen—to give up his woman rather than risk his own life.

Rædan pushed the man down into the chair, holding him fast. And rather than unbinding the ropes around his wrists, he began tethering the Saxon Lord to the seat. 'So you don't get any ideas about coming after us… Tell your men to ready the gold and silver,' he added. 'And when I return her to you tomorrow, I expect the deeds to the land to be drawn up.'

Then he reached out and removed the sword from Rebekah's hand, prising her fingers away from the hilt. 'You won't be needing this, my Lady,' he said, before gripping her upper arm.

She gasped, staring up at him, stricken. Had she felt the same searing heat that had shot through his body as their skin made contact? He tried to steady the unusual rapid beating of his heart as his eyes blazed down into hers, sending out a warning, as if to say don't make a scene—not now, not yet…

Chapter Two

The Northman's large hand encircled Rebekah's arm, propelling her forward, and it was as if she'd been struck by one of the fire arrows from earlier, heat rippling out across her skin. She *knew* that touch. It was those fingers, now coarse and roughened, that had stroked and soothed over her body that night, driving her to distraction. She knew it with every beat of her hammering heart.

It *was* him.

'Come with me. Do exactly as I say,' he barked.

He was so close, she could feel the warmth radiating from his large body and his outdoorsy, leather scent filled her lungs, making her dizzy. It was amazing she could walk at all. She couldn't believe this was happening, that she'd offered herself up to him. And she couldn't believe Atol had let her go.

He was leading her out of the hall at a pace, much to the alarm of the people, who were calling out in distress at what was to happen to her, drowning out the Saxon Lord's raging demands to get some guards in the hall, to secure the gates.

The Northman's strides were so long and powerful, she struggled to keep up. It was as if he wanted to get her away from here as fast as possible and fear mingled with a dangerous flicker of excitement at the thought of being alone with him again.

'Keep up,' he ordered.

When he had suggested she trade someone for Lord Atol, she had instantly known that he had meant her. A strange, responsive heat had burned low in her stomach and something had compelled her to speak out, to say she'd go with him. She knew she was playing a dangerous game—that if the Northman didn't harm her, if she survived the night, then Lord Atol certainly would. He would make her pay for this.

She would have to plead with him that she had offered herself up to save him and pray that he would be lenient, just this once. But she would worry about that later. Right now, she needed confirmation this man was who she thought he was, and, if he was, then where the hell had he been all these years?

But when they reached the courtyard, now bathed in twilight, she knew she'd made a monumental mistake in agreeing to go with him. Her footsteps faltered, for the scene was one of total devastation. There were little fires burning everywhere, swirls of smoke stretching up into the sky, leaving behind carcasses of destroyed buildings. Animals were running wild and injured men were strewn about the place, groaning—the aftermath of today's bloody battle. And outside the gates, the heathens still surrounded the Saxons.

'Captivity—a punishment worse than death, don't you think?' the deep, familiar voice from beside her said.

She reeled. The boy she once knew would never have caused this destruction. He would never have been this cruel. She swung out of his grip and rounded on him, suddenly angry. 'We had a deal. You promised to let the men go.'

If she had to give herself up in exchange for the safety of her people, just for one night, then so be it. She would step in where her Saxon

Lord had failed. But she didn't want anyone else to be taken captive—she had heard of the miserable existence of those taken as slaves.

She took in the warrior's beautiful, wild grey eyes and formidable face as he bore down on her, the sheer breadth of his shoulders, and she studied the thick silver chain and peculiar-looking amulet round his neck, shaped like a hammer. There was so much to take in. She thought she could stare at his face all night long and still be fascinated, still have so many questions…

She wanted to scream and shout and pound her fists against him, demanding answers, but instead she just stood there, her hands on her hips, her eyes blazing up at him. She didn't dare bring up the past until they were alone, unsure of his character and what he wanted.

He stared back at her, a cold, reprimanding look on his face, before turning to speak to his fighters in the Danish tongue, an authoritative, hard edge to his voice. Moments later, his right-hand man reappeared with some horses from Lord Atol's stable and, to her utter relief, the rest of his fighters began to slowly fall out, to leave the fortress and their Saxon prisoners behind.

'Happy now?'

She released a long, shaky breath. 'Hardly.' But he had stayed true to his word. At least the yielding of herself was not for nothing. Her daughter would now be safe—from these Northern brutes at least.

She prayed Gytha would be all right for the night. It was the first time she'd ever left her daughter in seven years and she was concerned. Gytha was only a few years younger than Rebekah had been when her parents had died and the last thing Rebekah wanted was her child growing up with the same nightmarish memories of losing a parent to raiding Northmen.

The horse beside him, who she knew to be called Colby, began nickering and nudging the man before her, trying to rest his head on his shoulder, and she gasped. Of course! Colby had been one of the horses in Rædan's stables. She remembered them grooming and mucking out the horses together, as if it was yesterday, falling on to the hay in a tangle of limbs, kissing. And it seemed the stallion had not forgotten this man either.

A flash of recognition crossed the Northman's face as he stroked Colby's nose, to calm the animal, and he gave her a knowing, heated look. Was he having the same memory?

He reached out to grasp her fingers, to help her up into the saddle, and the feel of her hand in his was almost too much.

'Ready?' he asked.

Once, his touch had given her strength and reassurance, now it was both melting her insides and scaring her to the core at the same time. But it was nothing compared to how she felt when he mounted the horse behind her.

She froze, shocked to be back in his arms once more. 'What do you want from me?' she whispered, her voice thick with emotion.

'You volunteered to come with me, remember?' he said, grinning into her ear. And he ruthlessly pulled her back into his chest, leaving her in no doubt of who he was, how much he'd changed and that she was his captive for the night.

His large, muscled thighs pressed against hers as he spurred the horse into action and she tried to steady her breathing, gripping the reins tight and focusing on the movement of the animal, not the way she felt in this man's strong embrace, and she steeled herself for every backwards thrust. She trained her eyes on the river in the distance—the point where she hoped she would be able to escape the Northman's arms, for this ride was torture. Her senses were in overdrive and she was acutely aware of every movement, each part of her body reacquainting itself with his.

His warm breath feathered against her cheek. 'I'm curious. Why did you offer yourself up?'

She realised she'd made this far too easy for him and she cringed, thinking back to her words in the hall.

I will spend the night with the Northman.

The statement sounded even more brazen now she was in his arms, the words seeming to hang in the air between them.

What *had* she been thinking?

'Because I didn't want anyone else to suffer.'

Liar, she told herself. Because she had wanted to come with him, hadn't she? She had needed to see him again, to look him in the eyes and ask him what had happened all those years ago.

Eight long years. How they had dragged…

She had made this journey over the wild meadows and farmlands many times during that time, when she'd needed some distance from Ryestone's callous leader, to clear her head and regain her strength for another onslaught.

As her captor finally began to slow the horse as they made their descent to the water, Rebekah realised she would need to dig deep and find some of that courage now—especially when she saw the foreboding fleet of long-ships lining the sandy banks. The dragon heads carved into the prows looked to be mocking her, because she was a fool—for she had agreed to this, even suggested it. But she'd had a gut feeling he wouldn't hurt her.

'And—and because you remind me of someone I once knew,' she muttered.

The Northman finally brought the animal to a stop and she felt overwrought, her cheeks flushed.

'Who?' He brought his hand up to cup her chin and turn her face towards him as they sat atop the still horse.

She stared into his eyes. 'A stable boy who used to work for my uncle.'

He dropped his hand and removed his arms from her body, swinging himself off the animal. Taking hold of the reins again to steady the horse, he took a step towards her, his eyes blazing up at her. Her body trembled in response. Did he realise how imposing, how formidable he was?

'But perhaps I've got it wrong. You can't be him. He was a good person. He certainly wouldn't have caused the destruction I saw here today…'

She watched a muscle flicker in his jaw. He held out his hand to help her down and she accepted it, reluctantly. Heat shot up her arm again and, her impatient curiosity getting the better of her, she found herself reaching out to touch his cheek, to check he was real. She had missed him desperately.

There had been so many times she'd wanted to turn to him and tell him about her day, about something funny Gytha had said… She had longed for this very moment, picturing it in her dreams. Her heart was pounding so hard she thought it might burst out of her chest, but the instant her fingers met his warm skin, he stiffened, stepping back, recoiling from her touch. And the hurt from eight years before came crashing down over her again.

'One of your uncle's workers…?' He gave a short, hollow laugh. 'Is that how you remember me? I have to admit, I remember our relationship rather differently.'

He had been handsome, but just eighteen the last time she'd seen him. And he was right—their relationship had been intense from the start. An instant, inexorable attraction, a whirlwind romance that had taken her heart by storm, making that summer shine.

He'd taught her to ride and she had asked him to show her the scenic routes during her lessons, so she could learn more about the beautiful land where they lived and more about the boy she was falling in love with. She'd wanted to make their journeys and conversations last. He had filled her days with light during that warm, sunny season and made her heart swell with happiness.

Deep down, she had known her uncle wouldn't approve of the match, as Lord Cynerik had hoped she would one day marry his son, Atol. She knew it was a good match—Atol was one of the wealthiest and most powerful men in the land and could offer her status and security, and she, too, was heir to her late father's wealth and lands. But she had wanted to marry for love, as her parents had, and for that reason it had been impossible to stay away from Rædan.

Her mind flew back to that one perfect night, when they had finally crossed the line to being lovers. He had tried to do the right thing, to slow things down, saying they should wait—

but in the end, their passion had taken over. She felt her face heat at the memory.

'So you do remember…' His face was dark, his voice mocking, his eyes following the colour spreading across her cheeks. Rædan made a gentle tut-tutting sound. He stepped closer and her back hit the horse's side. 'Why deny it?'

'Why would I want to remind myself?' she bit back, her pride returning with full force, remembering how she had felt when she'd woken the morning after he'd taken her virginity— her honour—to find he'd left Ryestone, like a thief in the night. She'd thought that her feelings were mutual, but he'd left her, after she'd given herself to him so completely, so easily. And then days later she'd been informed he'd stolen from her uncle, fled—and was captured and killed.

A part of her had died that day. She had been inconsolable. It had felt as if someone had thrown her down a deep, dark well and she was unable to see the light, incapable of climbing out—and she hadn't even wanted to.

'I can think of a few reasons, Bekah…'

Bekah… Her stomach turned upside down. Only he had ever called her that.

An invisible, silken cord wrapped around them, connecting them, as if he was a part of her, and yet that cord had been frayed, damaged beyond repair, and there was no way of mending it back together. She felt a ripple of anger shift through her and she wanted to lash out at him for leaving. She wanted to know why—to hear good reasons—and she also, perversely, never wanted to let him out of her sight again.

'You're looking…well,' his silky voice murmured, his eyes raking over her body.

And for a moment, she felt exposed. She wondered what he must see when he looked at her. She was no longer the fresh-faced beauty from when they first met. She felt every one of those long summers and winters he'd been away in the fine lines around her tired eyes, from the responsibilities of being a mother, a protector of Ryestone and the constant tension—and fear—that came with living under Lord Atol's cold-blooded rule.

'I'm so glad you noticed.'

His full lips curled upwards. Lips that had moved over her so gently that night, whispering words of reassurance, melting away any worries. But how could a man who had touched her so tenderly, as if she was precious, now be this brutal barbarian standing before her? She had never been afraid of him before, but now she was.

'This is the part where you're supposed to say it's nice to see me, too.' His mouth smirked, but his eyes remained hostile, cold.

'But it's wrong to lie,' she said. 'You appear to have turned your back on your people. Your homeland.' *As well as her.* She had been inconsolable those first few weeks, moping around, barely eating or drinking.

How was it possible that he could be one of them, a Northman who raided and pillaged and filled her people with dread? How could he have come back here and attacked his own home? Danish warriors killed her family. He *knew* what had happened to her parents. He *knew* she despised them.

'You even abandoned your father... He was devastated when you left.' *She* was devastated when he left.

His face darkened, and he brusquely took her elbow and pulled her over to where his men were setting up camp, taking woollen sheets from the boats and erecting various shelters. With their large muscles, snake-like long hair and inked skin, communicating with each other in another language, she felt the difference between them in every pore of her trembling body, in every inrush of nervous breath, and she tried not to think about what might come next, what he was planning to do with her…

He led her inside the shelter closest to the water and her heart was in her mouth, wondering what was going to happen. She knew the worst of what men were capable of and she knew she must stand her ground. She shook herself out of his grasp and braced herself, turning round to face him, ready for a fight. She immediately went on the attack.

'Why have you brought me here?' she asked, glancing around as if her surroundings would somehow give her the answers she was looking for.

There was a makeshift bed with a scattering of animal skins and one side of the shelter was open, overlooking the river, a small crackling fire just getting going on the outside. She determined to give it—and him—a wide berth.

'Was he killed?' he asked, his voice strained, toneless, his hands on his hips.

'Who?'

'My father. How did he die?' he demanded.

'You don't know?' she asked, shocked.

'No.'

'He died asleep in his bed…' She shook her head a little, her brow furrowing. 'After you left, he was a broken man. He deteriorated quickly. He became too frail to work the land and earn his keep,' she said accusingly. 'Every day he hoped you'd come back to us.' Every day they'd been disappointed. The old man had given up on living, as had she…

He nodded, but his face was hard to read, his unusual ghost-grey eyes haunted by something she had no knowledge of.

There had been a time when she'd known what Rædan was thinking, from the way his lips widened into a smile or his eyes flashed. Now, he was a mystery to her. This man seemed so cold, so remote.

'He was given a proper burial, next to your mother. I made sure of it.'

His nose wrinkled slightly and her breath stumbled.

She knew someone else who did that…

Behind her, the flames of the fire began to spit and hiss as it came to life and she baulked, backing further away. She didn't want to show any sign of weakness, but it was an ingrained response to an old fear.

Almost instinctively, Rædan went over to it and stamped it out and it was that small kindness that nearly broke her. Was it possible that he hadn't forgotten that she was scared of fire? She'd told him the story of how her parents' home had burned for days after being set alight by Northmen, while she lay trapped. Was the boy she once knew still inside this fierce warrior somewhere?

The evening was drawing in, with just the pale light of the moon now streaming through the shelter. She took a deep breath, finding confidence in the darkness to pursue her questioning. Enough was enough. She had so many questions, she didn't know where to begin. She needed answers. Now.

'Rædan, why have you come back now, after all these years, and like this? Why did you torch the fortress?' she said, her words full of accusation.

'Your men fired the first shot. It was their flame arrows that set the walls alight.'

'But you came here to attack us!' She shook her head. 'Rædan… Where have you been? What happened to you?'

How did he get that scar across his brow? How had he become so strong? And why was he posing as a Northmen, commanding this hateful army who were invading his Saxon home?

'As if you don't know.'

She lifted her hands up in exasperation. 'I don't! Lord Atol told me you stole silver from Cynerik. They said you were caught and killed.'

Thinking the best of him, she'd thought perhaps he'd stolen the silver for her, as he'd wanted to make a better life for himself. *For them.* She had known he had no land or titles to his name. And deep down, it was easier believing that version of the story over the possibility that just maybe he'd got what he wanted from her—taken her to bed—and then decided to leave. It had been the best night of her life, but the memories had since been tarnished.

'And you believed him?'

'Why would he lie?'

He stepped towards her, a dark, reproachful look in his steely gaze. 'You moved on pretty quickly—I believe Lord Atol reaped the benefits of that.'

His accusatory tone was like a knife to her heart. She swayed slightly, her arms folding across her stomach. The years had hardened him, she thought. And his words made her feel as if she was one of Lord Atol's many whores. But didn't she deserve it? After all, everything he was saying was true.

But she'd had no other option. And she still had a battle on her hands, even now, to keep her title, her pride—for the sake of her daughter.

Suddenly, anger flared inside, because he was the one who'd let her down. He'd abandoned her, leaving her vulnerable and with little choice but to take whatever security Atol could provide. Everything she had suffered had occurred because he'd left. She'd thought he was dead—but here he was, very much alive!

'I searched for you... I *mourned* you,' she whispered bitterly, brimming over with hurt, her rage erupting now.

There had not been a day that had gone by in the years since that she hadn't thought of him. 'And yet now you're standing here, still living and breathing!' Her words were laced with disgust and blame.

'Sorry to disappoint you,' he retorted. 'Although I'm sure Atol helped you get over your short-lived grief.'

She gasped. 'It wasn't like that,' she said, her fingers coming up to her throat.

'You married him!'

'I didn't,' she said, shaking her head.

'What?' His voice iced over.

'We're not…married.'

'But I *saw* you. I watched you announce your engagement.'

'You were here?' She felt ill. If he had been here, in Ryestone, why hadn't he come to her? Why had he let her get engaged to Atol? How could he have been so heartless? 'We never…'

The words felt shameful on her tongue, even as she spoke them. Shortly after she had been told Rædan was dead, her Uncle Cynerik had set in motion the marriage arrangements for her and Atol. Grief-stricken, she'd accepted her fate, realising she would never be happy again. She had told herself the wedding would please her uncle and that, although she didn't care for him, Lord Atol was a good man.

But she'd had no idea what suffering was to come… When no one else was around, she had soon learned of Atol's quiet cruelty, his hidden, darker side. And despite the shame that had followed, the invisible cage she now lived in, at least the wedding had never taken place…

'You have not shared his bed?'

Sickness swirled as the walls of the shelter began to spin, closing in on her. *Never willingly.*

She wanted to tell him no, she *wished* the answer was no. If only she could turn back the years… But she also knew she couldn't lie. She slumped down on to the furs behind her, her silence deafening.

'Well, then he got what he wanted.' His voice was deadly. And the cool reproach in his icy gaze made her shiver. His arms came across his chest, his body closed to her, and he stalked over to the open side of the shelter, to look out over the water. He hated her, she could see it in the set of his jaw, the cold, hard flint of his eyes.

'He insisted I leave this place…my home, my father—you—so he could make you his and you played right into his hands.'

'What?' Her head snapped up. She held her hand up to ward off the truth. 'No! You're lying.'

He turned to look back at her over his shoulder. 'Are you sure about that, Rebekah?'

It couldn't be true. Could it? His disappearance was around the same time that her uncle had begun pressing for her and Atol to marry… and when the Saxon Lord had first made his desires towards her known.

She shuddered, running her fingers over the

soft threads of the animal skins, seeking comfort. 'Did he offer you a bribe? To leave here?' she asked.

'Let's just say it was made very clear I wasn't welcome here any more.'

If Atol had done what Rædan was accusing him of—pressing him into leaving so he could have her for himself—her Saxon Lord was even more despicable than she thought. He had ruined her life.

Suddenly she felt overwhelmingly angry with him, but with Rædan, too. Because if he had been alive all this time, where had he been? If it was true that Atol had contrived the situation and sent him away, why hadn't Rædan at least sent her a message, if only to let her know he was all right?

'If you'd just let me know your whereabouts...' she whispered. She would have followed him anywhere. He'd even revealed he'd returned to Ryestone and seen them announce their engagement. Why hadn't he come to her then? How could he be so cruel as to let her go through with it? And now the void between them was so great. Bitterness burned in her stomach. This man she had once known better than anyone was a stranger to her.

* * *

'So you didn't steal Cynerik's silver?'

'No!' Rædan couldn't believe she thought he was guilty—that he might actually have stolen from her uncle. Just because of his lower station? Had she not known him at all? His grip on the post of the shelter tightened.

It had been some time before he'd realised Lord Atol was the man who had ruined his life. He'd often wondered how Atol had found out about Rædan's feelings for Rebekah and decided to get rid of him, so he could claim her for himself. But the bigger question had been— had Rebekah known what Lord Atol had done to him? It had been one of the thoughts that had tormented him these past eight years.

Staring down at her now, he fought to keep hold of his resentment and loathing. It seemed that she did not and yet she had still gone to bed with the man willingly, out of wedlock, and it sickened him.

Rædan watched as her fingers ran over the soft furs and he recalled how her fingers had once trailed over his skin in wonder, as if she cared about him. Had she really—or had he merely been a distraction, until someone better came along? Someone with wealth and a fortress?

And yet she had told him she'd buried his father with his mother and he was grateful for that. How did she make him feel this mixed-up jumble of emotions? He usually prided himself in not feeling anything at all! He was probably weary from the long journey here, from the fighting and negotiating, but he was surprised to find he still felt the pulse of attraction pounding in his groin, the need to touch her again.

Disturbingly, he had wanted her from the moment he'd seen her again—and when she'd stepped forward and agreed to spend the night with him, it had only escalated his desire. It had been almost unbearable holding her in his arms, between his thighs, on the short ride to the river, and now she was in his tent, sitting on his bed. Perhaps he should just take her and be done with it, to finally rid himself of this red-hot anger and longing that was tearing him apart inside.

She shivered and he realised that now he'd stamped out the fire—remembering how afraid she was of it—she must be cold. Reluctantly, he moved to get a blanket from the bed and handed it to her. Muttering her thanks when she took it from him, their fingers brushed, branding his skin. *Damn.* How could she still affect him so? He wished she didn't.

She tugged the fur around her shoulders and he noticed her hands tremble. His gaze travelled to her mouth—soft, with a fuller bottom lip that she was still biting down on. Was she afraid? He had the disturbing desire to reassure her, to tell her he meant her no harm, but instead he kept quiet. Up until now, she'd been brave, caring more about protecting her people than herself, offering herself up as part of the bargain. But was that the only reason she had volunteered to come here? Had she really been prepared to sacrifice herself for Lord Atol? Or did she have burning questions, just like he did?

'You still haven't told me where you've been all these years,' she said, shrugging a slim shoulder, drawing his eye to the pale skin at the base of her neck. 'Why didn't you send word to me?'

Because he hadn't been able to! Because he'd seen her in the arms of another man and felt all hope was lost. Because he'd been kept against his will. That night, he'd been savagely beaten by Atol's men and handed over to a slaver and transported across the sea. No one had listened to his words of despair. No one cared for his anguish. Lord Atol had made sure he'd had his life and his dignity snatched from him. For years, he'd been at the mercy of his captors. But his pride would never allow him to reveal that—not to anyone. And especially not to her.

'I've lived a somewhat nomadic existence, until recently, where I've settled in the north.' It was a version of the truth he was comfortable with admitting, the one that caused him the least humiliation. The barbarity he had suffered was indescribable anyway… He had made several attempts to escape over the years, but each time he had been caught and beaten to within an inch of his life. Each time they'd worn him down. And he was ashamed of his weakness. No, she didn't need to know those details—he didn't want her pity.

'But—'

'The rest is none of your concern, Rebekah, not any more,' he snapped, turning his back on her again, ignoring her sharp intake of breath.

'So why come back, after all this time, and like this?' she asked, matching his angry tone.

Because you had to see her again, didn't you? a voice mocked him. He smoothed a hand over his face. That's what this was really about.

And pride. Always pride.

He had been away for so long, he'd tried to forget his past, to put it all behind him, but when his Danish Lord had suggested this latest raid to the English Isle, and proposed coming further inland, Rædan had been eager to hear of the plans and take charge. He was Jarl Knud's best warrior and he owed him his life after Knud had rescued him from the slavers.

'When I heard the men from my settlement were coming here to raid, I saw it as an opportunity to get revenge on the man who ruined mine and my father's life. I want him to live knowing everything important has been taken from him.'

Her eyes were suddenly two huge balls of anger. 'And let me guess, you see me as a way to get it?' She laughed bitterly. 'Is that why you negotiated for a hostage? Is that why you brought me here? To take me to bed—to get even with Atol?'

Heat pooled in his groin at her words and the visions they conjured up. But she wasn't finished.

'Well, I'm sorry to ruin your plans, but in case you hadn't noticed, he may be possessive and controlling, but he doesn't care what happens to me. Only himself.'

Rædan didn't understand how that could be true. When she'd been his, he would never have given her up. Not for anything. Yet he'd witnessed what she was saying for himself. Lord Atol had handed her over to his enemy in his stead, without any regard for her feelings or her safety.

Rebekah stood to face him, the blanket dropping to the floor, and his gaze was drawn to the smooth skin at her neckline, the gentle swells of the top of her breasts, then back up to her lips. Her hands were on her hips, accentuating her slim waist. He noticed her breathing was unsteady, her skin flushed. She was so incredibly beautiful. If she was his, he'd never want to share her.

He knew he should leave this place. He knew he should forget about her—and perhaps he could if he took what he wanted, purging his desires and ridding this need inside him once and for all...

Her green eyes glittered at him, almost daring him. 'Go ahead. Do what you like to me, Rædan, but just know it won't make the slightest bit of impact on Atol.'

Was that a challenge in her words? The rebellious heat in her eyes made him instantly hard. And angry.

'All right, maybe I will.'

It took two strides to reach her and less than an inward breath to wrap his arm around her waist and pull her right up against him in a tight, possessive grip. And when she gasped, her heart-shaped lips parting, he couldn't wait another moment. His hot, open mouth was on hers, his hands cupping her face, holding her head to his, hard, as his tongue urgently moved between her lips, wildly—totally unrestrained and unapologetic.

She made a little startled sound of disbelief from the back of her throat and he told himself, if she'd struggled, he would have let her go, but instead of resisting, the moment his lips met hers she'd seemed to give in, to melt into him, as if she'd known this was going to happen, as if she was just as helpless as he was to fight it, her fingers fanning out against his chest in submission.

As he ravaged her mouth with his tongue, he curled his palm over her long braid of hair and slowly twisted the plait around his hand, winding it tighter, gently tugging her head back, giving his lips access to her jaw, her neck…

Driven by a desire he didn't understand, he wanted to touch her everywhere, to explore all her soft curves again, with his hands, then his mouth, to feel and taste her. He wanted to brand her with his touch, to wipe all thoughts of Lord Atol from her mind, to make her his once more. And he felt himself unravelling, the blinding hardness of his groin overshadowing all thoughts. He had never wanted anyone like this. He had to have her. Now.

His lips found hers again, his tongue delving inside her mouth once more, and her knees seemed to buckle under his plundering, swirling kisses. He hooked his arm around her waist, walking her backwards to the bed and toppling her on to it, his large body coming down over hers—and she froze.

'Rædan, stop!' she gasped, pushing at his chest. 'What are you doing? Get off me!'

He pulled back, staring down at her, his gaze hooded, his breathing ragged. Her green eyes were wide and startled, her face flushed, and he felt her perfect body tremble beneath him, as if she was afraid.

She was saying no. She didn't want this. Why the hell did he?

She'd completely and utterly disarmed him and anger lashed through him, furious with Rebekah—and himself—for still wanting her. After all, spending one night with her had led to his life being in tatters. Why was he willing to do it again? But there was no way he'd take her if she wasn't willing. He wasn't a monster.

His face grim, his jaw set, he tore his mouth away from temptation, withdrawing his body from hers, launching himself off the bed and backing away, disgusted with himself for being so weak. He carved his hand through his hair as he watched her pull herself up to a sitting position, her shaking hands smoothing her hair back into its braid.

A memory filtered back to him of that night, of her lying naked in his arms, when she'd said she hadn't wanted to leave him and yet he'd told her she must go. He'd been the strong one. He'd been determined to ask her Uncle Cynerik for her hand in marriage, but in the meantime, he had been concerned about her—in case she'd been found there, in his home, in his bed, before they'd made their relationship legitimate.

To think he'd been the one worried about *her* reputation!

Had she ever intended to marry him, or was she just a tease? Would she really have wanted to be a poor man's wife, given her privileged upbringing and status? He had known a prospective husband had to pay money or give land for a lady's hand in marriage and he'd had nothing to give. But he had decided he would spend his life saving for her bride price somehow. He had thought she'd been worth every silver bullion he could find in the world. He had thought she was special.

The way his body reacted to her was dangerous. It had got him into trouble before and, if that kiss had proved anything, it could get him into trouble again. What had he been thinking? He still could not trust her. And he damn well couldn't trust himself around her.

'You're right. There's no need to prove my point any further. I think we've already determined what you're like, Rebekah—you'll burn up for anyone, a Saxon peasant, a lord, or even a Northman.'

Chapter Three

Rebekah watched Rædan storm out of the tent, pressing her fingers to her swollen lips, a sob rising in her throat. She had thought she'd never see him again, let alone kiss him again! She sank back down on the bed, stunned by what had just happened, how easily she'd let him take her in his arms, even after the shocking events of today. But she had gone up in flames at his persuasive touch and she'd *wanted* him to hold her. She'd even challenged him to do so. And when his mouth had crashed down on hers, it had been so carnal, so possessive—it had felt so right. She hadn't experienced these feelings for years—not since the night she'd conceived her child.

Rebekah wrapped her arms around her stomach. The touch of her Saxon Lord caused her pain. It made her crumble, as if reducing her to ashes, yet this Northman's touch set her ablaze. How could it be that she still wanted him, like that, after all these years? After all that she'd suffered at the hands of men? And yet when he'd held her to his heated body, tumbling her on to the bed and rearing over her, she'd stiffened in shock and panic. She'd been afraid.

She would be a fool if she hadn't detected the anger simmering beneath his passion. She couldn't be sure why he was kissing her. What were his motives? What would he use her for?

Thank goodness she'd had the sense to stop this time. Would he have continued if she hadn't?

Rædan didn't realise the night she'd spent with him before had impacted her whole life. It had had consequences he didn't know about. She'd realised she didn't know anything about him either, not any more, so she'd hastily pushed him away. And the disdain and judgement that had blazed in his glittering grey eyes as he'd looked down at her lying beneath him had been chilling.

Yet, if he hated her, why had he brought her here? Did he really mean to use her as a way to get revenge on Atol? If that was the case, he would have just taken her when he'd had the chance. He was far stronger than her, after all. But when she'd told him to stop, he hadn't used force, not like her Saxon Lord.

She should have been relieved that Rædan had stopped kissing and touching her, that he'd left the tent, leaving her alone with her misery, but a part of her was also scared to let him out of her sight, afraid he might disappear again. And she wondered—if she'd stayed with him that night all those years ago, might he never have left? If she'd kept a grip on him, and they'd gone to see her uncle together, might she have been able to prevent Lord Atol from sending him away, like Rædan had told her he'd done?

She still didn't understand exactly what had happened between him and Atol. How he'd made Rædan leave. And had he really done it so he could claim her for himself? She realised now that he had. She didn't know why she'd doubted Rædan, it was exactly the kind of thing Atol was capable of.

She sat up straight, willing her strength to come back to her, for she knew she must go in search of the boy she'd once known, a Saxon turned Dane. She still hadn't got all the answers she craved, just a passionate kiss that had left her breathless and achingly unsatisfied, wondering where it had all gone so wrong. So she'd have to be brave.

She had just one night with this man to uncover what had really happened between them and, if they both explained, perhaps they could part ways in the morning having learned the answers they needed to put the past behind them. She knew she could never be happy, not in this life that had been forced upon her, but knowing the details of why Rædan had left might just give her some peace.

Drumming up some of her courage that had brought her here in the first place, she willed herself to her feet. She exited the shelter and a burst of cold air hit her. She shivered, pulling the blanket tighter around her shoulders. More tents had now been erected and groups of Northmen sat around campfires, talking and laughing.

She approached apprehensively, searching for Rædan among the crowds, and a number of warriors turned to look in her direction over the glowing flames. She nearly lost her nerve and was about to head back to the shelter, when one of the men with half a shaven head stood to greet her.

'I'm looking for Rædan. Have you seen him?' she asked.

The man smirked, coming towards her, looking like trouble, and his friend joined his side. Then another. 'You mean Halfdan? That's his name, you know,' the ringleader jeered.

Unwittingly, she seemed to have sparked their interest, as other men began to rise to their feet, all surrounding her, leering, while she tried to back away, the cold feeling of dread trickling through her. Some were short, some tall, but all of them were well built, inked and wild-looking, and every one of them was stronger than her. Plus, she was defenceless—she'd left her sword back at the fortress.

Fear crept into her heart as they closed in on her, beginning to push her between them, bandying her about, laughing at the sport they were creating, delighted to have a woman in their midst. She wrapped her arms around her waist, wishing she'd never left her tent. She certainly did not want to inspire any feelings of desire in these pagan warriors—she knew what brutes men could be. Lord Atol's ruthless treatment of her in the bedroom had made her fearful of a man's touch.

In blind panic she tried to escape, but every

which way she turned she came up against a huge, solid male body. One of them grabbed her by the wrist, the next pulled her into his arms—and she instinctively kneed him in the groin. He doubled over in pain and the rest of the men snorted and laughed derisively. When she was grabbed by the hair, she gasped, wild with panic, trying to struggle out of the man's grasp, staggering around, feeling helpless.

Suddenly, one of the men was wrenched backwards and Rædan was there, stabbing his sword into the ground, looking furious, and all eyes turned to stare at him. 'Stand down!' he roared, storming inside their circle and gripping Rebekah by the arm. She almost wilted in relief.

'*Ekki spilla skemmtun okkar.* We're just having a little fun here, Halfdan,' the one with flinty eyes who'd started it all said. 'She's quite a prize. Surely you're not going to keep her all to yourself?'

'No one is to lay a hand on her.' Calm, cold rage laced Rædan's voice.

'I thought we had a rule of no captives, no slaves? Now that we have one among us, you can't expect us not to play with her, just a little?'

'Which is exactly why we have that rule,' Rædan bit.

'So it's all right for you to break it?'

'Are you challenging my orders, Ogden?' His voice was lethal.

'I'm just wondering why you get to have all the fun. You can't expect us to come all this way only to leave the fortress without any spoils of our own? The men won't stomach leaving for home empty-handed.'

'Of course not, which is why I have secured us a going-away gift from the Saxons. The gold we won is to be taken back to our Jarl. But, Erik, fetch the silver we claimed from Ryestone today. Distribute it between all the men—after all, they've earned it.' He looked around from man to man. 'You shall all be well rewarded for your efforts today.' And then he turned back to Ogden. 'It should be more than enough to satisfy your desire for *spoils...*'

Erik brought out the coinage and the men crowded him, their interest greedily shifting from the woman to the treasure, wanting to check the purity and weigh out their portion. When their backs were turned, Rædan took Rebekah by the elbow and, seeming incensed, he roughly led her away from the group, heading towards the boats.

'What the hell do you think you're doing

wandering around camp? It's not safe for you out here.' Was he angry with his men, or her? Well, she was just as livid!

'So it seems—not safe from your men…and not safe from you either!' she retorted, trying to mask how shaky she felt.

He stopped abruptly and turned to her. 'I won't touch you again, you have my word.' His face was grim, his eyes full of regret as they met hers.

She felt a slight deflation in her chest and told herself it was relief, not disappointment. His full lips had been firm as they'd come crashing down on her mouth and she hated to admit it, but it had felt so good to discover that this man still desired her. Was that why she'd goaded him? But even more shocking was that, in that moment, she had *wanted,* too. Even though Rædan was now her enemy. She had never thought she'd want a man like that again. She had thought Lord Atol had put her off for life.

She tried to steady her breathing, taking in the view of the moon shining down on the gently lapping water, the outline of the large, intimidating longships at odds with the familiar tranquil scene.

He raked a hand over his beard. 'And I'm sorry. About my men. Are you hurt?'

She shook her head. 'No.'

'They're not all like that.'

'No?'

'No. They're just frustrated—mainly with me because I halted the fighting today. They took it out on you.'

At least he had got them back under control. She could tell he had their respect—she'd seen him in action today, on the battlefield, and how they'd dropped their weapons on his command. He was obviously a great leader as well as a great warrior. She imagined he and his men would have grown close on long voyages such as theirs and yet he was keeping his distance from them now. A lone wolf in the pack. Why was that? she wondered.

They approached one of the ships moored on the shore and he dropped her arm and threw himself up and into the vessel in one swift move. He stood at the prow, staring down at her on the bank, as if debating something. His lips twisted. 'It's bad luck to have a woman on board a ship. It angers the gods.'

She gave him a suspicious stare. 'Since when do you believe in the gods?' Determined to confound him, she took hold of the rope on the side of the ship, assessing how best to ascend it. 'Luckily for me, I don't…' And she began to attempt to clamber up. 'I think I'd rather take my chances with them rather than your men.'

He sighed, resigned, and, reaching forward, he gripped her arm, tugging her up towards him into the boat. His touch triggered another ripple of awareness through her body, but this time, he was quick to release her, stepping backwards, putting some distance between them.

'I'm aware I've put you at risk, bringing you here.'

'Then why did you leave me alone?'

'You know why,' he said, his heated gaze meeting hers. 'But I will make sure no harm comes to you tonight.'

Then she was safer than most nights at Ryestone, she thought bitterly.

'How? Are you planning to stay awake all night and keep watch over me?'

'It wouldn't be the first time,' he muttered beneath his breath.

'What?' Goose pimples prickled along her arm.

'Nothing.'

Looking around the ship, she thought it was

impressive. Made out of raw timber, it was big enough to seat thirty or more men quite comfortably. And she realised from their position on the boat, he had a good view of her shelter. He would have been watching as she'd left the tent and spoken to his men round the fire, which explained how he'd reached her so quickly.

Standing there, staring at him now, she took in the wolf pelt around his neck and watched as he pushed up his sleeves before folding his arms over his chest, and her gaze dropped to his wrists, taking in more of the swirls of ink that were etched there. They were all new, she thought, just like the deep scar to his face. She opened her mouth to ask him about it, wondering how he'd got it, what he'd been through, but bit her lip. She shouldn't ask. As he'd told her earlier—he was none of her concern.

The atmosphere was tense between them and she struggled for something to say.

'These ships are even bigger up close than I thought,' she said. She could see how their narrow bottoms allowed them to travel along rivers and pull up easily on to land, making for a speedy attack and quick getaway.

'They're fit for purpose.'

'And what is that—more raids and conquests?'

He slanted her a look of contempt and she
instantly regretted attacking him again. She
sat down opposite him on one of the sturdy
benches, keeping her arms and legs tucked in,
away from him, scared of her reaction when
they touched.

'So you didn't take Cynerik's silver, but
you do ransack Saxon fortresses. How many
of these raids have you been on?' she asked.

'A few.'

'And you enjoy it?'

He shrugged. 'I do it for the glory.'

She could tell that was important to him—
that his pride ruled him. She could see it in
the way he held himself—tall, impressive and
controlled. She didn't remember him caring so
much about that before. Did he feel as if he had
something to prove?

'So—you attack, take treasure and return to
wherever it is you've come from a rich man?'

'I'm not rich—I've never cared for coin,
like *some*.' Did he mean her, or his men? She
couldn't be sure. 'Back home, I more often
carry a scythe, not a sword.'

Surprise had her raising her eyebrows. 'And

was that true, what you said to your men—that you don't take Saxons to sell as slaves?'

'Of course it's true.' His eyes turned to shards of ice—and she shivered. 'It is one rule I have about these raids. No thralls. That term was non-negotiable when the men agreed to come with me.'

'So what am I?'

'A Lady who offered to come here,' he reminded her.

She swallowed. 'It's just that we've heard of pagan raiders, like you, ransacking Saxon fortresses and taking people as well as jewels and gold.'

'Then they're not like us, are they? We don't. You know, Saxons are not innocent when it comes to trading slaves, either,' he said darkly.

Her eyes narrowed on him. 'Do you think this raiding is a good way to earn your way in the world?'

'I do it to see the world, to discover new lands and make a name for myself.'

'But you've seen this place before… What do you intend to do with the land Atol will give you? Why do you want it?' she said, gripping her hands together tightly in her lap, needing to know what his intentions were.

She had heard accounts of Northmen raiding Saxon lands and then not leaving, but instead staying to create settlements. Is that what he was planning? It would cause a lot of hostility if Rædan and his men did that. And it would tie her up in knots, seeing him every day. She had noticed how he'd asked for his old land back. How had Lord Atol not put two and two together?

'I haven't decided yet…'

'The Ghost, Draug, Halfdan…' she said. 'Why do the men have so many names for you? Why do they call you that?'

'You ask a lot of questions.' He sighed. 'Half-dan—it means half-Dane.'

She shook her head again in disbelief. 'I don't understand. How did you become one of them?' She had always hated their kind, especially after what had happened to her parents. And yet, she had once known this man better than anyone. What had happened to change him? Why had he chosen to be one of them, forgetting his Saxon origins?

Then a thought struck her. Had *he* been with other women? Her heart lurched. But of course he would have! It had been eight years. He was far too attractive, far too red-blooded to have remained unattached. Was there someone waiting for him back at home, wherever that was? A pit emptied in her stomach. And then another thought lanced her. Did he have a family of his own?

'I needed to start afresh and there's nowhere else quite like Nedergaard, with its towering mountains and deep blue waters. You can be who you want to be there.'

She had the feeling he was rushing through the past eight years, missing out all the important facts. But wasn't she an expert at leaving out vital chunks of information herself? Guilt rushed through her blood at the truth she was keeping from him.

'And you wanted to be a Dane?'

His slow smile at her question, his silver gaze burning into hers, made her stomach flip over. 'Is that so bad?' His wicked grin had always made her breathless.

'You know what happened to my parents…'

His face fell. 'I remember. But not all Danes are like that.'

'Didn't you prove today that they are?'

'Isn't it right to fight back if you've been dishonoured? My pride was ruling my sword today. Atol deserved it.'

'What about everyone else in the fortress? They're dispensable, I suppose?' If only he knew what precious cargo lay behind the walls of that fortress—would he still have attacked? And what about her? Would he have cared if she'd been hurt? She knew he tarred her and Atol with the same brush of betrayal and she hated it. It had her conceding. 'But you're right. If Atol banished you from your home because of me, he probably deserved it.' She didn't want Rædan to think she was like her Lord.

His dark brows rose in surprise. 'You're agreeing with me?'

'I know how heartless he can be. I loved my uncle—very much—'

'He's dead?' Rædan interrupted.

'Yes.' She nodded. 'He died not so long after you left, within weeks of your father. It was a terrible time,' she said solemnly.

'That must have been hard on you,' he said, his voice strained.

'I cared for him and the marriage was one of his last wishes before he passed. I thought you had been killed, Rædan. I did what I had to do to survive…'

She saw his hands stiffen, his long fingers

curl up on his thighs. 'I'm sure a life of privilege has been tough to endure.'

'I have certainly had to endure,' she said hotly, rising off the bench. 'You have no right to judge me. You weren't here.'

'You wouldn't know the meaning of suffering,' he growled.

'You're wrong. I have suffered at the hands of Atol's brutality many times.'

He went rock-still. 'He does not please you?' he asked, incredulous.

'No! He hurts me!'

Rædan let out a violent curse, anger clouding his features, and he rose to his feet to meet her.

Feeling unsteady, and so acutely aware of his nearness, she lowered herself back down on to the bench, so that she didn't have to look into his eyes. 'His temper is uncertain. Some Saxon men think that their women deserve to be beaten regularly...unfortunately, he is one of them.'

But she'd take the beatings over his unwanted attentions any day.

There were many times at night when Lord Atol had come to her, expecting her to fulfil her duties. It had started just after they'd announced their engagement. He came to her room late at night, but she'd rejected his advances, saying they should wait until they were wed. It had been just a fortnight since Rædan had disappeared and she was still heartbroken, grieving her loss—she couldn't bear the thought of anyone touching her bar him. But Atol had become angry and forced her backwards into the room, locking the door before dragging her over to the bed. Bile rose in her throat at the memory, even now.

She should have told her uncle, but it was around the time he had grown ill. And just weeks later, she had discovered she was with child. Atol had promised her marriage, legitimacy for her baby, but when her uncle died, none of that had come to fruition. Yet Atol would still take her whenever he wanted her, whether she liked it or not. And she definitely did not. She'd shut her eyes and try to block out the pain, a sick, empty feeling churning in her stomach when his sweaty hands roamed over her cold skin.

He'd made her his mistress, shaming her, having the power over her and her daughter anyway. They were his to do what he wanted with. At least thus far, she had managed to keep ownership of her title, if not her body.

After he'd taken her, Atol would often laugh and tell her that if she bore him a son, a male heir, he would honour his promise and wed her, but no other child had come along and she was grateful for that one small mercy.

It was ironic that she had put up with it all because she'd hoped he would be a good father. But even today, Atol had shown how little he cared for her or Gytha—he had willingly allowed a Northman to take her, as if he was throwing a piece of meat to a hungry dog. They were merely possessions for him to rule over.

Rædan took a step towards her. 'I should have killed him today when I had the chance.' His voice was thick, raw, and his smoke-grey eyes had darkened in fury.

'But you're not that kind of man?' She had seen the way he fought. It was lethal. When had he learned to fight like that? They both knew he could have killed Lord Atol there and then and had his revenge. Why hadn't he?

'Don't presume to know anything about me, Rebekah. Not any more.'

She winced. His words hurt, but he was right. She mustn't believe he was still the boy she'd once cared for. That would be foolish. They'd both changed and moved on.

She gripped her hands tightly in her lap.

'I did think about it,' he relented. 'The gods know I wanted to kill him. Yet in that moment, I felt an honourable death in battle was too good for him. It wouldn't be nearly enough suffering.' He raked a hand over his hair. 'Although it sounds like killing him would have made life a lot easier for you. Are you telling me you're not safe at Ryestone?'

'Apart from today?' she asked sardonically. And then she softened. 'He frightens me,' she said, gently shrugging one slender shoulder. 'He didn't always. At first, I thought he was kind, then he was cruel. He scares me even more now I know he sent you away. I knew he was hateful, but I didn't realise he was so corrupt, so capable of destroying someone's life for his own gain.'

Bravely, she reached over and placed her hand on his arm. 'Rædan, you must believe I didn't know anything about him wanting to send you away from here.'

He flinched at her touch and pain lanced her heart. She could not work him out. One moment he was kissing her so passionately, so desperately, as if his life depended on it, stealing her breath away, the next he was hostile, shrinking away from her. Did he regret kissing her? Yes, that was it. She could tell that he did. And she felt a lump grow in her throat.

Even though he withdrew his arm, his steady silver eyes held her gaze, penetrating her soul, and finally, he gave a curt nod, accepting what she was telling him.

'I believe you.'

Her heart lifted, just a little. She knew it didn't mean he had forgiven her for becoming engaged to Atol so soon after he'd gone, but it was a start.

'It's been a long day. I think you should get some rest now, Rebekah, if you are able. You can stay here, if you wish, rather than in the tent,' he said, laying a few animal skins down in the hull of the boat, his arm brushing against her knees, making her pin them together to quell the sudden, peculiar heat that had shot between her legs. 'It's going to be a dry night after the rain this afternoon.' And then he glanced up at her. 'Are you afraid now, with me?'

'I can't begin to understand your actions today, but despite that, I know you won't hurt me,' she said quietly.

'Good.'

'Where will you sleep?' she asked.

'I don't…sleep much.'

He motioned for her to make herself comfortable and, suddenly bone-achingly weary, she decided to do as she was told. She would probably need all her energy and strength to face whatever tomorrow would bring. There were bound to be more negotiations, more memories and emotions dragged to the surface…but she hoped no more fighting.

She laid herself down beneath the furs and stared up at the night sky. She had spoken the truth—she wasn't afraid he would hurt her, but she was afraid of the desire tearing through her body every time he came near… And lying there, under the watchful gaze of the stars and the Danish warrior with silver eyes, she was afraid of the things she had done, the secrets she had kept, all because of him.

Chapter Four

Rebekah, wrapped up in warm furs, woke to feel the sun shining down on her. She could hear the gentle lapping of water, the feeling that they were gliding. Was she still dreaming? No, she could feel the ocean breeze on her face, taste the sea air on her lips. She couldn't believe she'd managed to fall asleep, surrounded by all these Northmen, but then, she'd always known she could trust Rædan not to hurt her, even when he tried to break through the fortress wall yesterday…

She sat bolt upright, her thoughts suddenly hitting her. Sea air. Ocean breeze. Gliding on water… In dismay, she realised she was still on the boat—and to her horror, she saw the ships were moving. *Leaving.* They were no longer on land. They had travelled about a mile and were heading out to where the river emptied into the estuary.

In a flash of panic, Rebekah went to throw herself over the side of the boat, with no care for how cold or deep the water was, or how far she was from the shore. But Rædan was too quick—as if he'd expected this. His strong arms came around her, pulling her backwards.

'What are you doing?' she gasped, shocked again by his searing touch, the feeling of being back in his arms, but at the same time struggling against his hold. 'You promised you'd take me back…'

'I changed my mind.' His breath was warm against her cheek.

'You can't! I trusted you!' she said, despair and anger charging through her. 'Where are we going? Where are you taking me?' She was aware his men were watching, amusement in their eyes, but all the time rowing, each powerful stroke of the oars putting more distance between her and Ryestone.

Between her and her child.

'I'm leaving this place. For good. I'm never coming back.'

And he intended to take her with him? Panic exploded in her chest. No! This could not be happening. She began to lash out, struggling in his arms, but he held her fast, his large muscles straining to keep her under his control. 'What about the land you wanted? What about the deal we struck?'

He spun her around, gripping on to her shoulders. 'I never cared about that.'

Then what did he care about? Exasperated, fraught, she tried to calm herself, to take in a breath. 'Rædan, why are you doing this? What's in it for you?' Did he want to take her simply to enact the revenge he seemed so set on? 'I can't leave! I can't go with you. Please, you have to take me back!'

'To him? You want to go back to him?' he asked incredulously. His face was so close— and suddenly mutinous. 'When you told me that he *hurts* you?'

Was that what this was about? Did he think he was rescuing her? Surely not. He didn't care about her, not any more.

'There's something you don't understand,' she said, wringing her hands, making every effort to free herself from his hold, but his large hands were like an anchor, holding her in place.

'And you're not understanding either. Can't you see I've put you in danger? What do you think Atol will do to you when you return, knowing you've spent the night with me?'

She struggled against his hold, trying to resist his tight restraint. Yes, he was strong, but so was her determination. 'It's not your fault. I'll tell him nothing happened!' She was so worked up, and the nearness of his warm body, his intoxicating leather scent, wasn't helping.

'Don't you know by now what kind of man he is? Have you not been listening to anything I've said?'

'Yes, I know what kind of man he is,' she said, suddenly furious, desperately trying to free herself from his grip one last time. 'More than most. Which is why I can't leave her!' she said, her hands attempting to push him away, to escape his hold.

'Who?'

'My child!'

He released her then, so suddenly she toppled backwards, and his stricken face was more than she could bear. The shock in his eyes slayed her. She might as well have rammed a knife into his chest. Casting her usual good judgement aside, in her total despair, she saw her chance and took a risk. She threw herself over the edge of the boat and plunged beneath the deep water, desperate to get away from the hurt and censure on his face.

Thrashing her hands, she attempted to swim to the shore. But she hadn't counted on the strong tidal current, the icy coldness of the water and the heavy weight of her clothes. In a panic, she realised she wasn't swimming, she was sinking.

'Helvete!'

She heard Rædan swear from behind her. And in one swift move he threw himself in after her. When he emerged from underneath the deep water beside her, his face was livid. He gripped her waist firmly with one arm, supporting her body, pulling her into his hard muscles, and he showed her how to move her arms with his other.

'Move your arms, like this,' he barked.

And to her surprise, it worked. It was an effort, but with his help, they made for the nearest bank together. Passing through the reeds in the shallows, he pulled her on to the sandy shore, both of them panting harshly, trying to catch their breath, his arm still wrapped around her.

'Are you all right?'

She wasn't sure. Betrayal ripped through her that he had dared to take her away against her will. How could he? And what would she be—his concubine? But she was also angry at herself that she'd been foolish enough to throw herself into the water—and shocked that he'd rescued her! Now she was freezing and her whole body was trembling, her breathing ragged, and his large hand, smoothing over her back, stroking her through the wet silk of her dress, was only serving to make her feel more shaky.

'I'm fine,' she lied, jerking herself away from him, pulling herself up to sit on the sand, trying to squeeze out the material at the bottom of her dress.

He curled his big body up and came to sit beside her, wiping the water out of his eyes. 'What the hell, Rebekah?' he said gently, casting her a sideways glance. 'What were you thinking, jumping overboard when you can't even swim? You could have drowned!' he berated her, running his fingers over his long hair, tying it back up into a band.

With her chin to her chest, her arms wrapped around her shivering body, they sat in silence amid the whispering reedbeds. She had almost been separated from her child. A child he'd known nothing about. And now she knew there would be questions. Questions she wasn't sure how to answer.

'I can't leave her. I won't,' she said eventually.

He nodded. 'I'm sorry,' he said. 'I didn't know you had a child.'

And he thought it was all right to take her from here if she hadn't?

But a giant lump formed in her throat. She didn't want his apology, for she knew she was also in the wrong—and a prickle of guilt edged along her skin.

'She's all I have in the world. My *only* happiness.'

The water was still, calm, and she realised so much had passed between her and Rædan— how had it all gone so terribly wrong? Now it was over. He was a Northman and she was a Saxon. She couldn't go with him! She couldn't leave. She had a child. And he couldn't stay—

The shouting of his men interrupted her thoughts. 'Halfdan, we have to go. Now.'

She glanced up to see the expanse of water that lay before them and the fleet of ships was growing ever wider. Yet Rædan still sat by her side. She felt a pang of panic. Did he need to go? Was he about to leave her for the second time? She blinked furiously as her eyes filled with tears she didn't understand.

He drew a hand over his face, as if to gather himself together.

'Keep going. I'll catch up with you. I'll meet you at the peninsula,' he shouted back.

Rebekah's head swung round to look at him.

'The tides won't wait,' his men yelled back.

'I know, I'll be there.'

And they both sat and watched as the ships continued on their way to the estuary, leaving them behind. Why wasn't he leaving? What was he thinking?

'How old is she?' he asked finally, his hands raking into the sand at his sides.

'She's seven.'

His brow furrowed.

The whole world seemed to close in on her. When she'd found out she was with child, she couldn't be sure who the father was. It had been just a fortnight between her evening with Rædan and the night Atol had first forced himself upon her. But when the baby was born early, Rebekah had realised she must be Rædan's daughter. And when she'd seen the curve of Gytha's mouth, the straight line of her nose, it had further confirmed her suspicions. Her child had been created from love after all.

She knew Rædan deserved to know the truth—that he was a father. But if she told him now, it would have consequences. She couldn't be sure how he'd react or what he would do… and what good would it do anyway? He was leaving. This wild, fierce warrior wouldn't want to take up his fatherhood duties. And if he did, he might want to claim Gytha for himself.

Would he even consider taking Gytha away from her? She couldn't risk it. And what kind of example would he be anyway, after yesterday? Gytha must already have a warped sense of what men were like—she'd been at the end of Atol's harsh words too many times.

And how would her daughter feel, knowing her mother had misled her? How could she now turn to her and say your father isn't Lord Atol after all, but the Northman who raided our home and took me hostage? No, telling the truth now would only hurt everyone involved… She should stay quiet.

'Rædan, when you were gone… When you were sent away…' she corrected herself. Her voice didn't sound real. 'I felt so alone. I thought you were dead and life wasn't worth living for a while.'

'So you found comfort in Lord Atol's arms…' he said darkly.

She shook her head fiercely. 'Uncle Cynerik planned the arranged marriage and I wasn't myself after you left. I didn't care what happened to me, so I agreed. But Atol didn't want to wait for the wedding to…to…'

His eyes narrowed on her.

'When I discovered I was with child—it was the first joy I'd felt in a long while. There was hope again.'

'Damn it, Rebekah, why are you telling me this? Do you think I want to know the sordid details of what happened between the two of you?'

'You're not listening…'

'I am. I understand,' he said, launching himself to his feet, as if he didn't want to hear her words. 'You thought I was dead and Atol showed you some attention. You let him put a baby in your belly. I hear what you're saying. Loud and clear.' His voice was laced with disgust.

She gasped. 'I didn't *let* him do anything! I would have chosen the beatings over the other things he made me do. Things I didn't *want* to,' she said, not meeting his eyes. She'd never told anyone what Atol had done to her and the words felt shameful on her tongue. 'He forced himself upon me time and time again.'

She saw Rædan reel, but she couldn't stop now. She'd had to suffer it, so he had to hear it. 'You were gone. My uncle was ill and then he died. All freeing Atol up to behave how he liked,' she said. 'And when a daughter came along, he decided he would only marry me on the condition that I produced a *male* heir, not before.'

Her eyes bore into him, willing him to understand, as he stood there, his slate-grey gaze staring down at her, his hands on his hips, letting this new information wash over him, sink in. Finally, he shook his head. 'Is there no end to this man's cruelty?' he whispered.

Over the years, she'd started to believe that perhaps she deserved it, wondering if she had brought this punishment upon herself, for concealing the truth about her child's true father.

She tried to focus on the sunlight dappling the trees, the fish making ripples on the water, thinking that any decision she made now would have a rippling effect, too...

'I have tried to summon the courage to leave Ryestone many times and take my child with me,' she said, tilting her chin up to look at him. 'But Atol has always said if I attempted to leave and shame him, he'd hunt me down and take her away, and make sure I never see her again. I have often hoped he would father a son with one of his many other women, thinking that might change things, but he hasn't.'

Rædan paced along the sand, before coming back to her. 'Was your child in the hall yesterday?'

'Yes.'

'Dammit, I'm sorry.' He took a deep breath. 'What's her name?'

'Gytha.'

'Gytha,' he said, trying the name out on his tongue.

'It means gift. You were gone and she was to be the only good thing left in my life.' *A part of him.* 'I wanted my baby, badly, and I knew I had to give her a good life.'

'And is it?' he asked, his voice strained. 'A good life?'

Rebekah chewed her bottom lip, thinking how Atol barely had time for Gytha, having wanted a son, not a daughter. And yet lately, he had begun to think about Gytha's potential use to him, talking about finding a suitable husband for her for his own political gain, to strengthen his power. And Rebekah had been horrified. Gytha was far too young to be promised to a man. The thought of her daughter having to put up with the same mistreatment Rebekah had had to endure in just a few years' time was too much.

Rædan must have seen the dark thoughts cross her face and he swore again.

'He is cold towards her. He wants to use her for his own gain…'

The silence stretched as he took in all that she had told him.

Finally, he came back down to sit beside her on the river bank, at a distance. 'Why are you telling me all this? Why now, Rebekah?'

'When was I meant to tell you?' she said, her anger flaring. Was it wrong that she had wanted him to know him leaving had caused her pain, to explain to him what her life had been like since? 'Should I have waited till after you'd kidnapped me and sailed me across the ocean?'

'I was trying to protect you! Now listen to me very carefully, as I'm about to tell you what's going to happen next.' His hand reached out to take her chin in his fingers, turning her face towards his. 'I'm leaving for Nedergaard today and I will be taking you and Gytha with me.'

Rebekah stared into his beautiful grey eyes and gasped.

'You would be so heartless as to take my child away from her home?' she said, shocked, pulling away from him, getting to her feet.

'A home where she's not happy. You've just said so yourself. And by the sound of it, a home where she has to see her mother be mistreated, with a similar fate in store for her in the not-too-distant future. The alternative is that you can choose to return to Lord Atol—I'm sure he'll enjoy making you his again after thinking you spent the night with me.'

She reeled at his cruel words. How could he say such things? Yet she knew he was right. She'd known, since the moment she had agreed to spend the night with the Northman, that Atol would enjoy tormenting her when she returned. Even though nothing had happened, even though she'd saved her Saxon Lord's life, he would see her offering herself up to another man as a betrayal of him and he'd punish her for it. It was all a game to him. She'd learned over the years her protests just made things worse.

And the thought of going back to him, and putting up with more of the same—living every night in fear that he would come to her, hurt her again—made her feel nauseous. But what Rædan was suggesting was crazy. Although perhaps she should have predicted his response, knowing how much he despised Atol. He would know this would wound the Saxon Lord's pride and reputation more than anything else he could do. But it would also provoke his fury. He would no doubt come after them. Gytha was far too valuable an asset.

'You think you can just take her from Atol? And take me, too? He would never let it lie... He will hunt us, track us down. He thinks we belong to him, like objects...'

'But he doesn't care about you—I saw that for myself. And we'll be halfway across the ocean before he finds out.'

Rebekah couldn't deny that, lately, she had started to feel more concerned for her daughter's future. Gytha was growing up so fast. She was changing—in looks and personality. And it was bittersweet. Rebekah was aware that if Lord Atol ever discovered her secret, both their lives would be in danger. It played on her mind constantly. But what if Rædan was to discover the truth, too?

Rebekah stood and tried to shake out her wet hair and focus her thoughts, to think clearly. She had dreamed of this day for years—that Rædan would come back to her and steal her away from this place. Wasn't this the rescue she'd always desired? Only now she couldn't be sure of his reasons. Was this just fulfilling his great plan of revenge?

'What's in it for you?' she asked, her eyes narrowing on him.

He shrugged. 'I know what you're thinking and, yes, it would please me to cause injury to Atol. It's what I came here for after all. But there's also no way I can leave you or your daughter in the hands of that man for a moment longer.'

Did he really care about their safety? She might have known him once, but now he was practically a stranger. She couldn't be sure of his motives. She knew she couldn't trust him, not completely, as he had abandoned her once before and not looked back. So could she and Gytha really travel across the sea with him, to some foreign land, with ninety-odd Northmen? It was madness. What if he let them down again? She shouldn't even be considering it. And yet she was shocked to realise she was...

She wrung her hands. 'What's it like—where you've come from?'

Her question seemed to ease his determination a little and he steadied his voice. 'It's beautiful, as I told you last night. The sun stays up all day long in the summer. And the people are warm, kind.'

'I saw how kind they could be yesterday...' she said.

'Some men are warriors, yes. They want to make a name for themselves. Conquer lands. Many are also good, honest farmers, or traders. Some are all of the above, like me.'

'And what would happen when we get there? If we come with you, how will we be treated?'

Would they be safe?

'You will be safe under my protection.'

'As your mistress or your slave?' she bit. 'What should we expect—iron collars and shackles?'

The strangest, starkest look crossed his face and she shivered. She instantly knew she'd said the wrong thing. 'I would never do that,' he said, his words like acid.

'And how should I know what you would

or wouldn't do? As you said last night, I don't *know* you now. And I've seen what your people are capable of.'

'You know me well enough to know I wouldn't hurt you—or your daughter.'

She glanced away, hugging herself tighter. She knew what he was saying was true. But what would she say to Gytha? She'd taught her daughter to be afraid of these men. How could she tell her they were going to sail away to a distant isle and live with them? No, she couldn't. Yet she did want Gytha to know her real father.

But what would Rædan say when he saw her? Would he take one look at the child and know she was his? Would he ever forgive her from keeping the truth from him now she finally had the opportunity to reveal it? Yet she knew she must remain silent, at least for now, until she knew the heart of him. Deep down, she had longed for Rædan to meet their child. Wasn't that only right?

At that moment, the sun appeared from behind a cloud, warming her skin and lighting up a path across the water. Perhaps she did want to take her daughter away from this place. Her future seemed bleak if they were to stay. And there was no love lost between her and Lord Atol…she couldn't abide his touch any longer. Plus the moment he had a son with another woman, who knew what he would do with the two of them?

Recently, Gytha had started to ask questions about why her mother and father weren't yet wed, why her father was cruel to them both, why he spent some of his nights with other women… If she was honest, her daughter was dreadfully unhappy here and so was she. Could a fresh start, with the Saxon boy she once knew, be the making of them all?

Chapter Five

'What would you say if I said yes?'

Rædan took in a deep, cleansing breath, allowing some of his anger to subside, and rose to his feet to look into her eyes. Was she considering his plan? He lifted her chin up so she was staring into his eyes, meeting her wary green gaze, and his lips curved upwards. 'I'd say that cold water must have knocked some sense into you.'

She swayed slightly on her feet and he caught her by the elbow. 'Are you all right?'

She snatched her arm away from him.

He thought she must be in shock. Well, so was he. When she'd revealed on the boat that she had a child, he'd been stunned, the betrayal hitting him hard, winding him. He had not imagined anything like that—he'd been blindsided once again. Her slender frame hadn't given away any clues of a past pregnancy—how had he missed the signs? He'd felt duped. And his first thought was, *That child should have been mine.*

When he'd realised Rebekah was struggling in the water—that she couldn't swim—he'd dived in after her without thinking. Now she was standing there before him dithering, her dripping hair plastered to her face, her soaking wet dress clinging to her body, highlighting all her curves to him. *Damn.*

He couldn't understand why he felt so protective of her—he didn't want to feel this way. He was still trying to hold on to his anger. It was easier than admitting he might still feel something for her. And it was his feelings that had got him into trouble before. Well, never again. He would have to keep them tightly locked away.

He had felt nauseous at the thought of her lying with Atol, but it turned out Rebekah hadn't been as willing to share Atol's bed as he'd first thought—instead, she had been forced to do so and it sounded as if Atol had hurt her, badly. She had been honest about the suffering she had experienced and it made him sick to think of it.

He should have known Atol would have mistreated her. It wasn't enough that he'd sent Rædan away, banishing him to a life of brutality and subjugation, but he had done it so he could make Rebekah his mistress—and then he'd caused her pain, too? He wished he had rammed his sword through the man when he had the chance.

Things must have been dire if she was willing to leave with him and his men, giving up her status as a Lady, her lands and inheritance to travel to Nedergaard, rather than return home to Ryestone. What lasting damage had that man done to her—and did that have something to do with the way she held her body stiffly away from him and why she'd pulled back from his touch last night?

He felt the sharp stab of guilt at the way he'd behaved, kissing her so fiercely, pressing her down on to the bed... His actions had been out of character for him, as he scarcely wanted a woman these days. And it wasn't for lack of attention—many of the women in Nedergaard showed an interest in him and, on the rare occasions he took one to satisfy a basic need, it was functional, over quickly. He never stayed afterwards—he didn't want to talk, or share intimacies, despite their pleading protests.

With Rebekah, he'd wanted her so badly, kissing her as though his life had depended on it, devouring her lips. It was as if he'd been possessed by the mad, frantic, furious desire of the Norse god Óðr. It had felt incredible, the old attraction once again sparking into life and then burning so brightly between them.

But she must have been afraid of him after the way he'd acted—first storming the fortress, then her!

He'd been too harsh on her, thinking ill of her these past years. He'd been so focused on his own pain, his own experiences, he hadn't stopped to think about what she might have gone through while he'd been away. Looking at Rebekah properly now, for the first time he noticed her skin was pale and she had dark circles beneath her eyes—and he felt like a brute for his treatment of her.

Perhaps their lives hadn't been so different—they'd both been objects of someone else's will. She had loved and lost people, too. He swallowed. He regretted not being here for his father's final days. But he mustn't forget she, too, had lost her parents, her uncle, *him*… But had he even meant anything to her?

He hated the thought of her suffering and he wanted to make it better for her, to put it right, only he wasn't sure how. He could barely deal with his own past traumatic experiences. He felt his feelings warring inside. He was torn between wanting to take Rebekah and her daughter away from this place and its leader, but also thinking they would be better off without him in their life either.

Could he really take them from this life of privilege, in a fortress, to living life on a farm? Could he allow Rebekah to give up her title, for potential shame and ridicule in the future, if she were to ever find out about his past? Perhaps the best thing he could do was to stay away. Yet, there was no way he could allow that man to lay his hands on her again. And it was as if Rebekah had finally decided this, too, if she was prepared to leave with him. And leave he must.

'Do you have your own fortress in Nedergaard?' she asked.

Now he had arrived once more on these shores, he'd realised it was no longer his home. Now he longed for the immense skies and majestic mountains of Daneland. Nedergaard and its beautiful scenery and wonderful people had begun to heal him. Perhaps they could do the same for Rebekah.

'No, Jarl Knud rules there and there are no fortresses, merely farmsteads.'

Rædan would be for ever in Knud's debt for saving his life and for welcoming him into his settlement. When Knud had found him in that slave market, he'd been so close to death. Now he would spend his life trying to repay him. When he'd finally got his health back, he'd learned how to fight, as a way to release his anger, and he'd become Knud's best warrior. He'd focused on getting his revenge and, finally, they'd left for the west. But he had been so set on vengeance, so single-minded in his vendetta to destroy, he hadn't stopped to think about Rebekah's or anyone else's feelings. The lives of others. *Her child.*

He shuddered at what might have happened if his warriors had ransacked the fortress, destroying everything in their path. But what had happened to him in the past had changed him—made him behave like the warriors who had attacked the fortress last night. And he couldn't bring himself to regret it, because if he hadn't done so, he wouldn't be here with Rebekah now, offering to take her away from this godsforsaken place.

'Where would we live? *How* would we live? I would have nothing…' Rebekah trailed off, looking lost.

'When I first arrived there I had nothing, too. Now I have a home, on the shore. It's not like the grand fortress you're used to, with none of the luxuries, none of the servants…but it is more than ample. I have a small farm with animals, I grow my own crops. I have somewhere you and Gytha could stay…'

'But would you want us there? Wouldn't we be in the way?' And then she swung to look at him. 'Is there a woman in your life?'

He gazed down at her, enjoying the pink stains blossoming in her beautiful face. 'No. I decided a long time ago never to marry or have a family.' He refused to be bound to anyone ever again. After everything that had happened to him, all that he'd lost, he'd been reluctant to build relationships. He'd come to realise if you didn't let anyone mean something to you, you couldn't risk getting hurt if you lost them.

She nodded, seemed to release a breath she'd been holding. 'How would we live in such close proximity, when we're practically strangers?'

It would certainly turn his solitary existence upside down. And yet he found himself saying, 'We'll figure it out.'

It would be complicated having Rebekah and her daughter in his life—but what alternative was there?

The first thing they would have to do was stop blaming each other for the past and try to break down some of the mutual distrust between them.

'All right,' she agreed slowly. 'We will come.'

'I'm glad,' he said slowly. 'But from this moment on, we have to be on the same side. We work together.'

She inclined her head. 'So, what do we do now?' she said, cautiously dusting off her sandy hands, giving her something to focus on. 'Your men are leaving and Gytha is in Ryestone, probably still fast asleep.'

'I will have to get her out of the fortress.'

'How?'

'There's always a way.'

'I'll need to come with you, to show you a route in.'

'No,' he said firmly, damp strands of his hair shaking from side to side. 'It's too dangerous. Besides, have you forgotten I used to live there?

I know all the ways in and out, I used to sneak in all the time...'

Her beautiful brow furrowed. 'Why?'

He shrugged a shoulder. 'To check on you.'

The blush in her cheeks began to deepen. 'You could have been killed for doing such a thing!'

'It would have been worth it.'

'E-even so, I'm coming with you,' she stuttered, her stubbornness flaring.

'You're not going anywhere near that man again.'

She took a swift step towards him, prodding him in the chest. 'Another thing we need to get clear. You may have bargained for me as part of your deal last night, but this is where it ends. Lord Atol has exercised his power of ownership over me for eight years. If we come with you, I can't play that role again. I won't.'

She could have taken the words right out of his mouth, for he never wanted to belong to or be controlled by anyone again either. He refused to spend any more time at someone else's disposal. What damage this one man had caused them both!

'We must be equals,' she insisted.

He gripped the finger that was daring to poke him, covering her hand with his.

'Allies.'

And she inclined her head in acknowledgement.

But was it possible?

Her tone softened. 'Rædan, let me come with you. Gytha won't know who you are. Or you her. She will be frightened if a Northman appears in her room and tries to steal her away. You *need* me.'

His dark eyes studied her, his chest burning from her touch. Need was definitely the right word. But if she came with him, he would have to stamp out this desire.

He tried to focus on the task ahead of them. Rebekah's child was only seven years old and he didn't know what she looked like. He didn't know anything about her and the idea that she'd probably take one look at him and be afraid— that she'd hate him at first sight—made his heart slam in his chest. He realised Rebekah was right, he would need her with him.

He gave a curt nod, strangely loath to let go of her hand. 'All right then. We go now, while the fortress is quiet, while they're still asleep. Do you know if that underground sewerage tunnel is still there, the one they used to drain the marshes? It winds beneath the Keep.'

She nodded. 'Yes. But they might be guarding it.'

'Let's find out. We'll need to be quick if we mean to join up with my men before they reach the ocean, but first I want to make a quick stop. I want you to show me my father's grave.'

Rebekah showed Rædan the mound of earth where she'd had his father buried, under the old oak tree. It was a good final resting place, next to his mother. Rædan thought his father would be pleased. He retrieved a small, bejewelled dagger out of his belt and buried it upside down in the soil—the old man had probably had no worldly goods to be buried with him and he might need them in his journey to the afterlife. Better late than never… It felt strange knowing they were resting here and that he'd never be coming back to this island.

After he'd said his final goodbyes, they made their way through the now-abandoned farmsteads, following the route he and his men had taken to the outer fortress walls, keeping among the shadows, darting for cover among the bushes and trees. It was still early and everything was quiet, just a few soldiers standing guard. The Saxons wouldn't be expecting any intruders—the worst had already happened, so at least they had that advantage on their side.

He could hear Rebekah's rapid breathing to the side of him—from the exertion of the uphill climb or because she was nervous, he wasn't sure.

'Try to stay calm,' he whispered.

'Calm? This is my child's life that's at stake.'

He pushed up his sleeves and glanced around the edge of a farm building, scouting out a route to their destination of the old Roman sewerage tunnel.

The truth was, he felt the same trepidation as her—that cool trickle of unease. They were taking a huge risk. So much could go wrong. If they were apprehended by Atol and his men, Rædan would fight. He knew he could best most men in battle, but it was Rebekah he was concerned about. If she was caught with him, she would be seen as a traitor and there was no telling what Atol would do.

He couldn't believe that man had taken her against her will. It made him sick just thinking about it. If he'd been here, that would never have happened. Had she blamed him all these years, the way he'd resented her?

They ran on a little further over the uneven terrain of the farmland, him gripping her elbow, but it was hard being this close to her—he was finding her nearness distracting, heightening his awareness to every sound, every touch. And if he was finding this difficult, what would it be like having her in Nedergaard? Was he making a huge mistake?

Just then, a Saxon guard walked past and every muscle in his body tensed. Rædan ducked behind the hut, pulling Rebekah with him, using his body as a shield, her chest pressing against his. Every time their bodies collided a burning sensation rushed up his skin. Would it always be like this? he wondered. And could he share his simple farmstead with her, feeling this constant pent-up frustration?

Allies, they'd agreed. He would be responsible for their lives, in a position of trust, so he would have to do the right thing and keep his hands in check. Especially as he now knew she had every right to be fearful of a man's touch. But surely it would be torture being around her, knowing he couldn't go near her?

Her breathing was ragged, her cheeks

flushed—was she as aware of him as he was of her?

'Rædan—'

Instinctively, he placed his hand over her mouth to keep her quiet and her green gaze flashed up at him. When he moved it away, he couldn't resist reaching out and taking one of the loose tendrils of her hair and twisting it between his fingers. He'd always loved the colour of her hair. It demanded to be admired, touched. He stared down at her and saw her pulse quicken, her eyes darken. Did he imagine her leaning in ever so slightly? 'I'm sorry about last night. In the tent. I hope I didn't frighten you.'

She frowned. 'Let's just forget about it.'

'Good idea.' He tucked the strand behind her ear, out of his reach, out of temptation. From now on, he would have to suppress his attraction. 'Now when I say, we're going to run as fast as we can across the field to the hidden entrance over there.'

Her eyes followed his viewpoint and she nodded.

'Ready…now.'

He gripped her arm again, moving her with him at speed across the grass, towards the tunnel. Amazingly she managed to keep up with him and as they made it underground, she released herself from his grasp.

'You know, you don't have to manhandle me, I'm perfectly capable of walking by myself! Unless… You think I'm going to make a run for it, don't you?' Rebekah whispered furiously. 'You still don't trust me.'

'Can you blame me?' He didn't trust anyone apart from Jarl Knud.

They both took a moment to catch their breath.

'Now stay behind me,' he commanded. 'It's dark in here and hard to see where you're going.'

'Stop bossing me about,' she hissed. 'You don't need to treat me like a child.'

'I wouldn't know how to treat a child, since I have no experience in that area like you do,' he bit out.

They crept forward and she was silent for a long moment. 'You said you don't want a family of your own. Did you *ever* want one?'

He stopped walking and his abrupt halt caused her to crash into him. She gasped at the meeting of their bodies, her soft curves hitting his back. She muttered a strained apology. He took a deep breath.

'It would have been nice to have had the opportunity.'

All those years ago, he had hoped he and Rebekah would marry and go on to have children of their own. He realised he would need to work on releasing some of the resentment he felt. But now…if he were to have a child, he would no doubt bring shame upon them because of his past. It was one of the reasons why he'd decided not to have any. Plus the way he lived, all his expeditions, didn't exactly lend itself to a life of domesticity and fatherhood.

He wondered how he would feel when he saw Rebekah and Atol's child. Would he be able to warm to Gytha, knowing she was his enemy's flesh and blood? And how would the girl react upon seeing him? She didn't know who he was—would she be afraid?

They hurried down the dark corridor, trying to ignore the vile stench of the thankfully shallow rotten water beneath their feet, towards the steps and access door at the end, and Rædan cocked his ear up to the wood. They could hear footsteps padding along the floor above them and the hairs on the back of his neck stood on end. He reached for the hilt of his sword, apprehension swirling in his stomach. There could be any number of Saxon soldiers on the other side.

When the footsteps retreated, ever so slowly, he pushed up the trapdoor and, on alert, he checked the corridor. It was all clear. 'After you,' he said.

Rebekah tried to heave herself up, but couldn't quite manage it, so he gave her a gentle push, inadvertently curving his hand over the back of her slender calf. *Damn.* He hoisted himself up after her, then closed the door behind them.

'Thank you,' she muttered.

'Are you sure you still want to do this? Last chance to change your mind…'

She nodded, determined. 'We've come this far.'

Rebekah's still-wet skirts swished over the floor as they crept along, leaving a trail of moisture, and glancing back at her, Rædan realised the material was still clinging to her body, enhancing her breasts, her nipples pebble-hard—and he groaned inwardly.

He tried to keep his eyes on the empty corridor ahead, but when she overtook him at the next junction of passageways, showing him the way, he couldn't help but be drawn to her tiny waist and the graceful sway of her hips. The reaction in his lower body was instant. So much for getting his desire in check. This was going to be harder than he thought.

He was relieved they made it to the staircase without being seen and they quietly climbed up the steps. This was the way he'd always used to sneak into Rebekah's room and he remembered there would be a guard waiting at the top. Cupping her shoulder, tugging her back, he placed a finger over his mouth. Dipping his head round the wall at the top, he saw one lone guard manning the corridor.

He signalled to Rebekah to stay put and ever so quickly he startled the guard, knocking him unconscious, holding his body as it slumped down on to the floor. Rebekah staggered back in shock, but he gripped her arm, encouraging her to carry on. 'He'll live,' he reassured her.

He checked all around him for more soldiers, or anyone he might have awoken, but thankfully the people of Ryestone still seemed to be in their beds, probably sleeping off the events of yesterday.

After walking stealthily down another corridor, Rebekah halted by a door. He realised this used to be her room—did it now belong to Gytha? Did Rebekah share with Lord Atol now? His gut twisted. He didn't want to think about that.

'Did you really sneak in here, before?' she whispered, her hand on the doorknob.

'Yes.'

'Why?'

Because he hadn't wanted to let her out of his sight. Because he'd wanted to be with her all the time. 'I used to like to watch you sleeping.'

She swallowed, turning away and pushing open the door.

Rædan noticed she almost wilted in relief at seeing the little body curled up in the blankets, the girl's chest gently rising and falling. They entered the room and he silently shut the door behind them. He moved towards the bed, his heart in his mouth. He really did want to like her…

He stared down at the child and his eyes narrowed. He could feel Rebekah's eyes on him, saw her chewing her bottom lip. He studied the little face, softened in slumber, and he realised she was beautiful—the most extraordinary thing he'd ever seen.

'She looks just like you,' he finally managed to say. From her dark auburn wavy hair to her

long eyelashes resting against the creamy pale-
ness of her skin and her heart-shaped lips, she
was the replica of her mother.

Rebekah nodded. 'People often say that,' she
said, pleased.

If he were ever to have children, would he
want them to be like him? He wasn't sure. He
carried far too much self-loathing...

'You'll have to wake her,' he murmured, 'but
we don't want her crying out in alarm when
she sees me.' It was true what he'd told her in
the tunnel—he didn't have much experience
with children, but he knew he didn't want his
and Gytha's first meeting to be marred by fear.
He didn't want her to be afraid when she saw
him here.

Rædan stalked back to the door, giving them
some space, but he watched as Rebekah tenderly reached out to stroke Gytha's forehead
again, waking her gently, smoothing her auburn hair around her rosy little cheeks. And
as the girl's eyes opened, Rebekah put a finger
to her lips.

Gytha sat bolt upright. 'Mother...' She was
instantly awake and ecstatic to see her, throwing her arms around Rebekah's neck. And
Rædan felt his heart swell. She had her moth-

er's fern-green eyes and she was the most perfect thing he'd ever seen. From her little fingers to her delicate ears, to her pretty rounded face and wide smile—and then he felt the jealousy burn that she wasn't his. *Theirs*.

When Gytha saw Rædan standing over by the door, she gasped.

'It's all right,' Rebekah added quickly. 'This man is an old friend of mine. He won't hurt us.'

'But I saw him in the hall yesterday. He took you away from me.' Her bottom lip wobbled and Rædan hated himself more than ever.

'I volunteered to go,' Rebekah soothed her. 'I'll tell you why, explain it all to you later, but right now, I want you to do exactly as I say. I need you to get up and get dressed. Quickly now. Quietly.'

'What's happening? Where are we going?' the girl asked, but even as she was asking she began to pull on her clothes.

'No questions now. Just do as I ask.'

'You might want to pack a few things,' Rædan said, prompting Rebekah, and she nodded. 'And change, if you can. You can't go around in that wet dress all day.' He really hoped she'd change…he was finding it far too distracting.

Her eyes narrowed on him, but she seemed to heed what he was saying.

The girl was ready first and Rædan and Gytha stood there, by the door, waiting. He pushed himself away from the wood and came down on his haunches in front of her, wanting to put her at ease, but what to say?

'Hello. You're Gytha?'

The child nodded.

'I'm Rædan. It's nice to meet you.'

The girl was understandably wary, seeing this big, fierce warrior in her room. And she bit her bottom lip. 'You don't need to be afraid. I'm not going to hurt you. Do you bite your lip when you're worried?'

She nodded.

'Your mother does that, too.'

'How do you know?'

'Because I've seen her do it many times,' he said.

The little girl frowned. 'When?'

'I've known your mother a very long time. Since she was just a few years older than you are now. We used to go riding together.'

'You were friends?'

'The best.'

The little girl seemed to think about that for

a moment, before accepting it with a nod. How trusting she was. Had he been like that once? Possibly, a long time ago, before his world had been shattered. Now he mistrusted everyone, with the exception of Jarl Knud. And with an ache in his heart, he knew he wanted things to be different for this child. He wanted her to have a better life than the one Rebekah or he had endured.

Still on alert, he checked the corridor again, the door creaking as it opened, and he reached for the hilt of his sword. He knew instantly he would give his life for Gytha and her mother. He would do whatever it took to keep them safe.

Turning around, he saw Rebekah had stepped behind a screen and he heard the heavy cascade of wet material before the dress came over the top of the wood, and his mouth dried. He turned back towards the door, trying to block out the imagined images of her naked body standing just inches away. He took a deep breath, trying to pull himself together.

'Hurry up,' he whispered.

Finally, Rebekah stepped out, dressed in a simple tunic and woollen breeches, with long, knee-high lace-up boots. The tunic was fastened tightly at the waist with a belt and the bottom clung to her shapely long legs. His mouth dried. She looked more like a Danish shield maiden than a Saxon ady. Was that what she had intended, so she would fit in more at Nedergaard? She grabbed up some trinkets from the top of a chest and a sword that had been decorating the wall, then reached in a cupboard and pulled out an already full bag. She handed it to him and his eyebrows rose.

'I told you, it's not the first time I've considered leaving.'

She picked up Gytha, hoisting her on to her hip, and they walked quickly out of the room, shutting the door behind them. Fortunately, all was quiet. When they crept past the slumped body of the guard, Gytha gasped and Rebekah shushed her. Rædan helped them both down the steep narrow staircase. When they made it back to the trapdoor, he rolled his shoulders, telling himself the same advice he'd given Rebekah—to stay calm. They were nearly there and soon they'd be leaving this place.

He jumped down into the tunnel and he looked up at them, glancing between Rebekah and the girl. 'Pass her to me,' he commanded.

Rebekah hesitated and the child gripped on to her tighter.

'Now is not the time to argue, Rebekah.'

Reluctantly, realising he was right, Rebekah handed her down, as if she was wary of what he might do to Atol's child. But despite Gytha clinging to her mother, he took her and he settled her on to his side. For a moment, he paused, looking down into the girl's wide eyes.

'You can't possibly be seven!' he said, gasping in mock horror.

'I am!'

He shook his head. 'No, you're far too tall! Far too heavy!' he teased gently, trying to put her at ease. 'You're almost as heavy as my dog back at home.'

'You have a dog?' she gasped.

He nodded. 'Yes, her name's Runa.'

'Runa,' the girl repeated. 'What's she like?'

'Well, she's an elkhound, a bit like a wolf. She's pretty big—grey and furry with pointy ears. And she's heavy—like you!' he said, pretending to struggle to carry her and the girl giggled.

'I thought you were the bad man,' she said, suddenly serious.

He felt as if she'd wounded him with a blade.

'No, darling. I told you, this man is a friend,' Rebekah whispered quickly, joining them in the dark tunnel and pulling the door closed behind them.

'I may have done a few not-so-good things in my life, but hopefully I'm not all bad,' he said. 'Have you ever been naughty, Gytha? I bet you haven't.' She looked like an angel.

She thought hard about his question for a moment. 'My father says I'm bad all the time, but I don't think so…' His heart felt as if it might shatter. 'I did steal a pancake from the kitchen once,' she said and clamped her hand over her mouth as if to say she couldn't believe she'd admitted her crime to him. 'I felt very, very bad afterwards.'

He grinned. 'I bet it was worth it, though.'

'It was. It was delicious.' And she smacked her lips together, causing another quiet laugh to erupt from his mouth.

He hoped he was doing the right thing, taking the child away from her home and all that she knew. What would Gytha say when she realised? The journey was a lot for him and his men to take on, let alone Rebekah and a seven-year-old child. But the alternative was leaving them here in the hands of that man, which was unacceptable to him.

He knew he would have a fight on his hands

to keep Rebekah and Gytha safe and his mind was beginning to whirr about how his men would feel about him bringing them on board the ship, and how the people of Nedergaard would respond to their arrival. But there was no way he could do anything other than this.

'I can take her back now,' Rebekah said.

'She'll be too heavy for you to run with,' he said, ignoring her and continuing on towards the daylight of the exit. And he was surprised when he began to move and Gytha's little hands wrapped around his neck.

'What's that smell?' Gytha asked him, wrinkling up her nose.

'You don't want to know,' he said, crumpling his own nose to match.

She giggled.

Glancing round, he realised Rebekah had stopped. She was standing there, watching them, a look of consternation on her face.

'Well, are you coming?' he asked.

She nodded.

Reaching the clearing, he knew they would be out in the open. They'd have to make a run for it across the field again. Could they make it without being spotted? It was a chance they had to take.

'Where are we going?' Gytha whispered.

'Do you like horses?' he asked her.

'Yes, but Mother says I'm not old enough to ride one.'

'Would you like to today?'

She turned to Rebekah, her face lighting up. 'Can I?'

Rebekah tried to smile, nodding.

'Then, yes, please. Only, I don't know how,' she said, her face falling.

'I can help you,' Rædan said. 'But right now, I need you to keep quiet, close your eyes and hold on tight, as we're about to go for a little run.'

Chapter Six

The warning wail of the oxhorn howled out over the ramparts and a torrent of arrows came raining down on them as they ran across the open field. They'd been seen and Rebekah's heart was in her mouth, as they pressed their backs against the wall of a farmstead, catching their breath.

'Saxon fools! Why are they shooting at their Lord's child?' Rædan roared, covering as much of Gytha's head and body with his arms as he could. 'They'll be after us. We're going to have to be quick. Stay in front of me. And keep to the shadows and the trees.'

They quickly scrambled from farmsteads to bushes, hiding behind the walls, staying low. They heard the sound of the old Roman gate being opened, the hooves of horses scattering out.

'Quick, get down, here,' Rædan said, crouching behind a pen of grunting pigs.

'They're on foot, my Lord, they can't have got far,' they heard a voice say.

'Find them, now! I want them brought back to me immediately. Kill any Dane you see on sight.'

Atol…

Rebekah and Rædan gave each other a look, fear crossing her face, and he tipped his head, as if to say 'follow me'. They scurried through the low brambles, Rebekah constantly looking around nervously, but Rædan seemed to know how to keep them well hidden. She couldn't believe it when they made it back down to the river, unscathed. Her blood was pounding in her ears. She kept glancing behind her, certain each time she did she would see Lord Atol's men right there, ready to scoop them up and take them back to the fortress. Fortunately the horses from the Ryestone stables were still grazing where the Northmen had left them and this time, to her relief, Rædan sat with Gytha, while she had Colby to herself, and they set off at a swift pace.

'We have to be at the peninsula by the time the sun is at its highest point in the sky,' Rædan told her. 'We're going to have to ride pretty hard. They'll be on our tail. Can you still ride like you used to?'

She nodded. That she could do. She knew there was no time to rest—it wouldn't be long before Lord Atol and Ryestone's soldiers realised the Northmen had set sail. And she knew, without a doubt, Atol would come after her and what he thought was his only child. She shivered at the thought.

How strange that in the space of a few hours she'd switched sides. Now they were running from their own people. She'd be deemed a traitor. She knew how Lord Atol treated his women, so God only knew what he'd do to a deserter... She flicked her messy braid over her shoulder and with it her terrifying thoughts, instead concentrating all her efforts into encouraging the horse to gallop faster.

It was strange traversing the landscape she and Rædan had explored together when they were younger, when they'd had their whole lives ahead of them. She followed him as they stuck to the riverbank at Ryestone, which meandered through the valley before joining the estuary and the sea. How different their lives could have been if Atol hadn't interfered.

She had thought she would marry for love and have many adventures, visiting new places, meeting new people, before finally having children, but she'd had the child and none of the rest. She couldn't bring herself to regret having Gytha, as she loved her with all her heart, but she felt as if she'd missed out on so much. How absurd that today she was finally going to travel, to see new lands, with the boy she'd once known and cared for more than anything.

With the father of her child.

And yet she knew things could never go back to the way it had been between them before. They could never get back what they'd lost.

She glanced back over her shoulder, taking a last look at her Saxon home and its commanding position on the top of the hill, growing smaller and smaller. She thought she might feel a pang of remorse, but there was nothing. She wasn't sad to be leaving, only apprehension at what lay ahead.

'Stop doing that.'

'What?'

'Looking back. Just concentrate on where we're heading,' Rædan instructed.

'There you go, being bossy again.' Still, she tried to do as she was told and not check behind her any more. And the further they got from Ryestone and the possibility of Atol's men catching up with them, the easier it was to breathe in the fresh air and take note of the scenery—and the man riding beside her.

She stole a glance at him, holding their child in his strong, protective arms, in total control of Gytha and the animal. It brought a lump to her throat to see them together—and the resemblance between them was actually uncanny. They both had a strong profile, the same straight nose.

When Gytha had wrinkled her nose up at him in the tunnel and Rædan had done the same, it had taken her breath away. She was now absolutely certain, beyond doubt, that he was her child's father and once again she felt the prickle of guilt that she'd lied to him. And to Gytha.

When Rædan had first looked down at the child asleep in her room, she'd wondered if he'd noticed the similarities between them, but he had only mentioned that Gytha looked like her and she'd been relieved. Rædan didn't strike her as the parental type—not with his formidable looks and skill with a sword, his love of navigating the seas and raiding. He'd even told her himself he didn't want a family, although she had always admired the relationship he'd had with his own father.

Was there hope for such a relationship between him and Gytha? She had been pleasantly surprised that he had attempted to win Gytha over in the fortress, showing his softer side, and Rebekah's heart had lifted.

He cast her a sideways glance to check she was still doing all right beside him, keeping up, but his gaze was impenetrable. He had been kind to Gytha, but would he ever again show some of that warmth to her?

She still couldn't believe he had decided they must return with him to Nedergaard—surely it couldn't be all about revenge? She still couldn't believe she'd agreed to it. That she was doing this.

Finally, late morning, when they were weary from galloping across the undulating countryside for so long and so hard, the open fields turned to marshland and, ahead of them, they spotted the fleet of ships out on the water. Rebekah's stomach began to churn with nerves. What lay in store for them across the sea? She was trusting Rædan, putting hers and her daughter's life in his hands. Was she doing the right thing? But it was too late to second-guess her choices now.

They began to bear down on the ships, which were hugging the rugged coastline, and when the warriors on board spotted Rædan, they whooped and bellowed loud cheers. She watched as one of the vessels began to break away from the rest to make its way over to the shore.

'Are we chasing the bad men?' Gytha asked.

'We're not chasing them, we're trying to catch up with them,' Rebekah explained. 'Rædan is going to take us for a ride on one of his boats.'

Gytha shook her head fiercely. 'I don't think I want to,' she said, her lip wobbling again. 'I think I've had enough riding for one day. My tummy hurts.'

'Ah, this will be very different,' Rædan said.

'Will it be as bumpy or as fast?'

'That depends on the winds,' he said. 'But I promise you'll enjoy it, it'll be fun. We might get to see seals and sea eagles.'

'I've never seen a sea eagle before.'

'No? Then you're missing a treat. Where I come from, we consider them a sign of freedom and strength,' he said.

'How apt,' Rebekah muttered.

They slowed their horses to a halt and dismounted, Rædan lifting Gytha down and placing her feet on the ground. But no sooner had he done so than the loud, scuttling sound of dogs running, panting, had them whipping their heads round. The animals were scrambling down the cliff path towards them, baying, alerting their owners who were no doubt close behind that their prey was nearby.

Rebekah gasped and turned to Rædan in alarm. 'They're Atol's bloodhounds. He's here.'

He turned to look at how the boat was doing. It was advancing upon the shore, but there was no way it would make it to them in time. Not before the dogs and the Saxon riders came.

'What do we do?' she asked, wild with panic.

'Both of you hide. Now. Over there, behind that rock.'

She nodded, picking up Gytha and carrying her over to an enormous boulder on the shore, tucking her underneath. 'Whatever happens, keep out of sight. You're not to move from here until Rædan or I come and get you. Do you understand?'

'But, Mother—'

'Just do as I say.'

She kissed the top of Gytha's head, then took hold of her sword, pulling it out of the sheath. She looked up and, against the backdrop of the midday sun, she saw the sickening sight of a small army of men at the top of the cliff. She couldn't believe Atol was here, not when they were so close to making it to the longships.

But even as she stared at them in horror, the Saxons were hastening down the hill towards them, the hollow sound of thundering horses' hooves making the ground beneath them shake. She looked around for a way out of this, but she knew their only hope was to stall the Saxons and wait for the Danes to reach them.

She made it to Rædan's side just as the dogs surrounded them, barking and snarling, spittle frothing at the sides of their mouths.

'I thought I told you to hide!' he said, his voice stern.

'And I told you I won't be controlled. Besides, I thought you could do with the help.'

'I can manage,' he said through gritted teeth.

'Against twenty men?'

'I've bested more before. Rebekah, don't be foolish. You're risking getting caught...'

A shiver ran down her spine. 'I'll take my chances,' she said, tipping her chin up. She was determined not to let Atol harm her again. She would defend herself, or she would die trying…

'Can you even use that?' he asked, nodding to her sword.

'A little. It was my father's sword.'

'Well, lower your weapon until we need it. Get behind me. Follow my lead.'

The riders from Ryestone galloped down on to the sand towards them before reining in their horses, coming to a stop in front of them, surrounding them, and Rebekah could taste blood on her tongue. She had bitten down on her lip so hard in fear, she must have drawn blood. She watched as Lord Atol removed his helmet, his furious face scowling down at them.

'What do we have here? I thought we had a deal, Heathen Wolf—land in return for my bride. Yet it looks to me as if you're attempting to leave, taking her with you. Surely you wouldn't be so foolish? Did you think we wouldn't be watching your ships and our coastline?'

'I thought you'd still be trying to get yourself out of those bonds,' Rædan mocked.

Atol's lips thinned, his nostrils flaring.

'My patience is waning,' he sneered. 'Hand

the lady over and our response will be merciful,' he commanded.

Cold dread swept across Rebekah's skin. Please, no. She couldn't go back to him. And she couldn't watch Atol hurt Rædan. Not now she'd found him again. She still wasn't sure what kind of man he'd become, but she knew she could never stand by and watch him die.

She saw Rædan's fingers bunch into fists at his sides, while a muscle flickered in his jaw. He lifted his arm as if to stop her passing him, but she was rooted to the spot anyway. Unmovable.

She glanced round at the ship drawing closer to the shore behind them. The men on the boat were roaring, waving their weapons, desperate to get closer, ready for some action, and Rebekah willed them to get here quickly. Her chest was brushing against Rædan's arm and she could feel the tension rolling off him. She knew he wouldn't give in to the Saxon Lord and it gave her strength. Neither would she. They were in this together.

Atol's brow formed a heavy dark line. 'Do as I say and I'll kill you quickly. Make this difficult and it'll be a slow, painful death.'

'No,' Rebekah said, shaking her head. 'You

will not harm this man. And I will not be coming back with you. Not today. Not ever.'

Rædan slanted her a glance in surprise, while Atol's face turned puce at her disobedience. 'If you would rather be a slave whore to a pagan than a lady to your Lord, you will never see your child again!' he spat.

'She will be neither,' Rædan interrupted, his voice simmering with anger.

'This woman belongs to me,' Atol roared.

'That's strange. She doesn't appear to be wearing a wedding band,' he said, reaching for Rebekah's hand and raising it to show the men. 'As far as I can see, she doesn't belong to anyone. She's free to do as she pleases.'

Her breath caught. Did he really mean it?

She saw Atol's gaze narrow on them, taking a closer look at his adversary. His eyes raked over them both and the dawning recognition had him grating his teeth.

'I thought I'd disposed of you once before, a long time ago…'

'Not well enough. I've heard there's a lot of things you don't do properly…'

Atol clicked his teeth. 'So somehow you've returned from the depths of hell.' He smirked.

'Does Lady Rebekah know where you've been, what you really are?'

Rebekah stole a glance at Rædan. What did Atol mean?

'She knows enough,' he said. Rædan was masking his anger well…but his secrets, too? What was he keeping from her and why? She determined if they were to survive this, she would find out what had happened to him while they'd been apart.

'If you'd like to try to dispose of me again, in a more satisfactory manor, why don't we settle this, man to man, just me and you?'

No! Rebekah had known he'd attempt something like this—that he would try to save her from fighting, putting himself in harm's way instead.

'Now why would I do that?' Atol replied. 'Why would I risk my life when I have these men to fight for me?'

'You never did have any honour,' Rædan said, shaking his head in disgust.

'You're the pagan attacking fortresses and trying to steal my bride away.'

'On the contrary, she volunteered to come. You let her go, remember?'

Atol growled and turned to his men. 'Kill him. And bring the lady to me.'

The men jumped down from their horses and began to move towards them, closing in on them, and Rebekah and Rædan raised their swords, moving so they were back to back.

'Perhaps you should hand me over,' she whispered, her mouth dry.

'Never.'

'You could swim out to the boat. Save yourself...'

'After coming this far? No,' he said, shaking his head. 'We're in this together. Like we said, allies...'

And then it was too late. The men erupted into action and she held up her blade to defend herself against the blows of the Saxons' swords, but it seemed the men didn't have the stomach to fight her too fiercely, instead focusing on Rædan. So she tried to help him, knocking down one man, then another. But her fighting prowess was nothing compared to his.

He was furiously violent, fighting without fear of death and warding off blows coming from every which way. It was almost animalistic, yet he needed to be, as the Saxons' strikes were coming down harder, faster, and he was only just about managing to hold them back when his warriors finally appeared from behind them, charging through the shallows, wielding their swords and axes, coming to life as if they'd been starved of amusement. Iron clashed against wood, sending shields and swords splintering, and bloodied bodies crashing into the water.

Yesterday, she had been but an onlooker, today, she was right there, in the fray, and it was more horrific than she could have imagined.

'Rebekah, get Gytha,' Rædan shouted over the noise of the brutal blows and clashing metal. 'Now.' And she saw her chance and took it.

She raced to the rock and bundled up her child, carrying her over to the shore where the boat lay in wait. The men began to cheer as the last of the Saxons began to run for their lives, back up the hill. But then Rebekah saw Lord Atol turning his horse around, charging towards her as if he couldn't bear for the heathen to win…

Her wide eyes met Rædan's and he raced Atol to reach her, sprinting across the sand, and when he got to her first, he didn't hesitate. He flung Gytha up and into the boat, towards his men who were clambering into the vessel.

And then Rædan leapt on board, holding out his hand to help Rebekah up into the ship too.

'Come on!' he shouted and she slid her palm into his and he hauled her up, just as some of the Northmen began to run along the sand, pushing the boat further into the water and jumping back in. But at the last moment Atol reached down and grabbed Rebekah's ankle. She screamed, but Rædan still held her hand, tight. She was like the rope in a game of human tug of war, and neither side was letting go.

'You're mine. You belong to me!' Atol raged.

The sword in his other grip, Rædan lashed out and the tip of his blade sliced across Atol's cheek. 'You're wrong. She never did.'

And in a final roar of anger and defeat, the Saxon Lord let her go...

The force of the release had Rædan reeling backwards into the hull, Rebekah falling on top of him, into his arms. And for a moment, they lay there in shock, Rebekah looking down at him, unable to believe what had just happened.

They'd made it.

His hands circled her arms, rubbing up and down her skin for just a moment. Then sitting up, righting himself, he placed her to the side of his body, steadying her.

'Are you all right?'

She shook her head. 'I'm not sure.'

'Understandable,' he said, his eyes full of concern.

It had been close. She'd almost been pulled back, reclaimed by her Saxon Lord, nearly parted from her child.

Gytha… She couldn't have borne it if an ocean had separated them, while she was left trapped in Ryestone with that monster. Shaking, she pulled herself away from Rædan's touch and turned her attention to her child. She gathered Gytha into her arms, cradling her tight, sitting with her on an empty bench near the prow.

Rædan cupped her shoulder. 'Can I get you both anything? Water?'

'Please,' she nodded. Her voice had dried up in fear. It was hoarse from screaming.

He moved with confidence inside the vessel, speaking to some of the men, giving them instructions, and then he clambered back over the benches towards her, all long limbs and imposing height, and handed her a flask.

Rebekah took a swig of the drink, her throat parched.

'It's over now,' he said and she nodded numbly.

'Mother, where are we going?' Gytha asked, her cheeks streaked with tears. 'Lord Atol...he seemed very angry. He scares me.'

'I know. But you don't need to worry about that now. We're going to visit Rædan's settlement for a while. To see if we like it there.'

'Where is that?' Gytha asked, turning to Rædan, as if her mother's answer hadn't been good enough.

'My home is called Nedergaard,' he said, coming to sit down opposite them. 'It's a pretty little town on the shores of a huge fjord. There are mountains covered in snow and sandy beaches.'

'Will Runa be there?'

'Yes,' he said. 'And she is looking forward to meeting you very much.'

'How long is the journey?'

'You ask a lot of questions—also like your mother.' He grinned.

'And you're so...unforthcoming!' Rebekah bit back, thinking about what Atol had said on the shore about Rædan's past, but now was not the time to ask him about it.

He ignored her, focusing on Gytha. 'By my

reckoning, about two, maybe three days, depending on the winds. We're at the mercy of the waves now—and the gods.'

'I'm hungry,' Gytha said. 'I didn't eat breakfast.'

Rædan rooted around in some of the luggage, before producing a bag of dried fish and fruit for them to eat.

'You like it out here, don't you?' Rebekah asked, almost accusingly. It was as if he was in his element.

He shrugged. 'It's what I know...' And then he frowned. 'Does Atol have any ships?'

She shook her head. 'Not that I know of. But he's not one to give up easily.'

He grimaced. 'Are you feeling any better? That was some fight. You handled yourself well. It seems you're not just a pretty face. I think you scared off Atol's men!' He grinned. Her breathing stalled. He still thought she was pretty?

'As did you. How is it you fight like that, without fear?'

'I ask Odin to give me courage. I didn't know you knew how to use a blade.'

She nodded. 'My uncle taught me, after what happened to my parents. I wanted to be able to defend myself if we should ever be attacked again.' She had just never expected Rædan to be the one who had come with an army, knocking at their gates. But today he had saved her from Atol. He had saved her life…

Her thoughts strayed to her mother and father and how different her life might have been if they'd lived long enough to raise her. They had been good parents for the short time that she'd known them and she hoped she was as good a mother to Gytha. She wondered what her parents would think of her travelling overseas now, with Northmen similar to the ones who had burned down their home. Was she betraying their memory?

She couldn't actually believe she was here, the rocking motion of the boat making her stomach churn—or was it fear? Surrounded by so many of these warriors, dressed in leather and chainmail, swords at their sides and shields decorating the sides of the boat, it all made her insides quiver. She couldn't be sure she'd made the right decision. Perhaps she was mad for agreeing to sail across the ocean with a man she barely knew. He had changed so much since she'd known him before, both in looks and his character.

'You've done the right thing,' Rædan said, as if he could sense her concern. And then he turned to speak to his men. 'This is Rebekah and her daughter, Gytha,' he said, introducing them properly, unlike the introduction she'd received at their hands last night. 'They'll be accompanying us back to Nedergaard. They're not to be harmed.'

There was a rumbling of voices as the men all turned and spoke to one another. She listened as Rædan said a few words in Danish tongue to his burly right-hand man, then grinned.

'What?' she asked.

'Erik agrees with me. He thinks having a woman on a ship is a bad omen.'

She rolled her eyes.

'Will you both be all right while I help the men row for a while—just until we get out into the ocean and can lift the sails?'

She nodded and turned her attention to Gytha, answering her many questions and trying to reassure her. But when Rædan swapped places with one of his men, it was hard not to look at him. He raised his arms to tie his hair back into a band, his muscles flexing. And then he picked up the oars and began to row. She was in awe of the strength in his mighty body, the power in every stroke, the determined set of his jaw.

When he followed the other men in removing their tunics in the heat, she almost swallowed her tongue as her eyes fell upon his honed chest, the large muscles in his arms and the new ink on his tanned skin. Her pulse picked up speed, heat flooding her cheeks. He had dark coils of ink over his wrists up to his elbows and the face of a huge lone wolf painted on his chest. She found the designs—*him*—fascinating. Did it represent how he saw himself?

She had certainly seen that savage, animalistic side when he'd been fighting. It scared her, yet she still had the strangest desire to get up close and run her hands over the markings, but there was no way she could ever do that. It was an effort to tear her eyes away from him, but it would be awful if he caught her staring.

The men told stories and sang songs to pass the time and Rædan called to Gytha, pointing out a few things—the sight of a seal basking on the rocks, and a heron and its haunting call—and her child seemed to be in awe, taking it all in, her little face lighting up at each new sight and sound. But Rebekah didn't dare look his way again. She didn't want him to see the interest in her eyes.

It wasn't long before they were far from land, when there was nothing in sight, just endless stretches of the deep blue ocean, and when the sails went up, catching the wind, Rædan came back over to them, pulling on his tunic. She almost sagged in relief. He allowed Gytha to steer the ship for a while, helping her over to the keel, showing her what to do, and she noticed he spoke in soft, gentle tones when he talked to the child and asked her questions about her life, as if trying to better understand her.

When Gytha answered, babbling away happily to him, he seemed to lean in and listen intently, and Rebekah felt ridiculously grateful to him for attempting to put Gytha at ease. If only she felt the same...

She had no idea what lay in store for them when they got to Nedergaard. She had no idea if they would be made welcome or not, where they'd be staying or how she would survive, day to day. It was overwhelming. But it was no surprise she felt shaken and confused—first the fortress had been attacked, then she'd been taken captive, now she was on a ship sailing away from her homeland.

And yet she also felt a little bit wild, a little bit free. She had stood up to her Saxon Lord and escaped his hold over her. She was out in the middle of the ocean, far away from him, and that had to be a good thing. But she knew her jitters also had a lot to do with the man she was sailing away with and the way he made her feel.

She tugged the band out of her braid and shook her long locks free, running her hand through the strands, rubbing her fingertips over her scalp as if to massage away some of her tension. In Ryestone, she was never allowed to wear her hair down like this, but she didn't think anyone on this ship was going to mind— or stop her. It felt rebellious and she liked it.

Their evening meal was more dried fish and Gytha soon shut her eyes and was breathing deeply on her lap. Rebekah stroked her forehead and thought how easy it was for a child to fall asleep in the security of their parents' arms. She hadn't experienced that feeling herself—of being protected, cared for—in so long.

'Is she asleep?' Rædan said, startling her. She looked up at him, set against the blanket of stars in the sky above them. She hadn't seen him approach in the darkness.

'Here, let me take her so you can get some rest,' he said. And before she could stop him, he was reaching down, his hands brushing her arms as he lifted Gytha out of her grasp, sending ripples of heat through her.

He'd been careful every time he'd touched her today, controlled, unlike the passionate kiss they'd shared in the tent last night. And she realised a part of her wanted him to do it again, to get swept away with that emotion. She wanted to see a glimmer of that eager intensity again, instead of this cool, controlled man—especially as her body was responding to him in ways it hadn't in such a long time.

He gently settled Gytha in his lap and she felt both thankful but also, ridiculously, a little bit jealous at the way he was cradling their child in his arms, so tenderly.

'I thought you said you had no experience of looking after children,' she said accusingly. Had he lied to her? Would they get to Nedergaard and discover he did have a wife and family of his own? He was excruciatingly attractive—and he must know it. Surely he'd had no end of female admirers over the years? She couldn't cope with sharing a farm, let alone a village with him and a lover. Seeing that would be more than she could bear. The thought brought her up short. When had she started caring again? Had she ever stopped?

'I don't. I must be a natural.' He smiled, winning her back round again all too quickly.

The temperature was dropping rapidly now the sun had gone down and she shivered.

'There are some furs over there,' he said, nodding to a pile of belongings.

She went to retrieve one and came back with two, laying one over Gytha in his lap, careful not to get too close to him, and covering her own knees with the other.

'It's beautiful out here, if a bit lonely,' she said, trying to steer their conversation on to safer ground. 'I can see why you like it.'

'You're lonely with all these men for company?' He grinned.

Her lips curved upwards involuntarily. Sitting so close to him in the boat, cloaked in darkness, there was an almost intimate quality to it and she felt the need to talk, rather than focus on the way his silver eyes shone in the moonlight.

'So how does it feel?' she said. 'Knowing you got your revenge.'

His eyes narrowed on her. 'Believe it or not, I'm doing this to help you, Rebekah…'

She swallowed, feeling ashamed. She must stop attacking him—it wasn't helping anyone. 'I'm sorry,' she said, clasping her fingers together in her lap. 'Everything just feels a little overwhelming right now.'

He nodded, his eyes softening. 'I understand. I know how it feels to leave your home behind. It's very brave of you to give up the dream—of having a title, a fortress, land…'

'That was never my dream.' *You were.* 'Everything that matters to me is right here in this boat.'

He looked down at Gytha resting in his arms. 'You know, if you want to get some sleep, I can watch her. You must be shattered after today.'

'Aren't *you* tired?'

'There'll be plenty of time to rest when we get home.'

Home.

She wondered when he had stopped thinking of Ryestone as home—and what made Nedergaard the place he now felt he belonged to? He obviously felt safe and accepted there—would she and Gytha, too?

'What can we expect when we get there?' she asked, focusing on a small tear on the knee of her breeches. 'How will we be treated? Did you mean what you said to Atol, about me being a free woman?'

'You'll have a lot more freedom than you did in Ryestone. There are rules, of course, but life isn't so regimented in Nedergaard. When we first arrive, there'll be a Thing—a gathering. Jarl Knud will feed the village and there'll be a celebration for a successful raid,' he said. 'He'll pay each of the men the silver he owes them— and we will have to present him with whatever treasures we have brought back with us.'

Her head shot up.

'He will then split up the loot evenly between the men.'

Alarm floored her upon hearing his words. 'Are we included in that treasure?' she asked, aghast. Why had he not mentioned this vital bit of information before? 'You promised… You promised we'd be safe.'

'Calm down, Rebekah,' he said. 'I will explain to Knud I don't want any of the treasure from our raid, just you and Gytha.'

She felt the blood drain out of her face. 'You make it sound like we're some kind of trinket, a prize to be rewarded with. And what if he says no? Is there a chance he won't agree?' She suddenly felt panic-stricken. Why hadn't she asked these questions before?

'Shh, you'll wake Gytha,' he whispered.

'If I had known it was in any doubt, we wouldn't have come!'

'Don't worry, he will agree.'

'How can you be sure?' She had known the Danes thought it was their right to own thralls, to use them for their own will, to trade them at markets. Maybe Rædan didn't…but what about his people? 'What if he thinks of us as thralls?'

A muscle flickered in his cheek. 'It won't happen,' he bit out, the steel in his voice not helping to settle her nerves. 'Jarl Knud is like me, we don't believe in treating people like cattle. I wouldn't have brought you with me if I didn't think I could keep you both safe.'

'But what if you're wrong? What if he says no?' Her mind began running away with her. 'If they say we're slaves and you can have only one of us, I want you to say Gytha. Promise me, Rædan.'

'Rebekah, stop it,' he said, his words cutting through her stampede of fear. 'If Jarl Knud doesn't agree to me taking you in, there's one very simple solution. I shall just have to make you my wife!'

'What?' she gasped, her green eyes wide with shock. 'I can't marry *you*!'

'Why?' Rædan asked, rage darting through him. 'Not good enough for you? Was Atol right—you'd rather be seen as a slave than a wife?'

'I'd rather be neither!' she fumed. 'You said I'd be a free woman. I believed you!'

Damn, but she was beautiful when she was angry. She was still the most stunning woman he'd ever seen. And although he knew she had probably sworn off men for life, as her green eyes flashed at him, he had the strong desire to change that—to show her that not all men were brutes, and that his touch could be enjoyable, as he had begun to do last night. Her loose auburn hair, cascading over her shoulders in fiery waves, made his heart race. His desire for her was greater than for any other woman. And surely there were worse reasons to get married?

'I could never marry one of your kind—a

Dane—especially after what had happened to my mother and father,' she added.

He blanched at her words, as they hit their target in his heart. She made it seem like marrying him was a fate worse than death and an old fury took up place in his stomach. Had she ever intended to marry him before, all those years ago? Had she ever thought he was good enough for her? 'You'd be safer as my wife.' He grimaced. 'You'd be protected under our laws.'

'But I don't even know you, not any more.'

'You know me enough to agree to leave Ryestone and sail all this way with me. To let me *rescue* you and your daughter...' he said, nodding to the child in his lap.

She shook her head. 'I told you, I never want to be ruled by a man. Ever again.'

He understood why she was protesting—he knew what she'd been through with Atol and what it was like to feel trapped, utterly reliant on a cruel master. He could understand that.

'You said so yourself—*you* don't even want to marry!' she continued.

She was right. He had told her that. Because he'd sworn he'd never be bound to anyone again and if they were to marry, she would own him and he her. But if marriage was the sacrifice he had to make to protect her, then so be it. Would she not make the same concession for her child's safety?

All of a sudden, the wind picked up and pellets of rain began to lash down into the hull, the weather matching Rædan's raging emotions inside. Gytha sat up in his arms, the water on her face waking her up, and he passed her back to Rebekah.

'We'll talk about this later…' he warned.

Rædan, Erik and Arne quickly made them a little roof out of one of the shelters they had erected on Ryestone's riverbank and Rædan told them to stay inside, while he saw to navigating the ship and directing his men.

The wind howled like wild beasts and the churning sea was comparable to his thoughts. Rædan wondered if his man had been right— perhaps having two females on board was a bad omen after all. They battled ferocious waves for hours, and the men had to cling on to the sides of the boat, drenched, cold and seasick. He thought the gods must be angry with them.

Rædan didn't mind the brutality of the ocean—and he'd seen worse storms. Yet concerned for Rebekah and Gytha, who were being flung about inside the shelter, like fish trapped in a net, he kept checking on them. But when a huge wave lifted up the ship, sending them all tumbling, he dragged his way over to Gytha, holding her tight. Using a piece of loose rope from the deck, he wrapped it around her waist and then Rebekah's, then finally his own.

'What are you doing?' she cried.

'So you don't get thrown overboard!' he shouted, struggling to talk through the lashings of rain.

It was something he'd learned during his years of living out at sea. He and his fellow bondsmen had been tethered together so they couldn't escape, but it had proved useful during bad weather. Too weak to cling on to the boat all night long, it meant you would have less chance of being claimed by the water. There had been times when he'd longed for a wave to take him down with the ship, though, hoping each next swell would be the one to end his misery, but not today. Now he had a purpose—he had to get Rebekah and Gytha, and his men, home.

'You said this would be fun,' Gytha said. 'But it's not fun, I feel sick.'

He nodded. He understood and he didn't want her to be afraid. He came down to sit beside them both in the hull and gathered them close, wondering how he could make the child less fearful of what was happening. 'You know, where we come from, we believe Hræsvælg, the giant eagle, beats his wings so hard he makes the wind blow.'

'A giant eagle?'

'Yes.'

'Well, can you ask him to stop it?'

He grinned.

If they survived this journey, he knew they could survive anything. Gytha had such character and Rebekah was tougher than she looked. She had to be to have put up with what she had done for the past eight years. And yet she hadn't lost her spirit. Atol hadn't broken her. There was so much about her to be admired—she was a wonderful mother and when she'd drawn her blade and begun to fight alongside him earlier today, a newfound respect had been born. Now if they could just weather this storm…

The thunder and lightning and driving rain lasted all night and most of the next day and they were all exhausted, having had no sleep. By the time the second evening rolled round, the storm had finally stopped but the mood on board had changed. The men longed for their homes, their women and their beds, and when he checked on Rebekah and Gytha at regular intervals, the child was tired and grumpy, and Rebekah had withdrawn into herself, barely meeting his gaze.

He knew she was livid with him, thinking he'd misled her, and he knew she was right to be concerned about what was to happen to them on their arrival in Nedergaard. Her invisible draw-bridge had come back up and she'd retreated inside an impenetrable wall.

He could see that they were both cold and their vulnerability reached out to him. He was also aware they were hungry. Food was something he was used to having a lack of, but he didn't like the thought of them going without.

Right now, there was still no sight of land, but tomorrow, if the weather stayed favourable, they'd be home. Over the past two years he had loved to explore different isles, each one offering hope, a new beginning. There was always something new to discover. Some lands had forests and beaches, some had grand monasteries and fortresses, and people who were ready to defend their homes with their lives. He'd come to realise that's how he felt about Nedergaard. It would be summer there now and he wondered what Rebekah would make of it. It certainly wasn't the grand fortress she'd experienced in Ryestone, with none of the luxuries, but it was a place that crept into your heart. Would she be able to make room in hers for his home?

Chapter Seven

The ship had been weaving its way through the majestic mountains and the deep blue waters of the fjord for a while, when finally, the small harbour of Nedergaard came into view and the men began to stand, cheering loudly, almost toppling the boats. When they sat down again, their rowing became more furious, fuelled by a fresh fervour to get home.

Rebekah was in awe of their achievement. They'd crossed the ocean, survived a great storm. They should be at the bottom of the sea, but instead the sun was shining down on them and although she was exhausted, she was elated they had made it. The men around her were laughing and waving to the crowds waiting on the shore, growing ever nearer, a sense of celebration in the air, but apprehension swirled deep inside her.

What kind of welcome would she and Gytha receive? She wasn't sure what to expect, or how she should behave, and she felt a knot tighten in her stomach. She sent a silent prayer up above that whatever happened to her, Gytha would be all right.

As the ships docked and the men began to throw themselves out of the boats and on to the wooden jetty, pulling women and children into their outstretched arms, Rebekah looked on in wonder and dread.

It was a bustling town of many simple buildings crowded together, smoke coiling out from the little holes in the roofs, and the people seemed in good spirits. Their clothes were different to those where she'd come from—they had thick furs and animal skins around their necks and both the men and women wore their hair in intricate braided styles, with beasts and serpents painted on their skin.

Rædan picked up Gytha, his eyes meeting Rebekah's over the child's shoulder.

'Well, are you coming?' he asked, tilting his head in the direction of the shore.

She gave a quick nod and, on shaky legs, she stepped out of the boat. She was in awe at the hustle and bustle, the women embracing their men, the ale being poured and the children running around on the sand, playing happily. Her heart lifted a little at that. There were other children for Gytha to play with. And yet there would be no chance of that if they were seen as slaves…

Rebekah's head swam. She still couldn't believe Rædan had suggested he should make her his wife! It was the last thing she'd expected. It was absurd! Following behind him, along the jetty, she felt as if her life was rocking out of control, just like the longship thrashing about on the waves in the storm. So much had happened in such a short few days and she stumbled along numbly, as if she was falling, spiralling, her head whirring in panic. She wanted to keep hold of Gytha, but Rædan had a firm grasp of her, so all she could do was follow.

She knew better than to make eye contact with anyone. She didn't want to draw any attention to herself—or her child. But it seemed there was no chance of going unnoticed, not with Rædan at her side, as the other men wanted to talk to him, to welcome him home, and the women seemed just as interested, trying to catch his eye. She could understand it. He was certainly a man who demanded attention. But they didn't appear happy to see her or the child he was carrying and apprehension engulfed her.

She was pleased when they made it past the crowds on the jetty and on to solid ground, and she halted as Rædan set down Gytha to embrace a tall, muscular man wearing elaborate furs and lots of rings, armbands and chains. She quickly deduced he must be someone important and that Rædan liked him.

The men spoke in the Danish tongue and then they glanced over at her and Gytha while talking.

'Heil ok sæl,' the man said, nodding in her direction. He was ruggedly good looking and yet still no equal to Rædan.

'Rebekah, Gytha—this is Jarl Knud. He rules here in Nedergaard.'

'Hello,' Rebekah said, attempting a smile, her heart hammering in her chest. If he was in charge, she had to make a good first impression. It was imperative that this man liked her...

'Let me take a look at you, child,' the man said, calling Gytha towards him in a thick accent. 'My, my, you're a beauty, aren't you?' he said, before placing a hand on Rædan's shoulder. 'They both are. Come, my friend. Come inside and warm yourselves by the fire and tell me all about your journey.'

Rebekah, relieved to take Gytha's hand in hers, followed the two men as they led them into a large, long building made of wattle and daub and a soaring thatched roof.

'This is the longhouse,' Rædan turned to explain to her and she nodded, her stomach in knots. 'It's the hub of the village.'

There was a central stone hearth and people sat around it on benches, relaxed, at ease, with none of the stiffness there had been in the great hall in Ryestone, and the space was filling up fast, the men from the ships and their families filtering inside.

She gripped Gytha's hand tighter. The tension was strumming through her body. Was this the gathering Rædan had warned her of on the boat? Was she to be paraded in front of all these people, or worse, thrown into a cage? Surely Rædan wouldn't allow it.

Someone handed Rædan a horn of ale and he passed it to Rebekah. 'Here, drink this, it'll help you relax,' he said. And then he signalled to a girl to fetch another and some water for Gytha.

Rædan mingled with the rowdy men, who pulled him into big bear hugs, congratulating him on his raid, and Rebekah felt so out of place, awkward and uncomfortable. She didn't know where to put herself. It was airless in here, too many bodies, too much noise.

She needed to get out, but she couldn't—she didn't even know where she was, or where she'd go. She was trapped. She had no control here. So much for the freedom Rædan had talked of. She was starting to think this had been a very bad idea. How could she ever fit in in a place like this?

She felt all eyes upon her, the women no doubt seeing her as a threat, competition, and the men's interest piqued at what prizes Rædan had returned with. Due to her position of being a Lady of Ryestone, she was used to people looking at her, taking notice, but this kind of attention was different.

It took her back to when she was a child and she'd awoken in a large bed at Ryestone, overwhelmed with sorrow for the death of her parents, scared by the brutality she had seen. Her uncle's armed guards had found her, barely breathing and with burns to her body. And that first day, when she'd been presented to the people in the Great Hall, she'd just wanted to curl up and hide, or run far away. While the grand feast had taken place, she'd sought sanctuary in the stables, much preferring the company of the animals to the strangers in the fortress.

If only she could run away somewhere now. Rædan had lied to her...he'd told her she'd be free, but she didn't feel free. She felt like a shiny silver bullion everyone wanted to take home in their pocket and her senses were on high alert. She'd been so foolish to believe him. Yet she didn't think he'd intended to deceive her—he'd told her he believed Jarl Knud would grant him custody of her and her child.

His suggestion of marriage was just a last resort, she reminded herself for the hundredth time. She could tell by the resentment in his voice when he'd suggested they wed that he didn't *want* to marry her either. Would he really go through with it, if he had to, despite his own objections to the institution, just to keep her safe?

Finally, Jarl Knud took up a seat at the top of the hall and the raucous Danes began to quieten down. Her fingers clung on to Gytha's shoulders, pulling her back towards her, holding her close.

Knud congratulated the men on their safe return and successful raid, saying the gods had been on their side. He thanked them for the treasure and, as Rædan had predicted, he asked them to place their hoard in the middle of the hall. All the men did so and Rebekah's eyes widened at the pile of loot. She didn't know Ryestone had such riches! They hadn't even stormed the castle, so had they taken them from the farmsteads or the churches? Why did they want it? To sell and trade?

Rædan mentioned the silver he had already distributed evenly between the men and he handed over the bag of gold Atol had given him. Then he was back by her side, his arm brushing hers. She hung on the Jarl's every word as he told every raider they could keep the silver as well as their earnings, plus take something of their choosing from the stash.

She watched as one by one the warriors stepped forward and the crowds stamped their feet and cheered until each man had snatched up a jewel or a silver goblet, or whatever had taken his fancy. And then it came to the turn of Ogden, the man with flinty eyes and half a shaven head, ink scrawled over his face, who had started the unpleasantness around the campfire the other night. He leered at her and her gut twisted. She knew he meant trouble.

'What about the thralls? What if we want one of those rather than this loot?' he asked, his beady eyes roaming over her.

She felt Rædan tense beside her, his fingers curling around her elbow, gripping her tight, and she was glad of his reassurance, even though she was still furious with him. She manoeuvred Gytha between them.

'They belong to Halfdan. They're not to be touched,' Jarl Knud responded firmly.

'So he gets two treasures?' the man sneered.

'Do you doubt he has earned them?'

'It just seems wrong to have a Saxon thrall in our midst and for each of us not to be able to have some fun with her.'

Rebekah turned her face into Rædan's shoulder.

'Heed my warning, Ogden. No one is to lay a hand on them. They are to be treated as one of us. Do you hear me?' the Jarl reiterated with force.

The man grimaced and took one last greedy look at her, before swiping up a silver dagger and backing away into the crowd, and Rebekah let out a long, slow breath. Was that it? Was it over?

It seemed as if it was when bowlfuls of piping-hot food began to be passed around and Rædan found them space on a bench, propelling her forward, still gripping her arm. She was glad to sit—her legs were like water. So did this mean they wouldn't be seen as slaves? That she wouldn't have to marry him? Was she free to be her own person? She wanted to plead with Rædan to give her answers, but she also knew this wasn't the right moment.

Once seated, he made sure she and Gytha had a serving of pottage each and they ate heartily, her appetite suddenly coming back with force.

'Do you always eat here?' Gytha asked.

'Only sometimes.' Rædan shrugged. 'I tend to eat alone.'

Rebekah noticed Rædan had left a little in his bowl—and her heart swelled when he offered it to Gytha, asking if she wanted more. But the little girl shook her head, yawning. Rebekah pulled her into her arms and that feeling of helplessness assailed her again—she couldn't put her to bed, she didn't even know where they would be sleeping.

'Ready to go?' Rædan asked and she looked up at him, grateful, tears of relief pooling in her eyes. He seemed to be putting their feelings first and it surprised her. She couldn't quite align the two sides to him. One moment he was a ferocious warlord, the next he was taking care of her child. *Their child.* Perhaps she had judged him too harshly. Perhaps he was still the same man she had fallen for before...

And the guilt hit her again that she should have told him that he was a father. She knew that every moment they spent together and she didn't tell him was a moment longer that he'd resent her for later, if she did eventually reveal her secret.

He gathered Gytha into his arms and, after signalling his goodbye to Jarl Knud across the hall, he led Rebekah through the heaving crowd and outside. She took a deep breath. It felt good to be back in the fresh air, away from all those strangers and prying eyes. To be alone, just the three of them again. And yet she also felt nervous.

'Where are we going?' she asked.

He quirked his head in the direction of a distant lone farmstead, more like a shack, on the beach. It was built from willow twigs and the roof thatched with rushes. 'That's my settlement. It's not much—not what you're used to—' he frowned '—but it's comfortable. And the views make up for the lack of other things.'

'It's stunning here,' Rebekah said, and she meant it. The sun was beginning to set over the mountains and the glistening water of the fjord was bathed in the amber glow. Yes, the shack looked primitive, but Rædan was right— its lone setting on the bay was breathtaking. She wondered why, if he had all this treasure from his raids, he lived in such basic lodgings like this. What did he buy with the trinkets he stole?

She felt so weary, it was an effort to walk across the sand to get there. And then, as they drew closer, an enormous wolf came bounding across the beach to greet them and sent Rebekah's adrenalin soaring. She froze, gripping on to Rædan's arm and squealing.

He laughed. 'I hope you don't mind dogs!'

After the encounter with Atol's hounds, she wasn't sure. But then the furry creature was there at his feet, jumping up at him, barking and wagging its tail. And she realised she hadn't heard Rædan laugh in years. It was a wonderful sound and she found herself smiling back at him.

'Runa!' Gytha squealed in delight, now wide awake again, and the dog began to dance around her, leaping up. Rædan put the child down and Gytha reached out to stroke the animal.

'That's a dog?' Rebekah asked, shocked. 'It looks more like a wolf!'

What was it with Rædan and wolves?

He laughed again. 'I told you, she's an elk-hound. A great guard dog, very loyal. And brilliant at hunting.'

'I think she's missed you.'

'I missed her.' He grinned, ruffling her fur.

'Who looked after her while you were away? Surely she didn't fend for herself…'

'I have some help on the farm—they kept an eye on her for me. Come inside,' he said, pushing open the door. 'Gytha, do you think you can keep Runa company while I show your mother around?'

The little girl nodded excitedly.

'These will be your new living quarters,' he said, stooping to get through the doorway, then standing awkwardly in the small space, raising his hands in explanation.

Rebekah took in the room with a little hearth and simple furnishings—a wooden bench and table. It was surprisingly cosy—or was it his nearness, his deep, gentle voice that had her feeling warm inside? Dotted all around, there were signs that someone lived here—a cloak hanging on a hook on the wall, clean spoons and bowls left out on the side and a pair of muddy boots by the door.

At the back of the hut, he cast aside a woollen curtain to reveal an extra living space with a large bed covered in animal furs. 'You and Gytha can sleep back here. Will that be all right for you both?'

'What about you? Where will you sleep?'

He tugged open a little door on the other side of the hut, which she'd thought was some kind of cupboard, but it had room for just a bed inside. 'I can bunk in here.'

'Is this—will we be sharing your home?' she asked, shocked. 'I thought you meant there was an outhouse, or separate farmstead you were going to put us in. I didn't think you meant we would be living with you.' Her voice sounded strangely high-pitched.

'You'll be safer in here with me.'

Safer, perhaps. But could she bear it, being this close to him all the time? Wouldn't it be dangerous, given the effect his nearness had on her? She'd be constantly on edge around him. And wasn't it rather intimate?

'Isn't it a bit close for comfort? Surely you'll need your own space?' she said, her heart pounding in panic.

'This is all I have. It'll have to do for now. Unless you'd rather sleep in the longhouse? Jarl Knud said he could make room for you there...'

She shook her head. 'No, no. This is fine.'

She looked around again, trying to imagine them all living in this perfectly comfortable but confined space. Was it proper? And then she almost laughed at her foolishness. Who was she kidding? Nothing about this whole situation was 'proper'. They were long past that. But she'd much rather stay here than in that cloying hall of strangers.

'So you're giving up your bed for us?'

He shrugged. 'Like I said, I don't sleep much anyway. Come on, I'll show you outside.' They stepped past Runa, who was now lying flat out on her back, enjoying Gytha stroking her belly, and Rebekah smiled at the happy scene. Rædan led her around the rest of the settlement, showing her a small outbuilding which he called a steam bath, puzzling her, and a farm with a selection of animals and crops. She could just about make it all out in the rapidly fading sunlight.

'You've grown all these yourself?' she asked.

'I like to be self-sufficient. I'm not good at relying on others.'

She didn't think that had always been the case. He and his father had always been close and she had fallen for Rædan's easy, laid-back charm. She didn't remember him having problems trusting people before. The years had changed him. She remembered his personality as being bigger than life itself. He'd been so sure of himself, always in good spirits. Now, he still had that same imposing presence and everyone was aware of him, but there was a seriousness about him that hadn't been there before—a dark, dangerous aura. What had happened to make him that way? What did Atol know that she didn't? Where had he gone after Atol had sent him away?

When they re-entered the hut, they found Gytha fast asleep on the floor curled up next to Runa. 'Well, these two bonded pretty quickly.' He grinned. 'She must have been exhausted.'

'That makes two of us,' she said.

Rebekah watched, helpless, as Rædan lifted Gytha and carried her over to the bed, laying her down on the furs, covering her up with another. The dog followed the child and hopped up on to the end of the bed, as if meaning to keep guard.

'Traitor,' Rædan remarked, but she could tell he was pleased.

Rebekah gave Gytha a kiss on the cheek and stepped away, and Rædan pulled the curtain back into place. She stood awkwardly in the small living space, the silence stretching between them. It was the first time they'd been alone in days and she felt uncomfortable, unsure how to behave as his guest here.

'Thank you for being so good with her,' she said, wringing her hands.

He shrugged. 'She really is a miniature version of you. Do you want a drink?' He headed over to a barrel and began pouring a cup of ale, then handed it to her. 'So what are your first impressions of Nedergaard?'

'The setting is lovely and the people are... interesting,' she said and he smiled.

'It's not always like that, in the hall. Only on occasions like these when a raiding party returns, or when there's something to celebrate. It's a much calmer place in the daytime.'

'You and Jarl Knud seem close,' she said, sipping the amber liquid.

'We are. He's a good man.'

'So, he said we were free, that we could stay here?'

'Yes, just like he did to me when I arrived on these shores.'

'I still don't understand—how you became a Dane.'

He shrugged. 'The people were accepting of me when I came here. I learned a lot from Jarl Knud. He took me under his wing, welcoming me into his family, and I decided to stay,' he added.

'Did you never want to come back?' she asked, sitting down on the little bench. 'To Ryestone?'

'At times, but it wasn't that easy. You need ships to sail across the ocean. I had nothing when I came here.'

She wondered how that could be. 'You haven't spoken much of your seafaring days. What did you say you did out on the ocean?'

'I didn't.'

She heard the light pattering of rain on the roof above and watched as he knelt down and began to light the fire, the tiny little flames creating flickering shadows across his handsome face.

'Are you all right with me lighting this?' he

asked and she noticed he was changing the subject. Why was he so averse to talking about himself? 'You'll freeze tonight if I don't.'

She nodded. 'I'll just sit over here.'

'Does it still bother you, like it used to?'

'The fire? A little.' She was still amazed he remembered that. 'I know it shouldn't.'

'Some things stick with you.'

Memories of that night when men from the North had attacked her family's fortress filtered through her mind. She'd been just twelve years old and her mother had hidden her under the floorboards. She'd watched through the slits in the panels of wood as huge, beastly men had stormed into the hall and attacked her parents and the other villagers, stealing anything of value and then torching the building.

She had been so scared, stuck beneath the ground, the heat and smoke almost taking her life. She still had the unsightly scars on her skin to remind her of the ordeal. And the fear of the flames.

She told herself to relax, that Rædan had this small fire under control. She was safe. But no sooner had they drained their tumblers, they heard male voices outside.

'Who's that?' she said, the hair on the back of her neck standing on end.

Rædan placed a finger over his lips and motioned for Rebekah to stay quiet, to go and hide in the back. Runa growled and leaped out from behind the curtain, back by her master's side. Rædan picked up his sword and went to open the door. Rebekah gripped his arm, her eyes wide with fear. 'Be careful.'

He nodded, staring at her hand encircling his wrist.

She crept behind the curtain, her heart in her mouth, and sat down on the bed next to Gytha. She wrapped her fingers round the hilt of her sword.

She could hear Rædan speak to the men approaching and she strained to listen to their low tones. With cold dread trickling through her, she recognised the voice of the one. It was Ogden, the man from the campfire and the longhouse—the one who had wanted to take her as his slave, rather than the treasure. By the sound of his slurring voice, he'd had far too much ale.

'You can keep the child, we'll just relieve you of the woman,' she heard him say and deep laughter erupted. He wasn't alone. She thought there must be two, maybe three of them. Rædan was outnumbered. She sat upright, her breathing shallow.

'Jarl Knud may think you deserve more treasure than the rest of us, but why should you have all the fun?'

'Ogden, I don't want to fight you,' she heard Rædan say. How did he sound so calm, so in control? Her heart was beating wildly, almost drowning them out. She'd seen him fight twice now. Surely they didn't want to go up against him? 'It wouldn't be fair while you're in this condition.'

'Then hand her over and you won't have to.'

'No. Go home. Go to bed and I'll forget all about this. Try anything foolish and you'll regret it.'

But it seemed the man was set on his goal as she heard the sounds of a scuffle, the scraping of metal on metal, and grunting. She was in half a mind to throw open the door and tell them to stop, to offer herself up. But she knew Rædan would never let her do that. And yet he shouldn't have to fight his own men on her behalf—this was his home. He should be safe here. What if something happened to him and it was all because of her? He had told her he'd been forced to leave Ryestone because of her all those years ago—and he'd never seen his father again. She couldn't bring any more suffering upon him.

She couldn't bear it if Rædan got hurt, not after they'd actually made it here. Gytha would be distraught—she could tell the child was already growing fond of him.

Rebekah could hear the men struggling, Runa snarling. She glanced over at her daughter, still sleeping soundly, and she was relieved she didn't have to witness this. Not on her first night here. There was a sudden cry of pain and then footsteps. Running. She heard the door to the hut swing open and she clamped her hand over her mouth, to stop herself screaming. Suddenly the curtain was pulled back and she gasped.

Rædan!

'Oh, my God, thank goodness. Are you all right?' she gasped.

'I'll live,' he said, his face like thunder.

'What happened?' she said, rising to greet him.

'The three brothers trying their luck. I wounded them—and their pride. Runa helped.

Hopefully they won't be coming back any time soon.'

And then she saw his face was bleeding. 'You're hurt!'

He put his hand to his temple. 'It's nothing, just a scratch. Although I think he also cut my shoulder open,' he said, grimacing, placing his other hand over his upper arm. 'The drunken fool.'

'Let me take a look. I'll clean it up.'

'It's nothing, Bekah, honestly.'

Her heart hitched at him calling her Bekah again.

She set about pouring some water and finding a cloth anyway. She needed to do something to keep busy, to distract herself from thinking about what had just happened—what those men would have done if Rædan hadn't chased them away.

'Sit,' she said, setting down the bowl of water on the table and motioning to the bench next to it.

'I said I'm fine.' He stood in the centre of the hut, stooping a little as he was so tall, his dark face scowling. His long hair had come loose from the exertion of fighting, wet from the rain, and her breath caught.

'I'll be the judge of that when I see it,' she said firmly.

'Who's being bossy now?'

'You don't want to drip blood all over the place—Gytha will be horrified when she wakes up!'

The thought must have swayed him, as with a heavy sigh, he reluctantly took off his chain-mail vest, casting it down on the floor. Next, he peeled up his tunic, pulling it over his head and shoulders, wincing. She sucked in a breath at seeing his magnificent body again up close. Honed to perfection, he had a dark line of hair ascending up—and downwards—from his navel. She was drawn to the dark ink that heavily covered his lower arms, stopped at his elbows, but continued over his chest. She studied the face of the wolf.

'Is it that bad? You're staring!' he said. Did he really not know how incredible he looked?

'Am I?' she said, flustered. 'Sorry.'

He had a bloody gash to his upper arm and she tried to focus on the task before her. She popped the cloth in the water and then pressed it to his skin, hoping he wouldn't notice her trembling fingers as she began to gently wash away the blood so she could see how bad the wound was beneath.

He scowled as the cloth made contact with the cut.

'Hopefully Ogden won't bother us again,' he said, ignoring her question.

'You said that already.'

'It wasn't exactly the welcome I'd hoped for. I want you to feel safe here.' His voice sounded gruff, as if he was still trying to stem his anger at his men.

She had the strange desire to reassure him. 'Well, now I know you can best three of your men, I do,' she said. But her fingers still shook as she reached out to wipe away another smear of blood. She couldn't be sure if it was because of what had just happened, or because of the way he was making her feel, his beautiful body so close, his piercing grey eyes glittering at her in the firelight.

'How is it that you're not afraid of anything?' she asked.

'That's not true.'

'I haven't seen you back away from a fight yet. Do you not feel any pain?'

He shrugged with his good arm. 'When you've been through a lot of pain, you become numb to it. Or at least I can tolerate it more easily.'

'Don't you care about getting hurt? Being killed?'

'No. We will all die, it's how and when that matters. There are far worse things than death, Bekah.'

'Such as?'

'Suffering. Shame...'

Her hand paused. 'What suffering have you endured?' Her gaze flicked over his chest, his arms, and back to his face—all ravaged by scars. 'Are they all battle wounds?'

'Most.'

Her eyes rested once again on the ink swirling over his lower arms. It was unusual—dark bands covering his skin. It was the same on his chest, merging into the wolf motif, and it was proving difficult not to stare and admire it.

'What are these?' she asked. 'They look new.'

'They're a talisman—they're meant to guide the bearer or ward off our enemies. But they also help to cover up some unsightly scars.'

'Do you have any alcohol?'

He looked up at her, surprised. 'Something stronger than the ale?'

'For your wound,' she said.

'Ah.' He reached into an alcove and brought out a bottle of clear liquid. 'Here, but it's a waste of good drink.'

She tutted and poured a little on to the cloth and pressed it against his arm. He raked in a breath.

Next she set to work on wiping the blood from his temple and his face was so close, she could feel his warm breath against her cheek. She had the feeling that he felt uncomfortable, that he wasn't used to someone nursing him back to health. Had he had anyone care for him these past few years? Jealousy smarted at the thought.

'Almost done,' she said, trying to help him relax. 'How did you get this one?' she said, brushing her finger across the scar through his eyebrow.

'That one was more a battle of wills.'

'You are very brave,' she said.

And then he reached out to grip her hand at his temple. She froze.

'That makes two of us,' he said. 'You were brave to come here, Bekah. To do the journey you just did. To leave your home…'

'Brave—or foolish?' she whispered.

His thumb smoothed over the tender skin on the inside of her wrist.

'Brave.'

She felt unsteady after the events of the evening, and goose pimples erupted all over her skin at his touch.

'Why *did* you decide to come?' he asked.

'You know why,' she stuttered, staring down into his eyes. 'I had to get away from there.'

And because I wanted Gytha to get to know you.

She bit her lip.

He nodded. 'Is that the only reason? That you wanted to escape?' His gaze seemed to penetrate her soul, as if he could see right through her.

'Yes. No.' she frowned. She didn't know what he was expecting her to say. Was it hot in here? Her cheeks were glowing from the warmth of the fire—or from being so close to him again.

She swallowed. 'What other reason could there be?'

He nodded, releasing her, and stood, moving the water and cloth to the side. 'Go to bed now, Rebekah. I'll clean this up.'

She noticed she was back to being called Rebekah again.

'Is that an order?' she said, annoyed at his command—and the loss of his touch from her skin. She felt a lump form in her throat at the sudden distance. She wanted to be as brave as he thought she was and speak the truth, to say he had been the reason she'd come here, that she wouldn't have left with anyone else, that she wanted to know him again. That she wanted Gytha to know her father. But he was already so angry about what he'd missed, what he'd lost, that fear kept her quiet. She was afraid of what he would say in return.

'It's a…recommendation.'

Resigned, she made her way over to the back area. She halted at the curtain, turning back towards him, watching him pull on his tunic, tugging it gingerly over his wound. When she hadn't answered his question honestly, she'd seen an old resentment creep into his eyes and she thought back to what he'd said on the longship. *What, not good enough for you?* Was that what he thought she'd felt back then, or now?

She realised he struggled to trust her. But even so, he had still opened up his home to her and Gytha. This place was all he had in the world and he was sharing it with them. If she wanted him to let his guard down with her, she knew she would have to do the thing she felt would be hardest to do in the whole world: she, too, would have to share something of herself to reach him.

Rædan lay in bed, thinking this was possibly the worst decision he'd made in his life. He was unaccustomed to having a woman in his house. And a child. How was he ever going to sleep again, with Rebekah in the bed just across the room from him? He'd known torture before, but this was far worse. He was still wound up from those men daring to come to his home and trying to take her for themselves. He had been so determined not to let anything bad happen to her, he'd been pretty brutal in his treatment of Ogden. But he would defend his home and its new inhabitants every night if he had to. He would do anything to keep them safe.

As she'd lingered on the edge of the long-house earlier, her head bowed, his heart had gone out to Rebekah.

She had been stoic on the journey here and then she'd had to face all those strangers staring at her, as if they'd never seen a Saxon woman before. Memories had crashed over him at how he'd felt when he'd first arrived here. He knew exactly what she was going through, as he'd once been in that position, too. He'd felt worthless and at the mercy of the people in that hall. Now, those people respected him. He hoped it would be the same for her. He would do whatever he had to do to make it so.

He hated that she'd had to suffer the humiliation of Ogden demanding her as his reward. The man couldn't take his beady eyes off her and Rædan wanted to kill him, just for looking at her like that. But she'd dealt with their greedy gazes and wild whisperings with strength and dignity. Glancing his way, she'd given him a tight smile and he knew she was concerned—for herself, but mainly for her child. He knew she would defend Gytha with her life. They both would. It was why he'd taken her arm in his, squeezed it tight, to offer her some of his strength. And he'd been glad when he'd finally got them through his door this evening.

He closed his eyes and her face filled his mind. She looked like a different person to the noblewoman who'd greeted him in the Saxon hall just a few days before. Now her clothes and her hair were all mussed up from being out at sea for days, her skin bronzed by the sun and the wind, and he knew she was exhausted. But even though her eyes were heavy and her lips taut, she was still the most stunning woman he'd ever seen. Tomorrow, he would source them some new clothes, he thought. He had come to realise how important clothes were to feeling as though you belonged, as something to shape your personality. Having none while on that slave ship had made him feel degraded, worthless.

He threw the furs off him and padded over to the curtain and peered round it. He hadn't been lying when he'd told her he used to steal into Ryestone and watch her sleeping. Always in his thoughts, he'd needed to know she was all right and it was the same now. He had vowed to hate Rebekah, but how was it that she was winning him over with a smile, a word, a touch at a time?

He saw they were both fast asleep, curled up like spoons in the bed. His eyes travelled over Rebekah's face in the darkness, her radiant russet-coloured hair now loose and spread across the furs. He wanted nothing more than to kiss her forehead, to stroke her hair and wake her, as she had done to Gytha the other morning, to see her green eyes blink open and smile up at him. But if he tried it, the reality was she'd probably freeze in fear. She'd wonder what the hell he was doing and push him away, horrified.

He knew Lord Atol had hurt her and although there had been times over the past few days when he'd wanted to reach out to comfort her, touch her, he'd stopped himself, knowing he mustn't. She wouldn't like it. He couldn't ruin the fragile truce they'd made. Allies, they'd said.

She rolled over on to her side towards him and he stilled. He should go. He didn't think she'd appreciate waking up and finding him standing here, gawking at her.

He sighed. He wondered if they were both really so different. He always shut people out—he was used to only being able to rely on himself, he found it hard to trust and he had the feeling she was keeping him at arm's length to protect herself, too.

He padded back to bed, but not before noticing her breeches had been discarded on the floor and, instantly, he was hard. What was she wearing beneath those animal furs? He'd love to find out. But surprisingly, it wasn't just her body he wanted to explore. He was also craving her company and that was new. Up until now, he'd always preferred to be on his own, with just Runa for company, but tonight he had found it strangely comforting to have her here to talk to at the end of the day, to share his thoughts with by the fire. It had been...*nice*.

Damn, his feelings disturbed him—since when did he need comfort? He certainly wasn't someone destined for family life.

For years on that slave ship, no one had ever cared to listen about how he felt about things. No one had bothered if he was hurt, or hungry. The times they came ashore, he'd had to share a dirty floor with other pitiful creatures like him, but they'd often been too tired to talk.

He had arrived here after being rescued by Knud and the Jarl had made him the man he was today—he'd given him ships and allowed him the freedom to raid and conquer lands, bringing back treasure, proving his worth. He'd made a name for himself, and now people looked up to him, respected him, wanted to hear his opinions. Perhaps people would talk about him one day, when he was long gone. Only he wondered if they would still feel that way if they knew the truth about his past. He doubted it.

Jarl Knud and his sister had been good at keeping it quiet. They had been the only people he'd ever confided in and even they didn't know everything. It was disconcerting that he wanted to share his thoughts with Rebekah—but he wasn't sure he could ever tell her the full facts. He would never want her looking at him with pity in her eyes.

What was it about her that made him want to talk, to keep the conversation going—was it their shared history? She had opened up to him about her relationship with Atol and what she'd suffered. Did she deserve to know where he'd been and what had happened to him? It would mean letting her in, deconstructing the walls he'd built up around his heart. No, he wasn't ready to do that. Some truths were best left unshared.

He tossed and turned, trying to get his body to relax, to get some sleep, when he heard the gentle pull of the curtain, the sound of bare feet on the floor, the scraping of pots being moved about. Damn. He threw the furs off him again.

'Can't sleep?'

Rebekah jumped, startled. She spun round and his body hardened at the sight of her in her thin cotton tunic. So this was what she was wearing and it barely reached the top of her thighs! He'd got his wish—and his comeuppance, for his mouth dried and his groin throbbed with the heavy pull of his arousal.

'You scared me,' she said, her hand over her chest.

'Sorry.'

He took in her wide green eyes, her flushed cheeks. He wanted to rake his hands through her long fiery locks, all the way down to the tips. He swallowed.

'I was just going to get a drink, but I can't reach the cups,' she said. 'I didn't mean to wake you.'

He stretched up, close to her, his naked chest brushing against her arm, and brought down a wooden tumbler, handing it to her. 'You didn't.'

'Thank you.'

She poured herself a drink and he went to go. He knew he ought to leave, now, before he did something he'd regret.

'Rædan,' she said softly. And he wavered. Slowly, he turned around. 'Did you come to some kind of an arrangement, with Jarl Knud, about the treasure?' she asked. 'Was I given to you instead?'

'You were never his to give,' he said carefully.

Her brow furrowed.

'And do you think Atol meant what he said, about coming after us?'

Were these all the things she was worrying about, preventing her from sleeping? She chewed her bottom lip and he wanted to run his thumb along it, to reassure her and wipe her fears away.

'Possibly. But it will take a while for him to secure a fleet of ships and to navigate his way here...'

'What will happen if he does?'

'We'll be ready for him.'

She nodded. 'Aren't we putting others at risk?'

'Let's worry about it if or when it happens. You're safe now. You should try to get some sleep...' He turned to go.

'Rædan, wait. When you asked me before, why I came here... I wasn't exactly truthful.' She stared down at her bare feet. 'I came because I knew we couldn't stay with Atol any longer—he was making us both miserable. But I also came because...'

He crossed his arms over his chest. 'Because...?'

'Because although I was angry with you, for attacking us, I wanted to know you again,' she said, toying with the cup in her hands. 'Because every day that you were gone, I missed what we had.'

His breathing faltered and he just stood there, unsure what to say or what to do, how to react.

'Did *you* want me to come?' she asked. 'Or did you take Gytha—and me—purely for revenge on Atol? If so, I hope you won't come to regret it. I hope we won't be in the way.'

His silver eyes held hers across the room and when he spoke, his voice was thick with emotion. 'I would have brought you here, Bekah, child or no child. Does that answer your question?'

She took a step towards him. His gaze dipped to the loose material of her tunic, gaping around her neck, and he wondered if she wore anything beneath—and he grew harder. Too much creamy flesh was on show. It would be dangerous if she came any closer.

She reached out and placed a hand on his folded arm. Her green eyes were huge and she was so beautiful, it hurt to look at her. And then she was leaning in, coming up on those pretty little bare feet and her lips pressed against the corner of his mouth in the sweetest, gentlest kiss. 'Thank you, Rædan. It's strange, I was exhausted before, but now I don't feel tired. My head's whirring with all these thoughts so I can't sleep.'

He felt the same, but now she'd kissed him goodnight, perhaps he would be able to. No, who was he fooling? He'd probably never sleep again.

Slowly, he released the barrier his arms were creating and his hands came up to cup her cheeks, his large thumbs caressing the corners of her lips, and he couldn't believe it when she moved closer, almost pressing her body gently against his. Almost.

'Is there anything else I can get you?' His heated gaze held hers. His voice didn't sound like his own. 'Anything you want?'

She took the final step towards him, closing the distance between them. 'You could kiss me back,' she whispered bravely.

And there was no way he could deny her.

Finally, he allowed his fingers to rake through the hair around her ears, clasping her head in his hands, and he gently pulled her face towards him. He dipped his head and saw her eyelids flutter shut as he covered her lips with his. He was careful not to crush her mouth as brutally as he had the other day, but instead tried to rein in his control, tentatively sweeping his tongue intimately between her lips, coaxing her to open up, to let him in.

And she did, drawing his tongue into her mouth, sliding her own against his, the never-to-be-forgotten fervent flick of her tongue making him shiver. His hand at the nape of her neck gathered up her incredible hair in his palm, drawing it away from her skin, giving his mouth access to trail down her throat, and she trembled beneath his feather-light touch.

Her fingers ran over his chest and clung on to his shoulders for support and he tugged her closer, tightening his other hand around her waist. His mouth drifted to place light little licks along her jawline, quickening her pulse, hardening his arousal, and he couldn't resist grazing his hand down over her breast, his hand splaying out over the soft swell, tenderly squeezing it in his palm, desperate to explore her body again—and she gasped, tipping her head back, giving his mouth access to the bare expanse of her neck.

His excitement hitched when she groaned at the pleasure he was creating. He dragged the material of her tunic downwards, exposing one beautiful swell and its rosy tip to him and he cupped her in his hand, reverently, lifting her up as he brought his lips down to take her silky hard nipple into his mouth. She shuddered and her fingers curled into his hair, clinging on.

He could be inside her in a heartbeat, he thought, as he pushed his knee between her legs and her eyes flicked open in awareness. Urgent with need he hadn't felt in years, he slid his palm along the smooth skin of her thigh and roamed upwards, his hand splaying out over the smooth, creamy flesh of one buttock, tugging her lower body against him. He wanted her to feel the hard length of him. He wanted her to know what she did to him. But when he heard her sharp inhalation of shock, the pressure of her hand increasing on his chest, he knew he'd pushed her too far and then the sound of a little voice came from behind the curtain, all cutting through his desire.

'Mother?'

Gytha.

He abruptly disentangled himself, pushing himself away as fast and as far as he could across the room.

'You'd better go to her,' he whispered, trying to ignore her shocked, heated look, as she tugged the material of her gown back into place, a flush burning in her cheeks. And then she was gone, out of his reach behind the curtain.

Damn it, why did it always come to this? He felt like the most base, senseless animal. After everything she'd told him she'd been through, how could he have touched her so brazenly? And in such a hurry? And what did he think he was doing, seducing her with her child in the other room?

He listened to her movements on the bed, her soft tones as she soothed Gytha back to sleep, and he poured himself an ale and drank it in one go, bracing his hands on the table. Did he have no restraint? It would seem not, not where Bekah was concerned. He went back to his bed and threw the furs over himself, trying to get the racing of his heart back under control, his mind a jumble of thoughts. It was her first night here and he'd tried to seduce her, when she'd probably just needed a few words of comfort from him—not a lesson in seduction.

Damn him, he was such a fool. What would she think of him now? Had he broken the fragile trust they'd begun to build up between them? And yet she had asked him to kiss her. He should have said no. He knew it was a bad idea. If they were to have any chance of making her living here work, he needed to get his hands and his control in check. Perhaps he deserved to be shackled after all.

Chapter Eight

When Rebekah next woke, Gytha wasn't in the bed beside her and she leapt up in a panic. She threw back the curtain and found the hut was empty. Gytha and Rædan were nowhere to be seen. She rushed out the door in her tunic, distraught—to find two startled faces and a dog looking up at her.

'Mother!'

'I—I thought something had happened,' she said, ashen-faced, her hand clutching her chest.

'Everything's fine,' Rædan said, continuing to dig his tool firmly into the soil over and over again. 'We thought we'd let you sleep off the events of the last few days.' She noticed he didn't meet her gaze.

'Oh,' she said, flustered, her thoughts instantly on the kiss they'd shared last night.

How she'd practically begged him to kiss her. 'What—what are you two doing out here?'

'Rædan is showing me and Runa how to plant cabbage,' Gytha said, rushing to speak. 'We've done three already!'

Rædan continued to explain something to Gytha about the ground and the child listened to his every word with rapt attention, nodding her head enthusiastically, asking questions. And he was very tolerant, answering each one.

'I hope she's not being a nuisance,' Rebekah said, standing watching them awkwardly, as if she was in the way.

'Not at all. You don't mind—me looking after her?' he asked, and she couldn't believe he was seeking her approval. She couldn't believe he was giving up his time for her at all. She thought he'd spent more time with the child in the space of a few days than Atol had done in seven years.

She shook her head. It was good to see they were getting on, but she couldn't help wanting to be a part of it, too. She bit her lip.

'Do you want some help?' she offered tentatively.

His eyes widened in surprise. She knew he had always seen her as a precious beauty, something to be lauded and admired. But she wanted to show him she was more than that, that she didn't mind getting her hands dirty. She wasn't afraid of hard work.

'I don't expect you to provide for me, Rædan,' she said sharply. 'I can weave and cook, and I know how to look after animals—and the land.' Why did she feel she had to explain herself?

Feeling out of place, she turned to go. She didn't know why she felt envious of their new-found rapport. She should be pleased, shouldn't she?

'We were just about to make some breakfast. You could help with that?' Rædan asked, halting her retreat, and her heart lifted. He could have asked her to clean out the pig pen with them and she would have been delighted just to be included.

'Thank you, I'll just get dressed,' she said.

'Did you sleep well?' he asked, finally meeting her eye when she stepped out of the back room. Gytha was setting the bowls out on the table, Runa following her around wherever she went.

She nodded. 'Surprisingly, yes. Eventually. You?'

He shrugged. 'I got a little... What do you want?' he asked.

Her head shot up.

He motioned to the bread and eggs on the side.

Anything else you want? He had spoken those words to her last night and she'd told him she wanted him to kiss her. She couldn't believe she'd been so bold. But when he'd taken her in his arms and pressed his lips to hers it had felt wonderful. She'd forgotten what it was like, to be held and kissed so passionately. Yet then she had felt the hard ridge of his arousal nudging into her hip and the reciprocal, languid heat pooling between her legs...and she'd been relieved Gytha had interrupted them.

It wasn't so much his, but her own brazen response that had shocked her. She remembered the feel of him before, when he was younger, but now he was all man, all muscle... And she had wanted... She realised she had wanted him again from the moment she'd seen him on the battlefield at Ryestone, his face turned up towards her, his boot on Lord Atol's chest. But now she was embarrassed. What would he think of her, pulling him close one moment, then pushing him away the next? She felt the heat rise in her cheeks at the memory and his eyes narrowed on her.

'I can do it,' she said, busying herself with the pans.

He raised an eyebrow. 'Have you ever cooked before?' The smile tugging at his lips was irritating. Infuriating.

'Of course I have,' she said, swiping a spoon out of his hand.

'I thought, being a Lady and all, you'd have maids to do that kind of thing for you.'

'I'm more than capable.'

A while later, Rædan and Gytha sat at the table eating burned eggs. Gytha was pulling a face, both of them wrinkling up their noses, and Rædan couldn't contain his grin.

'All right, so I might need you to show me how to make a few things.' Rebekah shrugged.

'I can do that,' he conceded. It was strange seeing him in his natural habitat. He seemed at ease, content here. 'But first, I'm going to show you where we bathe.'

'What?'

'I thought you might want to freshen yourself up? And then I want to go to the market to get you both some new clothes.'

'Is that really necessary?' she asked.

'What? The bath or the clothes?'

'Both!' she said, throwing her hands up, exasperated.

He looked her up and down. 'I think so, yes.'

Rebekah blushed and Gytha giggled.

'Well, here,' she said, tugging off her rings and her brooches, flustered. 'Take these.'

He frowned, looking at the pile of precious metal, and shook his head. 'Keep them.'

'No. I noticed you didn't get to take any of the treasure in the hall yesterday. I want to pay our way—be that working the land or selling my jewels.'

'I've got more than enough,' he said, looking up at her. And hope blossomed within her.

'These rings would fetch a good price. And I don't need them. Please.'

He sighed, reluctantly tucking the trinkets into his tunic. 'Very well. Thank you. Right, come on, everyone outside. In Nedergaard, we tend to all bathe together on Laugardagur— a Saturday. You have a lot to learn about life here.' Would he enjoy teaching them, sharing it all with them? 'But there's nothing stopping us from going in the fjord now.'

Bouncing up and down, her eyes wide and round, Gytha was suddenly excited. 'We're allowed in the water?'

'Yes. If it's all right with your mother. But I warn you, it's very cold.'

'The church prohibits people from public bathing,' Rebekah said and Gytha's face fell. 'Don't you remember?'

His eyes lit up with wicked amusement. 'What, they think it could lead to immorality?' He grinned. 'It's a good job we can *swim* any day of the week then, isn't it?' He stood and offered her his hand. 'Are you up for it?'

She sighed, resigned. Gytha looked so excited at the prospect, she didn't want to let her down. In Ryestone, her daughter had walked around as if she wanted to go unnoticed, timid and pale. Right now, she had a strong colour in her cheeks from their journey and a smile on her face. It was such a turnaround in a short few days.

'All right,' she said, relenting. She really did need to bathe. She took his hand and he helped her to her feet, her fingers tingling from his touch. Every time he touched her, her body went up in flames. Did he know what he was doing—how he was affecting her? 'What do we wear?'

'I'll find you something.'

Last night, after she'd soothed Gytha back

to sleep, there was a disturbing part of her that wanted to go back to him, to see if he would pull her close again. But thoughts of what would happen if he did had held her back. She had grown to fear a man's hands on her skin. Yet Rædan... He'd treated her well since she'd been in his company again, proving the boy she'd once loved was still in there somewhere, beneath the exterior of the fierce man he'd become. He had reminded her just how pleasurable his touch could be.

Yet it wasn't that stable boy that now had heat blooming low beneath her belly, it was this strong warrior who was getting her all hot and bothered, whenever she thought about letting him put his hands on her body again. She knew she wanted him, but she was afraid. And surely it wasn't a good idea. She had Gytha to think about.

She had chosen to involve him in Gytha's life—although she wasn't yet ready to tell him or her child what they were to each other. She'd seen the natural way he'd had with Gytha, so was she worried he'd let her down? Or did it have more to do with her own feelings? For didn't she fear that if he knew, he would claim the child as his own...and then what would that mean for her?

* * *

Rædan found her one of his tunics to wear and it was so huge, it swamped her. He was pleased. The less of her body on show, the better. It might just help him to keep his hands in check.

He stripped off his tunic, leaving his trousers on, and sunk beneath the cool water, soaking his tired, aching body. It felt glorious. He'd missed this. When he'd first arrived here, he'd bathed in the fjord for hours, not caring about the cold, wanting to wash off the stain of the past years of his life. And he did believe the water here had healing powers. He determined he would take Rebekah up to the hot springs one day soon, so she could experience that, too.

Gytha loved splashing about in the shallows and he showed her how to move her arms and kick her legs in the water, as he had done with Rebekah the other day when she'd thrown herself out of the boat. He still couldn't believe she'd done that—she had fire in her, this woman. It seemed like an age ago. Now she was here, bathing with him.

His eyes glittered at her across the clear blue water. She was so beautiful, lying back and soaking her red hair, which was splaying out around her. She was more beautiful than the sea goddess Rán. More beautiful than any woman he'd ever seen. But he should have known better than to touch her last night. He knew he ought to apologise.

Wading over to her, she righted herself in the water, chewing her bottom lip again. Checking they were out of earshot from Gytha, he still lowered his voice.

'I wanted to say I'm sorry, about last night,' he said. But her request for him to kiss her had been too tempting. He'd wanted to show her that he was trustworthy, that he could be gentle—and then he'd got carried away, pushing his knee between her legs and bringing her up hard against his arousal.

'Don't be,' she said, a blush creeping into her cheeks. 'It was all my doing.'

'Really? All on your own?' He smiled.

'Can we put it down as a mistake?'

'Easier said than done. But probably wise, given the circumstances.'

'It's so knotty,' she said, raking a hand through her long hair, changing the subject. 'I haven't combed it in days.'

'Do you want some help washing it?' he asked.

Her gaze swung up at him, disbelief in her eyes.

'I have soap,' he said, holding up the bar by way of an explanation. 'Turn around.'

Slowly, apprehensively, she did as she was told. 'I'm not used to wearing it down. It's getting a bit unmanageable. Maybe I need to cut it.'

'Don't do that. It would be a tragedy.'

He gathered her hair in his hands around the base of her neck, lifting it away from her skin, and she shivered at his touch.

He paused. 'Is this all right?'

She nodded, so he continued, running the soap over the wet tendrils.

He became excruciatingly aware of her back almost touching his chest. It would be so easy to pull her up against him, to mould her curves to his hard ridges. But he mustn't. When was he going to learn his lesson?

'It feels good to get clean again,' she said.

'I know.'

'What is that around your neck?' she asked.

He glanced down to look at the pendant resting on his chest. She hadn't even been looking at him, so her question took him by surprise. 'It's Mjolnir—Thor's hammer. It's a symbol of power and protection.'

Once he'd soaped up her hair, he told her to lie back in the water and he held her head, washing out the suds. When he was done, she rose out of the water to stand again and he was glad his lower body was beneath the water, so she couldn't see what effect she was having on him. He soaped up his hands again and smoothed them over her shoulders, then over his own, before swiping his finger over the smear of dirt on her cheek and she froze.

He instantly removed his hands.

'All right. You're clean enough. We can get out now.'

They waded back to the shallows and he saw Gytha was playing with something on the sand, cupping it in her hand.

'What have you got there?'

'A little crab. Look!' she said, holding up the creature, its legs flailing beneath.

'Fascinating,' he said. 'But you should put that back where it belongs.'

Her face dropped. 'Why? I want to keep it.'

'Maybe so, but I'm sure that crab doesn't want to be stuck in your hands when he can be out crawling around on the sand, free. No creature wants to be caged. It's not right.'

'Sorry,' she said and reluctantly tumbled it

out on to the shore. They watched as it scuttled away, sideways.

'Good girl,' Rebekah said and took the child's hand and led her up the beach to the farm.

Rædan couldn't help but rake his eyes over Bekah's body. He'd told himself not to, to give her some space, but the dark material of his tunic was clinging to her breasts and her stomach. You would never know she had carried and nurtured a child for nine moon cycles. She looked incredible.

Charging ahead of them to get dry, Gytha raced inside to get dressed, already excited for the market, their next adventure. But Rædan took Rebekah's arm, tugging her back.

'How was the birth?' he asked quietly. 'I never asked you.'

She glanced up at him, surprised, as if no one had ever asked her that before. 'Painful,' she admitted truthfully.

'And afterwards? Did you recover well?'

She nodded. 'Yes. It was only Atol who caused any lasting damage...'

He felt his face darken. 'Do you want to tell me about it?' he asked, his voice strained.

She glanced over at the door, to check Gytha

couldn't hear them, but the girl was now playing happily with Runa inside.

'It might help if I know more about it,' Rædan pressed.

She shrugged, closing the door and walking back out to the fence, leaning against it. 'There's not much to say. He'd come to my room at night, drag me out of my bed by my hair, and take me on the floor, like I was some kind of dog.'

His brow formed a harsh line and he closed his eyes, as if the images she was describing were too horrific to imagine. 'Did you ever tell anyone about it?'

'Who would I tell? My uncle had died and there was no one else who would listen or care. When I had Gytha, I thought he might leave me alone, but that was just the beginning. He had this hold over me. It was always a blessing when he found himself a new mistress for a while—it meant he wouldn't come to my bed. I'd have a reprieve from his brutal touch.'

'I'm so sorry, Bekah.' It made him sick to think of what she'd had to suffer. This man had caused them both so much damage—would they ever be able to recover from it?

Just then, a little robin landed on the fence

next to them, bobbing its head up and down. 'I swear that bird follows me around,' she said. 'I used to think it was you, or my parents, visiting me.'

He raised an eyebrow. 'Perhaps like is attracted to like,' he said, running a strand of her red hair between his fingers. 'Here in Nedergaard, they do call robins the firebird.'

'I'm hardly that, not with my fear.'

'Oh, I don't know... I was thinking more about your fiery temper!' he teased. And her passion...

She grinned. 'I'm sorry, too, about last night,' she said, and then sighed. 'It's just...he's taught me to believe a man's touch isn't meant to be gentle. That it's not meant to please a woman...'

He took a step towards her and stroked his thumb over her cheek. 'That's not the way I see it, Bekah.'

'All right, shall we head to the market?'

'You go,' Rebekah said. She longed for a bit of space to get her thoughts in order. She needed some distance from him, as her nerves were in overdrive, her body still tingling from the way he'd stroked and washed her hair in the water, helping her to get clean. And then the words he'd whispered to her outside…

'Would you mind if I didn't come? If I stayed here?'

He frowned. 'I think you should come with me. I don't feel right leaving you here on your own,' he said, suddenly serious.

'I'll be fine,' she said. 'I've got my sword. Haven't I proved to you I can defend myself by now? Besides, surely you can't always be here to watch over us?' She hoped not—she thought she would go crazy under his constant heated gaze. 'Plus you said you wouldn't give me orders.'

He seemed to think about this for a moment. 'Very well. But do you mind if I take Gytha?'

She bit her lip.

'I'll guard her with my life.'

'Please, Mother? Please may I go?' And the new glow in her daughter's eyes made her concede.

'All right. But be careful. Stay with Rædan.'

Runa and Rebekah watched them go, the two of them strolling along the beach, and Rebekah felt her heart might burst when she saw Gytha's little hand curl up into his. She couldn't believe how easily she was trusting him with her child…but she had relented because Gytha had wanted to go with him so much. And he had been careful with her so far. As he had been with her…

Again she found herself wondering if she should tell him. She knew it was wrong to keep this enormous secret from him, to deny him the knowledge of knowing he was a father. But the truth was, she was afraid of how he might react. She didn't want to give him cause to be angry with her, not when they were getting on so well.

She watched them as far as she could and when they had disappeared from sight, she pottered around the settlement, getting to know the animals on Rædan's farm, watering the crops, sweeping the floors, acutely aware she felt a strange sense of contentment in this little place. It was homely and she found herself chattering away to Runa, plus she also attempted to grind the grains for their bread the next day. She'd show him she could cook! Back at Ryestone, she'd been responsible for running much of the fortress, as Atol hadn't cared much for any type of work, instead spending his time hunting or bedding other women. But she had been glad of it, to keep her mind busy.

* * *

It was mid-afternoon when she saw a figure heading towards her across the sand. Raising her hand to shield her eyes from the sun, she tried to make out who it was. It couldn't be Rædan. If it was, where was Gytha? When Runa started growling, a pit emptied in her stomach. She knew this couldn't be good. The dog set off in search of her foe and Rebekah hurried inside, swiping up her sword from the side, closing the door and leaning back on it, her eyes darting round for anything else she could use to ward someone off if she had to.

The rattling of the door made her heart lurch and she bit down on her lip to stop her crying out. Where was Rædan? Surely he would be home soon? She suddenly felt foolish for not wanting him to boss her about, being too stubborn and saying she'd stay here on her own. She didn't know this place, or what the people were capable of. She'd been too bold, too soon. She'd forgotten all too quickly how fiercely the men had stormed Ryestone's fortress. She'd tried to forget about those men coming to the farm last night…

When she heard the man's footsteps retreating, she released a breath. Perhaps the visitor had realised no one was in and was about to make his way back across the beach. But then the door swung open at force, smashing into her and slicing open her forehead, causing her to crumple on to the ground. She tried to focus her gaze on the large boots swimming in front of her as the man stepped into the room, kicking the door shut behind him, then two rough hands gripped her dress and bundled her upwards.

The room was spinning before her eyes and she was aware of blood trickling down her face, of being hauled on to the table and dread pounded through her veins, her whole body trembling. Her vision cleared to see Ogden, the man from yesterday, rearing over her and he was unbuckling his belt, undoing his trousers.

Fear lodged in her throat. 'What are you doing? Let me go!' she whispered. 'Rædan will be back any moment.'

He punched her in the face, knocking her backwards.

'I'm going to show you what we do to slaves around here. What you're good for.'

She felt sick, her mind racing. She struggled to sit back up again, to fight him off, but he was looming over her, pushing her backwards, try-ing to spread her legs, forcing his large body between them. And she tried to claw him off with her hands, kick him away, to remember all the tricks her uncle had shown her, but he was just too strong.

Something was wrong. Rædan knew it the instant they made it halfway up the beach and Runa didn't come bounding along to meet them. Despite all the goods he was carrying, he picked up Gytha with his other arm and set off at a pace over the sand, trying to keep calm despite the alarm racing through his blood. He'd been eager to get back to Rebekah, to check she was all right. They'd had a good afternoon browsing the stalls, the little girl delighting in all the colours of the materials and trying out all the spices and different textures of food. But the moment he saw Runa in a crumpled heap on the shore, near the entrance to the hut, it was all forgotten. He checked the dog over, saw the wound to its stomach and told Gytha to stay with her.

And then he sprinted towards the shack, his pulse thundering. 'Bekah?' he shouted.

He heard the sound of pots crashing, the bench scraping, and he reached the door and kicked it open. Bekah's head shot up and her body sagged in relief when she saw him. He took in the scene at once—Bekah fighting off Ogden, blood to her brow, the man looming over her, his trousers undone. And he saw red.

He reached for his sword and the man went for his. But Rædan was too quick. He bore down on him, the man raising his hands in defeat. And he raised his blade to finish him—but Bekah's hand on his arm stalled him.

'Stop,' she said. 'I'm all right. Leave him.'

But his anger was blinding him, he couldn't think straight. He hauled the man to his feet and threw him out the house, kicking him on to the sand, knocking him unconscious with the hilt of his sword. Quickly binding Ogden's wrists with some rope, Rædan tied him to a wooden boundary post.

He turned back to the hut, to Bekah. 'Are you hurt?' he demanded, his blood pounding, aware his voice was far harsher than it should be. He stood before her as she sat up on the table and he quickly checked over her forehead and looked for any other signs of injury. He felt sick to the stomach.

She shook her head. 'I'm fine. Just a little shaken. Where's Gytha?'

'She's outside. She's all right.'

'Runa?'

'Hurt.'

Bekah gasped, her eyes welling with tears. 'This is all my fault. I should have listened to you—come with you to the market. It was foolish to stay behind on my own.'

He gripped her head and pulled her into his chest, closing his eyes and sending a silent thanks up to the gods. He would never have forgiven himself if something had happened. If something *worse* had happened. Her body was trembling in his arms and he hated himself for having left her, for not being here to look after her.

'I'm never letting you out of my sight again.'

And she laughed into his chest, sniffing. 'Ever?'

'No.'

He kissed her forehead and went to fetch a cloth, to patch up her wound as she had done for him last night.

'I'm fine,' she protested. 'Let's check on the girls.'

He wavered, before nodding, deciding Runa might need more urgent attention. He followed her as she staggered out to the beach, wobbly on her feet, past the limp body of the knocked-out brute, to where Gytha was stroking Runa as the dog lay on the sand, its breathing laboured.

Bekah gasped as she sank down on her knees before the animal.

Rædan stroked away some of her fur, to take a better look at the wound, and the dog cocked its head, its ears twitching. 'Gytha, run and get me something to patch this up with, will you? A sheet or something.'

The little girl nodded, before running off, and Bekah looked at him, concerned. 'Will she live?'

He nodded. 'I hope so.'

'Thanks goodness. I think she tried to protect me.'

'I wouldn't expect anything less.'

Moments later, Gytha came dashing back towards them, handing Rædan the sheet, and he tore it up with his teeth, making bandages to wrap around the dog's body, to stem the flow of blood.

'Is she going to die?' Gytha asked him, her little face crumpling.

'No, she's tougher than that. She'll be fine. But she'll need plenty of rest and lots of looking after by you.'

'I can do that.'

He gathered the dog up in his arms and Runa struggled and whined, but he managed to get her inside the hut and laid her down by the hearth. Gytha loyally sat by her side.

He came back to Rebekah, touched his fingers to her brow. 'Now you. Sit down.'

Dutifully, she did as she was told, the shock seeming to have set in now and she began to dither. He wrapped a blanket around her and lit the fire, before beginning to clean up the mess of her face.

Despite her wound, she was still achingly beautiful. He didn't know how he could have left her alone for a moment. He vowed to himself he would never do it again, not if she was at risk. Damn it, he thought he'd warned those men off last night. He was such a fool to believe they'd heeded his or Jarl Knud's warning.

His hand to her brow, he was as gentle as he could be, but he knew each swipe of the cloth smarted. He could see it in the bracing of her jaw, the widening of her eyes. But she still let him do it, trusting him.

When he was done, he came to sit down beside her, his arms opening to hold her, gathering her close. He pulled her into his shoulder, his hands smoothing over her hair, giving her the comfort she needed. The kind of comfort he should have given her last night, instead of trying to seduce her. He was glad when she didn't pull away, but instead rested her head in the curve of his neck. Perhaps she didn't think him too much of a beast.

After a while, she finally pulled her head away to look up at him.

'How was the market?' she asked.

The little girl stopped stroking the dog and jumped up, suddenly pleased to share some good news.

'Rædan brought you some new clothes!' she said, nodding over at the material stacked up on the side. 'And me!'

'I thought you'd need them for your new life here. That is, if you still want to stay,' he said slowly.

Would she still want to? Or had the events of today, the awful attack, put her off this place for good?

Gytha showed her the new garments and Bekah smiled.

'They're all different shades of green!'

'To match your eyes,' Rædan said.

'Try them on!' Gytha said, excitedly.

And when Bekah pulled back the curtain to

show him and Gytha her new Danish attire, his eyes grazed over her, admiringly. He stalked towards her across the small space and, reaching up, he unclasped the chain around his neck and, turning her around, he fastened it around hers instead. Her breath caught.

'To keep you safe,' he whispered.

She looked up at him, fingering the little silver hammer. 'Thank you.'

'I will see that he's reprimanded,' Rædan said, a scowl carving into his face, taking her chin between his fingers. 'Ours is a culture of honour here in Nedergaard. I could have killed him for what he did—without risking punishment myself. You should have let me.'

'You can't kill every man who hurts me, Rædan. Atol, Ogden—who's next?'

No one. Ever again, he thought. He must never let anyone hurt her again. Damn, but he was so worked up. What was it about this woman that stirred his feelings as well as his body? He wasn't sure he liked it.

Right now, he never wanted to let her out of his sight, but keep her as close to him as possible, if she'd let him. Last night, when Rebekah said she'd thought he wasn't afraid of anything, she was wrong. He wasn't scared of fighting, getting hurt—certainly not death. But now he had something so precious, something to protect. Now he had something to lose—and that made him more afraid than he'd felt in years.

'An assault against one of our women is an assault against the community.'

She placed a hand on his arm, perhaps to calm him. 'Is that still the case, even if your people see me as a slave?'

'You're not my slave!' he gritted out, his eyes blazing into hers.

'*I* know that…'

'Then we'll have to make them see exactly what you are, won't we? Enough is enough. We're getting married, Bekah. As soon as possible.'

'But you don't even want to get married!' she gasped, pulling away from him. 'And neither do I!'

'I'm prepared to endure it—let's call it penance for what happened between us all those years ago… If I hadn't made my feelings towards you so clear, if I hadn't taken you to bed…' He, too, stole a look at Gytha, but the child was stroking the dog, seemingly unaware of his comment '…perhaps Atol wouldn't have reacted the way he did…sending me away, making you his fiancée…hurting you.'

Bekah visibly recoiled and he knew he'd hurt her, as she had him in rejecting his offer. But the more he thought about it, the more he realised this was the only solution. Marrying her would help to keep her and Gytha out of danger—it was that or she'd just have to suffer his constant company, which wasn't very practical, especially when he wanted to bed her every time he looked at her.

And now he'd decided, there would be no changing his mind. She would just have to get used to the idea. 'If a marriage between us is what is needed to keep you and Gytha safe, then that's what's going to happen.'

The longhouse was bustling with people as they entered that night and, as Rædan shoved his prisoner before Jarl Knud, forcing him down on his knees, everyone stopped and stared. The Danish Jarl took in the man in bonds, the wound to Rebekah's forehead and the blazing anger on Rædan's face and he swore.

'Ogden, damn you! I told you they were not to be harmed. You will be punished for this.'

Rebekah was shocked the man believed them, no questions asked. He was on their side.

'But she's just a thrall,' the man protested. 'She has no rights!'

'Whatever she is, she's not yours to touch. I told you she belonged to Halfdan. I'll deal with you later.' He motioned to one of his housecarls to take the swine away and Rebekah sank down on to a bench in relief. She hoped she'd never have to see him again.

A woman with long blonde braided hair came over to her and poured her a drink. She took her chin in her hand and tilted her head up, inspecting her wound. 'You'll live,' she said kindly.

Rebekah nodded, surprised by her overfamiliarity, but instantly liking her at the same time.

'I am Brita, Knud's sister. This is your daughter?'

Rebekah nodded. 'Yes, this is Gytha.'

'Then she must play with my children. They are of the same age. Come,' she said, encouraging Gytha to go with her. Rebekah went to protest, to hold Gytha back, but then she saw the children happily playing up the corner and Gytha tentatively approach. Rebekah's heart lodged somewhere in her throat as she watched the children scrutinise her child. For a moment, she held her breath—and then they happily welcomed Gytha into their game, all of them wanting to sit next to her, trying to get to know her. Her palm pressed against her chest and she sagged into her seat.

How easy it was for children, she thought. They weren't old enough to form any preconceived opinions—they just accepted someone on sight. She knew what everyone thought of her—that she was a slave who belonged to Rædan and that she was fair game. Would marrying Rædan really change their opinion of her and make them treat her differently? She glanced around, looking for him, and saw he was deep in conversation with Knud, the older man's arm around his shoulder, trying to calm him down.

She couldn't believe he wanted to marry her. Well, *want* wasn't the right word for it. She couldn't believe he was insisting upon marrying her. She took a sip of the ale Brita had given her, enjoying the feeling of the alcohol warming her stomach and easing her nerves. And then the woman was back, stepping over the bench to sit beside her.

'Nice dress,' the other woman said.

'Thank you.' She was wearing one of the new ones Rædan had picked out for her at the market. They were plain, practical, but she loved all the different shades of green. When she'd tried them on and his eyes had raked over her, she'd felt her skin prickle with awareness. And when he'd given her his pendant, her breath had caught. In that moment, she realised he was still a kind man. He seemed to care for her and she him. And there was this thing between them that was making her insane with need. But that didn't mean they should get married!

'They are making the wedding plans for Frigga's Day,' Brita said, patting Rebekah's thigh, as if following her thoughts.

'Frigga's Day?'

'The goddess of Love and Childbirth,' she said. 'Tomorrow. Your husband-to-be is very keen,' she said with a knowing wink. 'You are very lucky. When you find a good man, you are right to keep hold of him. To make him yours. I lost mine to the sword a few months ago.'

'I'm so sorry,' Rebekah said.

'He left me with six children to rear. Six! I would not recommend you and Halfdan having that many.' She grinned. 'In the morning,

I shall take you to the hot springs to cleanse, before the ceremony. It is tradition here.'

Rebekah's head swam. She couldn't believe she had agreed to this, that Rædan was putting the plans in motion. She felt as if in the space of a week her life had been turned upside down, just like her and Gytha on the boat on the way over here. So much had happened in such a short time, and it was overwhelming.

Growing up, she had always had the foolish hope that she would one day marry for love, but those dreams had long been shattered. Now, in a strange twist of fate, she was finally going to marry the boy she had wanted to wed when she was eighteen. The father of her child. This was what she had always wanted—so why did it now feel as if her heart was breaking into tiny pieces? Was it because he had told her he never wanted to marry and spoken no words of tenderness? That she felt he was doing it out of duty, not desire?

She'd told him she'd never wanted to be owned by a man again, but when he'd pointed out it didn't much matter if she was his wife or his slave, that the people here thought she belonged to him anyway, she knew he was right. What difference did it make, apart from the fact that being his wife would keep her and Gytha safe?

'You were willing to marry Atol for far less than the reasons I'm giving you,' he had pointed out. And it was true. She had agreed to marry Atol in a haze of grief—but in the end, she had been relieved it had never come to pass.

She had never loved Atol and he had never cared for her. Could she now stand there and be bound to another man who didn't love her, to listen to him say vows she knew he didn't mean?

And if he wed her because he felt he had to, out of obligation, just to keep her safe, wouldn't he come to resent her for it? He had even used the words endure—that marriage was the atonement he would make for that one night they'd spent together eight years ago. She'd heard the resigned tone of his voice, his reluctance—and it had devastated her. And what would happen if they ended up hating each other? What would that do to their child then?

She knew there was this thing between them, an attraction that couldn't be denied. But she also knew that simmering desire wasn't enough to hold a marriage together. Not really. There had to be more to it—there had to be love and understanding, and most of all, trust.

But she didn't have a choice. It sounded like the date had been set, the plans put in place, and tomorrow, there would be a wedding.

Chapter Nine

Rebekah's morning had been a blur of getting ready. Brita had taken her and Gytha to the hot springs as promised and it had felt glorious to soak beneath the warm, bubbling water. It had been so wonderful she had almost forgotten it was her wedding day.

Jarl Knud's sister and her family had taken care of her, dressing her, plaiting her hair in a mass of intricate braids and painstakingly feeding little wildflowers through the knots, and now she was just about ready. Or as ready as she'd ever be.

As she walked up the aisle and saw Rædan standing there at the altar, her heart lurched. He, too, had bathed, his still-damp hair washed and swept back off his face into a band, his beard neatly trimmed. He had lost his warrior attire, instead wearing a dark tunic and trousers that clung to his muscles, highlighting the silver shards in his eyes, making her mouth dry.

Her eyes were drawn to the tanned skin at the top of his chest, the open tunic giving way to the tips of the swirls of ink that she knew lay hidden beneath. He had no equal in her eyes—she had never seen a more strikingly handsome man. But instead of smiling as she moved towards him, his brooding face was unreadable, his shuttered eyes trained on her as she approached.

She had often dreamed of this moment, in her youth, but how different it was in reality—how the circumstances had changed. She wasn't walking up the aisle in her parents' church—or even in the chapel at Ryestone. But she was on a beach, on the shores of a vast fjord in Daneland. How did she get here? she wondered.

Rædan wasn't forcing her to do this exactly, for she had agreed—but she knew there was a fair amount of trepidation about it on either side. And surely it was no longer necessary? The threat had been dealt with. Brita had told her there had been a Thing this morning, at which it had been decided there would be a holmgang. When Rebekah had asked Brita what this meant, she'd said it would mean Ogden would be made an outlaw, banished from Nedergaard for ever, and she'd been relieved that it was over.

When she and her bridesmaid, Gytha, reached him, the child gave her mother's hand to him, grinning, and he thanked her, winking, and Rebekah's smile quivered.

Then he turned to her, his penetrating gaze focusing on her face. 'You look beautiful,' he whispered.

When they'd arrived back at his home last night, they'd checked on Runa and put Gytha to bed, then he'd excused himself, saying he was tired. But hadn't he told her he barely slept? She'd lain awake for ages, her mind whirring about the day's events, the wedding plans—and what he'd said to her, trying to reassure her, about them not having to consummate their marriage. He'd promised he wouldn't touch her if she didn't want him to, that he'd stay away—and she thought she might die if that was the case. Being around him and never being able to touch him would be torture. She was all too aware he hadn't kissed her since the other night because he felt bad about his behaviour, but if he didn't do it again soon, she thought she'd go insane.

The pagan cleric began the service and, facing each other, he asked Rædan and Rebekah to take each other's hands and he began to bind them together with a crimson cord, representing the joining of their two lives together, as one. He spoke words of their intertwining lives, the union of their hopes and dreams, but when she glanced up, Rædan looked as if he was going to his execution rather than marrying the bride of his dreams.

The cord tightened around their wrists and his eyes darkened, his jaw was tense. He looked so disturbed, she almost begged the priest to stop, to put him out of his misery. She gripped his hand tighter, as if to reassure him everything would be all right. But she had the feeling his mind was elsewhere entirely. What nightmare was he reliving? She had been so wrapped up in her own worries, she hadn't stopped to think about what was going on in his mind. What demons haunted him?

She was relieved when the handfasting ceremony was over and the colour seemed to come back into his face. When it was time to exchange the wedding bands, she was shocked when he pushed her mother's gold ring on to her finger—one of the jewels she'd given him the day before at breakfast to take to the market. Her eyes shot up to his.

'I know it was your mother's,' he whispered. 'It's too precious to sell.'

She looked up at him, tears in her eyes. She was amazed he'd remembered the band had belonged to her mother and she was incredibly grateful to have it back. Her heart bloomed like the daisies in her hair.

'I have kept the rest of your trinkets safe for you, too.'

The man she was marrying certainly wasn't cruel. He had treated her kindly and shown her compassion. He had saved her life more than once. And she knew he desired her, as she did him. This thing had been raging between them since they were eighteen, like the flame of a fire that would never go out. And like all fires, it made her feel radiant and warm, but it also scared her. Fires could burn bright, but they could also die out…but either way, they could cause a lot of damage.

When the cleric said Rædan could now kiss the bride, he stepped closer, his eyes glittering down at her, his hands coming up to hold her face, and he placed a gentle, lingering kiss on her lips. The intensity of his touch sent a shot of heat down between her legs and she couldn't help feeling it was a promise of what was to come...

She wasn't sure how Jarl Knud and his sister had put on such an enormous celebration in the space of one day, but they had done a wonderful job. After the ceremony, there was a sacrifice, to thank the gods for bringing the couple together, and then, without warning, Rædan swung Rebekah up in his arms, his large hands firmly, but gently, holding the tops of her thighs, her arms and hip pressed into his chest, and he carried her into the longhouse. Her chest against his, her arms wrapped around his neck, smiling up at him, she actually felt happy—and she didn't want to let him go.

He stared down at her for a moment, not seeming to want to put her down either, but a huge feast had been prepared, which all of the people in Nedergaard had helped put together, and the rest of the villagers began to bundle into the hall, sweeping them up with them. The afternoon was a blur of singing and dancing, food and ale, and everyone was in fine spirits.

They had been so busy talking to their guests, the women now wanting to meet and get to know Rædan's new bride, the men wanting an audience with the groom, that she barely got to speak to him until later in the afternoon, when he managed to steal her away from Brita and some of the other women and led her outside.

'Are you having fun?' he asked.

'Actually, I am.' She smiled.

'Good.'

'Where are we going?' she asked.

'I wanted a moment alone with…my wife,' he said, taking her hand in his. Tingles erupted up her arm. 'And I have something for you.'

'Rædan, I don't need gifts. I have more than enough. Everything I need.'

'Still, you have to have a present on your wedding day—it's tradition.' Arriving at a gate, she saw they'd come to a field where a white stallion was grazing.

'I know how much you like to ride,' he said, motioning to the animal.

And she gasped. 'You got me a horse?' she

said, placing her hand over her heart. And then she laughed with pure pleasure. 'Rædan, thank you. It's an incredible gesture.'

Gytha came charging up the path after them. 'I helped to pick him. He looks like a Wilburh, don't you think?' she said.

Rebekah laughed. 'Does he?'

'Can we call him that? Please?'

'If you insist.'

'He may need a rest before you ride him. He's had a long journey from the other side of the mountains. He will probably need a few days to adjust to it here.'

'Well, that makes three of us.' She smiled.

Back inside, sat together at a long table, they were presented with more gifts and so much honey mead she thought that it would last them a whole moon cycle.

'What's it for?' she leaned in and asked him.

'It's another tradition. To help the newlyweds get to know each other—and conceive a child,' he said.

Her heart stumbled.

'Don't worry, there are no expectations,' he said, his cool, striking gaze studying her.

From him, or the villagers? she wondered.

He tipped up his horn of ale and said, '*Skol!* A toast to my beautiful new wife.'

But she frowned, not raising her own glass. She wanted to stay on the subject, it was important. 'I thought you didn't want children,' she said. She couldn't believe they hadn't even discussed this. But then, he hadn't discussed many of his hopes or desires with her and she couldn't help but feel it made a bit of a mockery of their marriage.

He shrugged. 'Before I came back to Ryestone, I had ruled out ever being a father. Gytha has made me realise I might actually be good at it...'

She turned to look at her daughter, who seemed to be having a wonderful time with her new friends. She had noticed how Gytha always clambered closer to Rædan, wanting to be near him at mealtimes, and she volunteered to help him with any tasks. So far he had been generous with his time with her and it was amazing how quickly they'd grown close. He was right, he would be a wonderful father, given the chance. She knew it now. And she determined she would put her fears aside and tell him and Gytha the truth. 'Why didn't you want to before?'

His features clouded over, taking another sip of his drink. 'It just wasn't what I thought I wanted.'

The party went on long into the night, and when Gytha fell asleep on one of the benches Brita insisted she stay with her children for the night, to give Rebekah and Rædan some privacy. Rædan tried to protest, saying it wasn't necessary, thinking Rebekah would be happier keeping Gytha in her sights, but then they were being propelled out of the longhouse and along the beach, amid all the merriment.

'What's happening?' Rebekah whispered to Rædan.

'It's custom for the newlyweds to be accompanied to the bridal bed on their wedding night—to make sure they consummate the marriage.'

Her head whipped around to look at him and her heart began pounding wildly.

'Don't worry, Bekah,' he said, placing his hand on her shoulder. 'They won't stay. Nothing needs to happen.'

She nodded, telling herself she was relieved. But did he realise what his touch did to her? Just like the movement of the water in the fjord, lit up by the moonlight, it sent ripples of heat through her body, making her long for things she knew only he could give her.

The revellers scooped them up and carried them through the door of the hut, placing them both in the bed, a riot of fun, offering their congratulations again, before leaving in a cloud of clapping and cheering, closing the door behind them. And suddenly, after the rowdiness of the day, it felt quiet, the faraway sound of the villagers' laughter causing Rebekah's throat to constrict, her chest to pound. They were finally alone.

Rædan went to move. He swung his legs off the bed, about to leave her, and she felt something urgent—a desperate need—take hold of her, knowing she couldn't let him go. She had never wished to lie with a man so much, not since that one blisteringly hot summer night with him before, when she had been in love and had felt so ready for more intimacy. A maiden then, it was strange to think she was more nervous now.

But back then, everything had been so much simpler. It had been spontaneous and felt so right. There had been no doubt in her mind that they would marry. She loved him and he her and she knew he would ask for her uncle's blessing. But now so much had happened, now everything seemed so much harder. They'd both been hurt and had never recovered.

She had never wanted Lord Atol to touch her, only ever Rædan. Now they were married and they were here, alone in his bed, and he was about to leave, to walk away from her, thinking that's what she wanted. But it wasn't. She trusted this man with her life. With her daughter. Perhaps she could trust him with her body, too?

'Don't go,' she said, her voice reaching him as his hand curled around the curtain.

Slowly, Rædan turned to stare at his new wife, his grey eyes smouldering at her across the room. She was the most beautiful woman he'd ever seen. She always had been. And he couldn't believe they were married. At last.

But still he kept his arms loose at his sides. He didn't trust himself to move, not until he was sure what she wanted. He wouldn't ruin this again. He'd promised her he wouldn't touch her and if she wanted him to leave, he would.

He raked his hand through his hair. 'Tell

me what you want, Bekah,' he said, his voice strained.

Kneeling on the bed in front of him, her green eyes glowing at him in the candlelight, she reached one hand out towards him. 'Stay,' she whispered. 'I want you to stay.'

He couldn't believe it. It was the only word he'd wanted to hear.

He stretched out his hand to meet hers, like a lifeline, entwining their fingers. His whole body went up in flames as she gently pulled him towards her. He came up on the bed, kneeling before her, his other hand rising to cup her face. 'Bekah, are you sure?' he asked.

And she nodded. 'Yes.'

His hand stole into her hair, curving round the base of her neck, drawing her head towards his, and he placed a soft kiss to the wound at her brow, before resting his forehead against hers for a moment, breathing in her floral, musky scent.

'I've wanted to kiss you all day, but wasn't sure you'd let me,' he whispered.

'When have I ever stopped you?'

He smiled and, now that he knew he had her permission, his lips came down on hers, his tongue sliding slowly inside her mouth, mesh-

ing with hers. And he thought if this was all
she would allow him to have of her tonight, it
would be enough. He would be satisfied that he
had at least kissed his bride goodnight.

But to his surprise, she moved closer, her
hands coming up to take his jaw in her fingers, and she lightly pressed her body against
him, her breasts brushing against his chest, her
stomach nestling against his groin, and his desire rocketed, his thudding heart racing. Her
fingers curled over the band around his hair,
at the base of his neck, and she tugged, releasing his long hair from its restraint, and boldly
slid her hands up into it.

'I like your hair like this,' she said. 'Longer.'
And she held his head to hers, deepening the
kiss, as if to say she wanted this. *Him.* And it
sent a throb of desire to his already heavy, aching arousal.

Her delicate fingers began to roam beneath
the neckline of his tunic, caressing the smat-
tering of hair there, and then she began tugging the material out of his trousers, bunching
it up. She was so eager, it surprised him, delighted him, and he helped her bring it over his
head, before tossing it on to the floor. But then

she pulled back a bit, biting her lip, studying his chest.

'How did you get so…big?'

Her words amused him, made him smile.

'From rowing out at sea, hard labour…'

'And what is this? Is it Runa?' she asked, her trembling hands drifting over the ink on his chest. Was she as nervous as him?

'No,' he said. 'It's Fenrir—a wolf.'

'Why a wolf?' she asked.

'We believe…fearing his strength…the gods bound Fenrir, but he longed to set himself free.' He shrugged a naked shoulder. 'The story resonates with me.'

'I like it,' she said, trailing her fingertips over his silky but hard skin, tracing some of the scars, over his healing wound from the other night, and he clasped his hand over hers, flattening her palm over his heart. 'Who did it for you?'

'Brita.'

'Was there something between you? Should I be jealous?'

He smiled. 'No. Nothing like that. You're shaking,' he said.

'You make me nervous.'

'In a good way?' he asked.

And when she nodded, he drew her trembling fingers up to his lips, drawing each one into his mouth, slowly sucking and kissing them as he held her gaze. She whimpered and kissed him hard on the mouth again, so passionately it took his breath away.

'Bekah, I want you naked,' he whispered.

She pulled away and looked up at him, hesitant, suddenly shy, and he worried he'd said the wrong thing. Had he pushed her too quickly? She slowly swung her legs off the bed and stood, and for an awful moment he thought she was leaving—that she'd changed her mind. Then she turned to face him, her cheeks burning.

'Rædan, will you undo it? My hands are shaking too much.'

He nodded, his mouth dry, and she turned around, offering her back to him. His fingers weren't much better, as they fumbled with the thin ties of her dress at her neck. When the cords finally came loose, he raised up her arms gently, before gripping hold of the dress beneath her waist and lifting up the material, pulling it over her head. He discarded it on the floor, before coming towards her to the edge of the bed and holding her in her under-gown, pressing her back to his chest for a moment.

'Shall we take this off, too?' he said, his large hands skating up her ribcage to hold her beneath her breasts.

She nodded, lifting her arms for him again.

Once it was gone, she stood with her back to him, her naked body exposed, and his breath stalled at the sight of her—the curve of her pert, rounded bottom, her long, radiant hair cascading down her bare shoulders. It was the colour of his desire for her. He knew the daisies in her hair were a Norse symbol of sensuality, motherhood and new beginnings—a reminder that he mustn't mess this up. He held her hips and bent his head, pressing a kiss to her lower back, just above the crevice of her buttocks, and she gasped.

'Why do I feel on fire wherever you touch me?' she whispered. 'Like liquid heat between my legs.'

And her words made him harder, gave him confidence to continue. Did she really want this as much as he did?

He drew her backwards towards him and his hands slid up to cup her breasts, revelling in their heavy weight, rolling the hard, silky peaks between his fingers, while his chin rested on her shoulder, his mouth beginning to leave a trail of kisses along her neck.

'Rædan, I don't think I can stand,' she whispered, so he pulled her with him to join him on the bed, laying her on her back, and he came to stretch out beside her, his head propped up on his hand. He was conscious of his powerful body, his strength, and he didn't want to crowd her, to scare her off. He knew he had to take this slowly. He knew Atol had abused his power and made her fearful of a man's touch. It made him feel special that she trusted him to touch her body.

He lifted her arm above her head and trailed his fingers along her skin from her wrist, down to under her arms, before feathering over the swollen swells of her breasts.

'You are so lovely,' he said. He thought he could look at her all night long. But wherever he looked, he wanted to touch and his mouth finally came down to steal her nipple into his hot mouth, his hand splaying out over her stomach. Her hand came up to cover her burn scars above her left hip, but he moved it away.

'Are you forgetting I've seen them before?' he said, reminding her of their past intimacies.

'Your body appeals to me in a way no other does. Don't hide yourself from me, Bekah,' he said, gently admonishing her shyness.

Her restless thighs parted slightly at his words and, as her hand stole into his hair, holding him to her breast, his fingers roamed down to thread through the delicate auburn curls covering her mound. She gasped, pressing her thighs together, stopping his descent.

His head came back up to hers and he kissed her gently again. 'Bekah, show me what you like,' he whispered, taking her hand in his, venturing their entwined fingers back down towards the secret parts of her he was desperate to explore.

'I don't know what I like,' she said. 'It has never felt like this. Not since the last time—the first time—with you.'

His brow furrowed. 'Never?' he asked.

She shook her head against the furs.

'Then we will have to find out together.'

His hand cupped her breast again, and he squeezed gently. He rubbed the pad of his thumb over her nipple, teasing her, before taking the rosy peak into his mouth, tugging it with his teeth, laving it with his tongue, and she groaned. 'Do you like this?' he asked.

'Yes,' she whispered.

His large hand smoothed over her stomach and down over the curve of her hip, caressing her creamy thighs, and then back up to linger over her mound, and she gasped again, but still she didn't part her thighs for him.

He rolled on to his back and tugged her on top of him, her back to his chest, his arousal nestled in the crevice of her buttocks, straining against the material of his trousers. And when his knees pushed her legs apart, holding her open, she uttered a shocked sound of disbelief. His one hand came up to knead her breast, anchoring her in place, while his other stole down between her parted thighs.

There was nothing she could do to prevent this onslaught of pleasure, for he held her fast, he had the control. Her head thrashed from side to side, incredulous, as his finger slid between her folds, finding her small, sensitive nub, and as he circled it slowly, she cried out, his lips kissing her neck, whispering into her ear.

'Does that feel good?'

'Yes.'

'You're very wet,' he whispered, grinning into her ear.

'Is that a good thing?' she spluttered.

'Yes, it means you're ready for me to do this.' And his fingers dipped lower, to her soft, silky entrance, and he gently, carefully, pushed a finger inside her. She gasped, tensing around him.

He drew it out, before pushing it back inside again, and her bottom writhed wildly on top of him, desperate for more, his cock hardening even further beneath her, and he groaned.

'Do you like that?' he asked.

'Oh, God. Don't stop, Rædan,' she choked. 'Don't ever stop.'

And he wouldn't. Not until she came apart in his arms.

She turned her head to the side and he kissed her, his tongue stroking hers as his fingers stroked her below. He spread her legs wider, increasing his speed, alternating between circling her nub and touching her inside again, intimately. Deeply. He wanted this to be about her. He wanted to show her that her new husband could be gentle, that he would not hurt her, but only give her pleasure. Always.

And then he felt her tensing around him, her body arching, spasming, and she cried out her long, spiralling orgasm.

Only when her body stopped convulsing did he withdraw his fingers from her heat and release her from his hold. He rolled out from under her and pulled her relaxed, sated body into him, enfolding her in his arms. He held her against his chest, stroking her hair.

Rebekah lay with her head resting on his magnificent chest, which was steadily rising and falling. Was he asleep? She lifted herself up on her elbow, brushing her damp hair out of her face, and took the opportunity to look at the handsome face of her new husband. Her husband whose skilled hands had just given her the most amazing pleasure, making her feel cherished and cared for.

She had vowed never to belong to a man again, but this man, he had been so gentle with her that it had made her trust him completely. And she wanted to be bound to him. That's why she hadn't fought him when he'd decided they would be married, she thought. She traced her fingers over the dark ink on his chest and his eyes flicked open, startling her. His hands came up to trail over her back.

'Are you all right?'

'Yes.' She nodded.

He had shown her what things should be like between a man and a woman, how beautiful touch could be. And she was just wondering if she could be brave enough to touch him, pleasure him, in return? She had no idea what to do and she bit her bottom lip, yet her fingers had a mind of their own, wandering south, venturing over the hard ridges of his stomach, and he tensed.

'Bekah…' he warned and the dangerous tone in his voice sent a fresh wave of heat between her legs.

She wanted to tease him, to drive him wild, as he had made her when he'd pushed her legs apart and touched her with his masterful hands.

Her fingertips grazed lightly beneath the waistband of his trousers, stroking lower, her hand curving over his hard, silky arousal, and he groaned. He pushed the material down his legs, kicking the trousers off, so they were finally both naked, and she curled her bare leg over his thigh, starting the exploration of his incredible body with her hand once more.

'Have you slept with many women, since me?' she asked.

He stopped stroking her back. 'Does it matter?'

She shrugged, before encouraging him to

continue grazing her skin with a wiggle to her shoulder. 'I'm just curious.'

'A few,' he said, his hand stealing down to curve over her bottom. 'But I'll promise you this. You will be my first—and my last, Bekah, if you want me.' And in one quick move, gripping her buttocks, he rolled her over on to her back, his welcome weight on top of her, pressing down on top of her, savage hunger in his eyes. He was perfectly poised to take her in one thrust.

He stared down at her and she knew he was asking permission to possess her body, giving her time to say no, letting her know it was her choice. But she wanted him. Badly. And by the feel of his hard cock throbbing against her sensitive skin, he wanted her just as desperately. She wrapped her hands around his back, bringing him fully down on top of her, wanting to feel his muscled body on hers.

'Bekah, can you feel how much I want to be inside you?' he said.

'I want that, too,' she whispered.

He parted her thighs wider with his knees, his hand coming down between their bodies to angle the tip of him into her sensitive flesh.

'There's nothing to be afraid of,' he whispered. 'I promise I won't hurt you.'

She bit her lip again and nodded. 'Then I'm ready. I want this. I want you,' she whispered.

She always had.

She lifted her arms to place her hands around his neck, pulling his face down to hers and he kissed her, deeply, as he guided himself inside her entrance. She knew it was just the tip, but he felt huge, sending waves of heat racking through her body.

'How's that?' he asked.

She nodded. 'More,' she whispered, wrapping her legs around his waist. 'I want more, Rædan.'

And he grinned, not giving her what she wanted yet, but gently circling his hips, driving her crazy by just edging in and out of her slick heat, giving her time to get used to him, to accommodate him. Pleasure floored her and she almost came undone right there and then. And when she gripped on to his bottom, hard, trying to anchor him in place, he finally gave her more of what she wanted, thrusting gently inside her a little bit further.

She gasped, burying her face in his shoulder.

He pulled himself away from her chest slightly, so she had nowhere to hide.

'Look at me, Bekah,' he said. 'Don't hide from me. I want to see the reaction in your eyes when I storm your body.'

'Oh, God,' she said, his words driving her crazy, her slick excitement allowing him to slide inside her a little bit more, before he withdrew again.

'Are you ready?' he asked.

And she nodded.

He fastened her to him in his steel-armed embrace and thrust harder, and this time he slid all the way in.

'Are you all right?' he asked, his ragged breath coming wildly against her cheek.

'Yes. You feel…amazing.'

And locked together, he began to surge inside her, over and again. And just when she thought it couldn't get any better, that she was going to shatter beneath him, his hips began to quicken, increasing the pressure, her pleasure—rocking into her in an intense, insistent way that was making her wild, causing her to thrash beneath him, frantic with need. The pleasure was mounting, so she clutched on to him tight, grappling with his shoulders, his buttocks, wanting to savour every moment of giving herself to him. And she knew they were almost there, right on the edge.

She held his jaw, gazing up into his intense, impenetrable face, wanting to look into his eyes as he came apart inside her. She bucked beneath him, clenching her internal muscles, wanting him to lose all restraint, to bury himself inside her, to give himself up to her completely. And he gave one final hard thrust in response and she felt herself scream and splinter as unbridled pleasure swept through her body and he roared out his own climax against her lips.

He lay on top of her for a moment, their bodies dewed with sweat, entwined together, their hearts hammering, and she tried to get her breathing under control. It had been amazing…he had been amazing. She felt satisfied, complete, and it was all his doing. He had just given her the wedding night of her dreams. And she loved him for it. She kissed him, tenderly, on the lips.

When saying their vows, he had promised to take care of her and he had told her she would be his only lover from now on. In return, she had just surrendered her body—and her heart—to this man. She had allowed him to possess her—totally and utterly—and it had felt so right.

'I never stopped thinking about you, Rædan,' she said. 'You were always in my heart.'

He looked down at her with hooded eyes, her words hanging in the whisper of a breath between them, and he kissed her again, tenderly.

'I have a wedding gift for you also...' she whispered.

'Something more than your body?' He grinned. 'I don't need anything else.'

'It's more something I need to tell you,' she said.

This was not how she'd envisioned telling him, lying beneath his naked body, a part of him still inside her. There had been so many times she'd imagined what it would have been like, sharing the news with him, planning their future together. Instead, she'd done all that with Lord Atol. But she knew she had to do this now. She was in love and she couldn't deny him the knowledge of knowing he had a daughter any longer.

'It's about Gytha...'

'What about her?'

'I haven't been completely honest with you about some things... I realise now how wrong it was to keep it from you…but I wasn't sure how you'd react, or what you were truly like, when I first met you again… And there was no way of knowing, I mean, I wasn't absolutely sure, until I saw you together…'

He frowned. 'What are you talking about, Bekah?'

'You look so alike, it's obvious now… I've always looked for signs of you in her, since the start,' she said. 'I hoped to see a hint of your smile or hear a turn of phrase that reminded me of you. You even both do this thing—this wrinkle of your nose.'

She did it, to show him what she meant, and he lifted himself away from her a little, suddenly realising what she was saying, what she was trying to tell him…

His brow furrowed. 'Gytha isn't Atol's daughter?'

She shook her head. 'No! I think I was already with child—*your* child—when he first forced himself on me.'

She kept talking to fill the silence, trying to explain, the guilt that she'd kept this from him rushing through her thick and fast now. 'It was a few weeks after that that I discovered I was with child. And I couldn't be sure who the father was. But then, when everyone thought she was a little premature, it allowed me to hope… It reasserted what I'd thought might be the case all along. She even looked like you. I see it even more now, when you stand side by side.'

Rædan was still staring down at her, his arms braced, his face hard.

'I've lived in fear that Atol would find out, that he would see her begin to change, to look more like you. And I know it was wrong to lie, but by God have I suffered for it ever since…'

His eyes were like steel and he continued to stare at her, not saying anything. It was unsettling.

She lifted her hand up to his face. 'Rædan…?'

'You're telling me I'm a father? That I—*we*—have a child together? That Gytha is my daughter?' he said finally.

'Yes.' She bit her bottom lip.

'A seven-year-old child—*daughter*—I have only just begun to know?' She could hear the accusation in his voice, feel his anger building. She knew she deserved it.

'Yes.'

He withdrew from her body and the sudden loss of him was great. He backed away from her on the bed.

'I have a seven-year-old child who's grown up thinking Lord Atol, the man I have sworn to hate, is her father?' The despair and hurt in his eyes was almost too much.

She nodded, her eyes welling with tears, sitting up and covering her naked body with the furs.

'Yes. But what else was I meant to do?' she said, suddenly feeling both ashamed and defensive all at once. 'You were gone! You were dead. And I didn't know if she was yours or Atol's until she was born... But we can tell her now...' She knew that Atol sending him away had changed him. Hardened him. And yet his strong streak of resentment seemed to overshadow everything else. 'Can't we begin to put what Atol did to us behind us? Try to forget about it?'

With a sudden, almost violent movement, Rædan was up on his feet, pulling on his trousers.

'Forget it?' he said, shaking his head. 'Never! Not after what he did to you. What he did to me...'

'I don't know the extent of what he did to you, because you won't tell me,' she said, exasperated.

But he carried on regardless. 'And now I find out that on top of being banished—having been sent away, lost all I held dear, my family and my reputation—that you've also denied me my legacy as well, not even letting my own child know I existed!'

'I'm sorry,' she spluttered.

'I'm going to get some air. Maybe take a swim.'

'Now?'

'You should get some sleep,' he said, his cool, reserved expression at odds with the passion of their intimate acts.

An icy draught passed over her and she shuddered. 'Stop saying that! Stop using it as an excuse so you don't have to talk, to open up to me. Maybe I don't want to sleep!'

'Bekah…' he warned.

'Rædan, please don't go. Stay. Talk to me. I know you're angry, but if we just talked about it…' she said, reaching out to touch his arm. But he shrugged her off, swiped up his tunic and stalked out of the room, leaving her all alone in the bed. She reeled as she realised he was an expert at making love and an expert at blocking his feelings, causing her the most exquisite pleasure and excruciating pain at the same time.

Would he ever open up to her? Would he ever forgive her from keeping the truth from him?

Rædan sliced his arms through the water, cooling his sweat-slicked skin from their love-making, and he felt like the world's worst fool. He didn't like himself much. Not that that was anything new. His wedding day had been the best day of his life, surrounded by his friends, his daughter, and marrying the woman of his dreams. And his wedding night had been even better.

When he'd made love to his new wife, she was all that he wanted and more. It had been mind-blowing, better than he'd ever known it to be. He'd buried himself inside her body, taking everything he could from her, giving her everything in return—and then she'd dropped that news.

He was a father! He had a daughter! It was the most extraordinary news. He felt moisture in his eyes and furiously tried to blink it away. Was this what it felt like to be overcome with emotion—and an instant, enormous sense of responsibility and protection? He thought of Gytha and his chest swelled with pride at what he'd created. *She was his.*

But it bothered him that he had missed the first important years of her life. His father had always been there for him, since day one. Was he too late to make an impact, to form a bond? He hoped not.

He had thought he'd learned to suppress all emotions—because he'd come to realise that if you never loved, you never lost, and that was a much safer way to live. But every moment of being with Rebekah, she was showing him how to feel again… And that scared him more than any journey across the sea, any battle.

But how could Bekah have raised her child to believe Lord Atol—his enemy—was Gytha's father, destroying Rædan's memory, his legacy? It was a terrible betrayal. She had lied to him—and her daughter. Could he ever forgive her for that? Yet, deep down, he knew she would have had no choice at the time.

He'd got her pregnant, out of wedlock, making her vulnerable, putting her at risk. Yes, he'd intended to stay by her side, to marry her, but when he'd been sent away, when she'd been told he was dead, she would have had little option but to seek a marriage and provide legitimacy and security for her child, even if she didn't know for sure who the father was. He wished he'd been there to see Bekah's swollen belly, carrying their child. He hated that he'd missed so much. And his heart went out to her and all she'd had to suffer on her own.

But why hadn't she told him in Ryestone, when he'd found out she had a child? Why had she continued to lie, keeping it from him? Did she not trust him? And yet, why would she? He'd attacked her home, he'd taken her hostage…and yet she had put her faith in him and come away with him. And now she'd married him and opened up to him, revealing the truth… And he'd raced from her arms as fast as possible.

He drove his arms through the water. Being so intimate with her again had made him realise what he'd been missing. And when she'd started telling him about their child, old wounds had resurfaced. Memories had come rushing back of the last time he'd been this close to her, then within hours his world had been destroyed. And although he knew it wasn't her fault, her words had brought it all back—the feeling of abandonment. Everything he'd lost. And how he'd determined he would never be a father because of the shame it would bring…

And yet, there she was, looking up at him

like that, telling him she'd missed him, telling him that he was a father.

It had him removing himself from the bed so fast, leaving her sitting there, wounded. And he hated himself for it. Because a pain burned in his chest when he wondered what would happen when Bekah discovered who he really was. She wasn't the only one who had kept the truth of the past hidden. How would she feel about him when she found out he'd been a slave? He knew he should have told her about it before he'd made love to her. Hell, before he'd forced her to marry him. But knowing it might change her opinion of him, he'd cowardly put it off.

After walking along the moonlit shore, he arrived back at the hut and roughly dried himself off before pouring himself an ale, looking out over the fjord. She was right, they'd come a long way. Perhaps it was time to put the past behind them. But he wasn't sure he was able. He couldn't forget it, like she'd said.

The memories haunted his dreams, they were at the back of his mind in every waking moment. And the last thing he felt like doing was explaining himself. She was also right that, despite the intimacies they'd shared, he would still find it a struggle to open up to her about his past. He would never be able to find the words to explain it…

He downed the drink before taking himself off to the other bed, knowing he probably wouldn't be welcome back in her arms, not now. He'd had the best sex of his life and then ruined it. He'd taken Rebekah and Gytha from Ryestone not only to get back at his enemy, but to protect them. He realised now everything he'd done, the way he'd behaved, it was all because he still cared about her, he always had. He'd never stopped thinking about her either, and fate had finally brought them back together. She was his destiny.

He threw his body beneath the furs and lay on his side, and his arm came across his forehead, wanting to shake the bitter words he'd said to her away, wanting to return to that moment after their lovemaking when he lay content in her arms.

He heard the familiar soft pull of the curtain, the padding of feet across the floor and he held his breath. Then the door to his little room creaked open and he felt the weight of her body come down on the bed. She lifted the furs and got in beside him, wrapping her arm around his waist. He tensed.

She planted soft kisses to his shoulder. 'I'm sorry,' she whispered. 'Please forgive me.'

He knew he should apologise, too, tell her his own secrets, but the words were suspended on his tongue. And yet her kisses were too enticing, melting his hardened heart, thawing his anger. He relented and turned over to face her in the darkness, pressing a kiss to her lips, her mouth opening, allowing him to deepen the connection.

'I should have told you sooner,' she whispered when they came up for air.

'I understand why you didn't...'

He was surprised to discover she was still naked, wearing nothing but the pendant he'd given her and her mother's ring, and he kissed her again, taking his time, making it the longest, deepest kiss. His hand roamed down her back, over her bottom, splaying out over her soft flesh, tugging her leg over his hip and pulling her closer, possessively.

'I realise why you wanted to wait. Why you might not have thought of me as being an example of a great father... I didn't exactly make a good first impression when we met again, bringing bloodshed to your door. And hell, if it wasn't for me, you would never have been in this situation in the first place. I should never have encouraged you to spend the night with me all those years ago. We should have waited.'

Her breath stalled. 'You regret it?' she said and he realised his words might have hurt her. 'What about last night?'

'No! Of course not. I don't regret it then or now. How could I? But...' he said. Why was this so hard?

'But what?' she said, raising her chin up in pride.

'I don't know how to explain it.'

'Rædan, please try.'

Rebekah couldn't believe Rædan was admitting that he felt he was as much to blame. Most men never did that. And she appreciated the fact he was sharing the responsibility of their actions. But she had never once regretted that evening she'd spent with him. Yes, there had been times afterwards when she had hated her life, but that was a night she held in a special place in her heart.

'I wouldn't change it,' she said carefully. 'How can I when I have Gytha?'

'She is pretty incredible.' He shrugged. 'I guess I'm finding it harder than I thought to put the past behind us. The memories of what happened. I want to, but…'

She nodded. 'It will take time.'

The dawn of a new day was beginning to seep through the smoke hole of the farmstead and she wanted this to be the start of a new chapter. A fresh beginning for their family.

Last night, when he'd launched himself from the bed, she'd felt distraught. She knew she'd hurt him, let him down, for lying to him and Gytha all this time. But it was a relief to hear he didn't regret their lovemaking back then, or now. Yet she still felt as if something was holding him back—that he was keeping a part of himself from her. She didn't know what it was, but she intended to find out. He had helped to heal her last night, being so gentle with her, and she would now do the same for him.

'I know you're still keeping secrets from me, Rædan—that you're not willing to open up and talk about your past. And I know you're struggling to trust me, but I want to show you that you can.'

A new determination had filled her. She would make him feel he could talk to her, open up to her, with words—and through her touch. However she could reach him.

She pressed her naked body harder against him and he grew hard in an instant. She tugged down his trousers and ruthlessly took hold of him, and he groaned, resting his forehead against hers, holding her arms and her body tight against him. He was so powerfully, beautifully built. A proper warrior, with broad shoulders, muscular arms and legs. She had loved him when he was a boy, but she adored him now he was a man.

'I don't regret last night, Bekah. I need you to know that.'

She nodded, pressing a soft kiss to his mouth, before trailing her tongue down his body, over his muscular chest and down, over his taut stomach. She knew what she was going to do. Staring up at him, kneeling over his broad thighs, she continued to hold him as he met her gaze and she drew him into her mouth. He raked in a breath.

'Bekah—'

He sounded tortured and she wondered if he wanted her to stop, but then his hands roamed into her hair at her temple, holding her to him, so she brought her lips over the top of him, licking and nipping his hot, silky skin. She had no clue what she was doing, she had just heard her maids discussing how they'd pleased their husbands back in Ryestone, and she wanted to please Rædan, more than anything. He tasted of sin and the salt of the fjord and she wanted more, taking him further into her mouth.

His head tipped back on the furs, his eyes closed, and he began muttering words she didn't understand. Good. She would break him down, a touch at a time if she had to, to discover how he really felt about her.

She used tender strokes of her tongue around the tip and then sucked down on him, hard, and she knew he was teetering on the edge, the muscles in his arms bunching, his fingers tightening around her head, his hips gently thrusting as she took him further into her mouth. And then she felt the release tear through his body, the rush of his orgasm on her tongue, the feeling of elation rip through her that she had given this incredible man the satisfaction and pleasure he deserved.

She sat back on her feet, drawing a hand across her mouth, staring down at him.

'That was incredible,' he whispered. 'Come here,' he said, tugging her towards him and wrapping her in his arms, holding her, and she knew she'd moved him. One touch at a time, she thought again.

'Well, my first wedding gift didn't go down so well, so I thought I'd give you another.' She smiled.

And he laughed softly into her hair, his chest vibrating against hers.

'Both gifts were more than I could have ever wished for… To find out you're a father on your wedding night is…unbelievable. But, even so, do you think we can wait to tell Gytha? Just until I've got used to the idea myself?'

She nodded. 'All right. You just tell me when you're ready and we can do it together.'

He stroked her back tenderly and she must have drifted off to sleep, as the next time she woke, Rædan was fully dressed, buckling his leather chainmail tunic. He bent down to kiss her on the forehead.

She sat bolt upright. 'Where are you going?'

'I have that holmgang with Ogden this morning. The boat leaves shortly.'

She shook her head in confusion. 'What exactly is a holmgang? Brita said that the whole thing was settled, that Ogden would be banished.' Had she missed something?

'I requested to settle the dispute with Ogden

through a duel of honour. He agreed to meet with me in single combat.'

'What? No!'

'It's how we deal with things here, Bekah.'

She couldn't believe that he had to fight for her again. She couldn't believe he'd kept this from her. But she knew why. He'd have known it would have overshadowed their wedding day. She would have spent the whole time worrying. 'What if you get hurt?'

'I won't.'

'What if you do?'

'It's a fight to the first blood, not usually to the death.'

'And if he wins?'

'I have to accept he didn't do anything to dishonour me. Or you…' A muscle flickered in his cheek. 'He would also get three marks of silver.'

'And if you win?'

'Sudden outlawry. He won't be welcome back in these parts.'

'Where is it?'

'It's on the island, over the fjord,' he said, placing his sword in its sheath.

'I'm coming with you,' she said, throwing off the furs and stalking to the other room to gather up her clothes.

* * *

They went to the longhouse to check on Gytha and she noticed Rædan studying their daughter in a new light. Was he looking for signs of himself in her? Did he see what she saw? He'd gathered the child into a tight embrace before they left and she'd noticed the unusual mist in his eyes. But then they'd piled into a boat to row over to the island and he'd visibly recovered himself, trying to focus on the fight ahead. She watched as Knud showed him the shields Rædan would be using.

'Why does he need three shields?' she asked.

'Each man gets to choose their weapons and has three shields for protection. They take it in turns to strike the other. When first blood is drawn, the fight is over.'

'And if someone is killed?'

'Then they'll have died in honour and will have earned their place at Odin's side in the great hall of Valhalla.'

Rebekah's mouth dried. Rædan's rightful place was at her side, not some Norse god's...

On the second ship crossing the fjord to the island, she saw Ogden and his brothers, who were readying him for battle. She felt sick. How could this be allowed to happen? It seemed so wrong.

Reaching the small island, she saw many of the villagers were already there and was grateful Brita had stayed behind with Gytha and her own children. This was not for their eyes. There was an ox hide stretched out, staked to the ground, and Knud began reminding the men of the rules.

'No one is to step out of the square. It will be deemed a sign of cowardice and the duel will be over. The other person will claim victory.'

She bit her lip, assessing Rædan and his opponent. Ogden was no match for him in terms of breadth and height, but the other man seemed agile on his feet and she was damn sure he wouldn't play fair.

The men took up their positions on the animal skin, squaring up to each other. She couldn't bear it if anything were to happen to Rædan. Not when this new chapter of their life was only just beginning.

Ogden was first to strike and he brought his axe down hard and Rædan lifted up his shield. The wood splintered, just a little, and the crowd jeered and heckled. Were they enjoying this? she wondered. How could they? It was torture.

Next, it was Rædan's turn and he swung his sword smoothly, slicing into the wood of Ogden's shield, cutting it in half. The man sneered and cast his first shield aside.

The people went wild, cheering, 'Halfdan! Halfdan!'

He certainly looked like a Dane, with his long dark hair, a scowl carved into his dark brow, his arm and leg muscles full of power. And he wasn't holding anything back, just as he hadn't held back during their lovemaking last night. He had so many different sides to him, she thought. He could be fierce yet gentle, tough yet kind…

The blows became more vicious, more savage as their turns went on, and they were pushing each other backwards, edging nearer to the boundary of the square, as they both became increasingly desperate to win and to end this. And no one wished for it to be over more than Rebekah.

Soon, they were both down to their last shields and she began to panic what would happen when they had no barrier between them, just metal against skin, when the tip of Rædan's blade sliced low and caught Ogden's thigh, just below the wood. The man roared in anger and lunged for Rædan, breaking the rules of the duel, slamming his body into him and forcing him down on to the ground. There was a tussle on the floor before Knud and Erik launched forward and gripped Ogden by the arms, pulling him backwards, announcing him *'nioningr'*. He was to be banished immediately.

Rebekah almost sank to the floor in relief, racing over to Rædan and throwing her arms around him, and he held her tight.

'It's over now. You're safe.'

'I'm so glad you are, too,' she said. 'If anything had happened…'

'It's all right. We can go home now.'

On the boat back over to Nedergaard, the mood was noticeably lighter. Knud and the men opened a barrel of ale and deemed they should have another day of celebrations, to mark Rædan's victory. They made Rædan laugh and she could feel the tension ebbing away, leaving his body.

'Come back with us to the longhouse,' Knud said, draping his arm around them both as they walked along the jetty.

'We will. But I need to get this armour off first, take a bath.'

'Oh, yes?' the men jibed, winking at Rebekah. And she enjoyed their teasing. She liked his friends. 'Don't be too long…'

Rædan nodded, grinning, and he took Rebekah's hand as they walked slowly back up the beach towards the farmstead.

'I was so worried,' she said, when they were alone. 'Never do that to me again,' she said, pounding her fist gently against his chest.

'I'm sorry I put you through that. But I saw no other way to make certain he would be cast out for ever. It's over now.'

She sagged into him. 'I think you need to make it up to me…'

'How?'

She looked around for inspiration. 'What's that steam bath you have outside?' she asked.

He looked surprised at the direction of her thoughts. 'It's a sauna,' he said.

'Show me?' she asked and began to tug off her clothes, giggling, heading over there. He watched her, as if he was unsure of what was happening, before taking a deep breath and following.

Inside, Rebekah sat on the little wooden bench and Rædan poured hot spring water over the heated stones. A swirl of steam filled the small room, enveloping them in its warmth.

'Did you make all this?' she asked.

'Yes. Like it?'

Rebekah stood and came towards him, wrapping her arms around his neck and placing a kiss on his lips. 'I'll tell you later.'

He eased her on to the wooden bench, so she was sitting down, and as he came before her on his knees she noticed his gaze was full of wicked intent. 'My turn.' He ruthlessly parted her knees with his hands, spreading her thighs so he could look at her.

'Rædan,' she gasped, her face heating. God, it was hot in here.

'What? Aren't I allowed to look at my wife? Besides, you said I had to make it up to you...'

And then he pulled her forward towards him and dipped his head, laying claim to her with his tongue.

His hands came round her to grip her buttocks, to fasten her to him, and he ravaged her with his mouth, his beard grazing her skin, his tongue teasing her tip. She spluttered at the intimacy, the insane pleasure ripping through her, as he hooked her legs over his shoulders and her fingers gripped his hair, pressing him closer, gasping out her almost instant, blinding climax.

She was just getting her breath back, the feeling returning to her tingling toes, when he pulled her down into his lap, so she was straddling his thighs, and she was aware of his new arousal, his sweat-covered body and the heat in his eyes.

'I think I'm beginning to figure out what you like.' He grinned. 'Are you sore this morning, after what we did last night?'

'No.'

'Good.'

And in one easy movement, he lowered her down on to him, impaling her, as she gripped his face between her hands, kissing him hard. He groaned, resting his head against hers as her tongue entwined with his, and she could smell her own raw scent on his lips.

He placed his hands down on the floor to steady himself as Rebekah began to rock on top of him, fire burning in her emerald eyes, running her hands down his arms. First, she would take ownership of his body, next, she would take over his heart, she thought. Her hands gently circled his wrists—to support herself or to restrain him, she wasn't sure—and as her fingers smoothed over more scars, she saw his brow furrow, the consternation in his eyes, and he faltered for just a moment, his arms pulling away. But then he was back with her, focused, gripping her bottom and thrusting inside her all the way. She threw her head back, marvelling at the feeling of him filling her up, driving inside her again, until the ripples of pleasure racked through her body, stealing her breath away, and she screamed out her orgasm as he came hard inside her.

The next thing she knew, Rædan was lifting her, throwing a cloak around her and then she was back in bed and he was pulling her into his arms.

Chapter Ten

~~~~~~~~~~~~~~~~~~~~

Rebekah's first week of married life had been mostly bliss. They worked the land during the day, ate and swam. She had been teaching Gytha to ride and they were getting to know more of the villagers, and at night, when Gytha was asleep, she and Rædan tasted, touched and soared inside each other.

In the bedroom he could give as much as she wanted, and she was greedy, taking it all. But it had been days and he hadn't once mentioned his feelings towards her, or opened up to her about his past, and she was becoming increasingly frustrated. She wanted to learn more about him—if only he'd share more of himself with her. They had what it took to make a successful marriage—become a family—but he wasn't giving it a proper chance.

He hadn't even revisited the idea of telling

Gytha he was her father. He was wonderful
with her, showing her how to do things on the
farm, telling her stories about his gods and even
making the time to play with her. She couldn't
understand what he was waiting for. What was
holding him back?

And then there were times when he'd disappear for a while, never explaining where he'd
been. Was he purposely trying to keep his distance from her?

Last night, in the longhouse, there had been
talk of another raid and he'd been asked if he
would lead it—and her heart felt heavy with despair. She didn't understand why he needed or
wanted to go. She could understand him coming back to Ryestone, wanting his revenge. But
why go elsewhere?

She could tell he got a lot of satisfaction from
discovering new lands—he took great pride in
it. But why did he need to raid and pillage? He
was a man who was excruciatingly conscious
of his own dignity and she was hoping, now he
had her and Gytha in his life, he wouldn't want
to go. That they would be enough to keep him
here. Clearly not and she felt angry. Let down.

She sat on the beach, watching the water of
the fjord lap the shore, admiring the elegant

egrets wading in the shallows, with their long necks and legs, and she wondered if she was like them—was she in too deep? Was she out of her depth with this lone wolf of a man, who she was struggling to tame? She was beginning to fall in love with this place he had brought her to—just as she was falling love with him all over again. Wouldn't he struggle to leave Nedergaard? *Her?*

She saw his shadow on the sand before he reached her, felt his approach. Her body always seemed to know when he was near and react with eager fascination, despite her mind telling her to keep cool. He'd been gone all afternoon. Where had he been this time?

'Hello. Have you had a good day? What have you been up to?' he said, cupping her shoulder as he sat down beside her.

She turned to look at him. How easy it was for him to ask questions and how freely she gave her answers. Why was it that he couldn't do the same?

'Gytha and I made a stew. And we took Wilburh for a long ride. You?'

'Here,' he said, handing her what looked like a comb. 'For your hair. I made it for you, out of deer antler.'

She turned it over in her hand. It was beautiful. Exquisitely made. 'Thank you,' she said, her face lighting up with pleasure.

'You kept complaining about your knotty hair, so I thought it would help.'

Is this what he'd spent the afternoon doing? If so, she'd been too harsh on him. 'I knew you were good with your hands, but this...'

'Really? How good?' He grinned wolfishly, wriggling his eyebrows, and she smiled. She was touched by the gesture. She loved the comb. But she still would have preferred his company today...

'You know, I used to go down to the river in Ryestone when I wanted to think, to be alone. But this place is even better for that.'

'Sounds ominous,' he said a little warily. 'What have you been thinking about?'

'I was wondering what you do with all the treasure you raid?'

She felt him tense beside her and he removed his hand from her skin. She couldn't understand why he would need to go away and steal more of it if he already had enough.

'You know what happens. We hand it over to Jarl Knud to be fairly distributed between the men. The rest goes to providing for the people of the settlement.'

'Yes, but I mean the treasure *you* take.'

'Why?'

'Well, it's just you obviously trade it, use it, as we live here, in this hut—but surely the quantity of treasure you take would allow you to have a home greater than this? So what do you do with the rest of it?'

She instantly knew she'd said the wrong thing when his eyes hardened, darkened. 'Starting to realise this place doesn't live up to living in a grand fortress, Bekah?' he asked, his voice icy.

'That isn't what I'm saying. Don't put words in my mouth. I've never cared for titles or land or silver...'

'No?'

'No! I love this place. More than I ever thought I would. I just wondered, that's all. But you're not going to tell me, are you?'

'What?'

'What you do with the treasure from your conquests? It's just one simple question. But one of the many things you won't share with me, isn't it?' she said, the hurt from the past week bubbling over now. She'd been trying so hard, and although he'd made love to her with his body, over and over again, she wasn't sure he was making love with his heart.

'I want to know why you choose to live like this, when you must have riches from your raids? What work did you do when you were out on that ship all those winters? And what happened to your face, your body, to be covered in all those scars?'

'Are you finished?'

'No! I want to know what your plans are—do you intend to go away again? To leave me and Gytha? How long for? And will it be dangerous?'

'I don't see why you have to know everything about me. Why do you probe and pry? I married you to keep you safe, not so you could know every single detail of my life.'

She reeled, crushed at his words. 'You *made* me marry you. I never asked for your protection.'

A muscle flickered in his jaw and she knew she'd angered him. Well, good, she was angry, too.

'No, but you got it anyway. But that doesn't mean I want to share everything about myself with you.'

She felt the sharp inrush of breath. It was happening, they were arguing and they were only a week in. She knew this would happen. 'I didn't want a fake marriage,' she said, suddenly feeling that that was what this was, and she felt empty inside.

She saw the barriers come up. She saw it in his spear-coloured gaze. The ones he used to shut himself down, to hide himself away from her.

'I came over here to ask you if you want to go to the longhouse,' he said, deliberately changing the subject, curling up to stand and walk away from her. 'It might be a bit warmer there than here.'

Sitting round the hearth with Knud, Brita and Erik, the children playing, Rebekah was pleased they'd come. Anything was better than feeling alone eating dinner back at the hut with a stone-faced husband who wouldn't look at her or talk to her.

She couldn't believe how quickly they'd settled in here and how welcome Rædan's friends had made them. She loved chatting to Brita about the villagers and the latest goods at the market.

She glanced across at Rædan, but he was sullen and brooding, hardly joining in with the conversation. She wanted to know what he was thinking, what was going on in that intelligent mind of his. He looked devastatingly attractive, the flames of the fire reflecting in the anthracite of his eyes, and she hated to admit it, but she would give anything to be in his arms again.

She knew that even though she was angry with him, if he wanted her, she would end up in his arms again tonight. How did he have this pull, why was she drawn to him so? How could she still want him, when she was so livid with him?

'Why do you need to know everything about me?' he'd said.

Because she loved him, she realised. And the emotion tore through her with the fervour and intensity of the fire. She would spend her life trying to get him to love her back, to feel an ounce of what she felt for him.

She knew he was angry with her for prying into his life, but why shouldn't she? He knew everything about hers. Why wouldn't he open up to her? What was holding him back?

Erik was chatting to her about his new boat

and she was trying to look as if she was interested, nodding her head, smiling at his witty comments. Then suddenly, Rædan stood. He threw another log on to the fire and she instantly felt its heat, reeling back. If he'd wanted to get her attention, he'd certainly got it. He lifted his gaze and their eyes met over the forking flames. He grabbed his cloak and left the hall. No explanation.

'What's up with him?' Erik said, rolling his eyes.

Her chest burned, the hurt sealing up her throat.

How could he leave her so easily, when she couldn't bear to let him out of her sight? Where was he going now?

Swiftly, she made her decision. After asking Brita and Knud if they could watch Gytha, she, too, grabbed her cloak and followed him. She knew it was wrong. She knew he would think it meant she didn't trust him. But still she couldn't stop herself. She had to do this, to better understand the man she'd married.

And then a thought struck her—was he going to see another woman? Her stomach churned. If that was true, it would be more than she could bear. But, no, surely not. He had told her she would be his first and his last.

Her heart was in her mouth as she followed his tall, proud frame along the pathway through the farmsteads, keeping a fair distance back. And when he reached the shore, she wondered if perhaps he was going home. If he was, why hadn't he taken her and Gytha with him?

But when he reached their settlement, he didn't stop and instead kept going. He clambered over a few rocks and disappeared out of sight, and once she'd done the same she stood, glancing around, wondering where he'd gone. The sun was beginning to set, casting everything into shadow, making it harder for her to see, and she willed her eyes to get used to the light.

'What are you doing?'

The sound of his voice startled her, making her jump.

Rædan.

He had come from behind a deserted fisherman's hut.

'Are you *following* me?' he asked, incredulous, his arms coming across his chest, his eyes like glowering balls of coal.

Her chin tilted up. 'Maybe,' she said, meeting his anger with her own.

He took a step towards her. 'Why?'

'Because I want to know where you go to every day,' she said, throwing her arms up. 'What's so important that takes you away from me and Gytha?'

He bore down on her in the darkness and he seemed taller than ever before. 'Don't you trust me?'

'Should I?'

'What do you think I'm doing?'

'I don't know—that's what I was trying to find out.'

'And you didn't think to just ask?'

'Would you have told me if I did?'

His eyes narrowed on her.

'No…' she laughed bitterly '…of course not. What is it—do you have another woman?'

'Are you crazy? You think I have the energy to lie with another woman after my nights—and days—with you?' He raked his hand through his hair. 'Do you think I *need* another woman, other than you? You're the only woman I've ever wanted.'

And as if to prove it, he hauled her to him, crushing her mouth with his. She pushed at his chest, turning away from him, still angry, but he tugged her back into his body, her bottom against his groin, as if he was mad for her. And she was glad. She wanted to see him lose control where she was concerned—it meant he felt something, too.

And the way he was rucking up her dress, tugging down his own trousers, in fierce, desperate urgency, she knew there was no other. He plunged inside her from behind, all the way in one hard thrust, and she whimpered. He felt so good. And with a groan of surrender he brought them both down on to the sand, pushing her forward slightly, as he drove inside her again, making her cry out in pleasure.

She spread her legs wider, wanting more of him, everything he could give, and he pressed her belly into the sand, thrusting harder, kissing her neck, her shoulder—the parts of her flesh that were exposed to him. He stroked his hand down the front of her dress, lifting it up so he could move his fingers between her legs, to caress her tiny nub as he continued to take her with his body. It only took one more surge for them to both come apart and he roared out her name into the night.

* * *

The feelings raging inside him were no less than anarchy.

What was happening to him? He needed her, wanted her, all the time. It was never enough. So much so that he'd even taken her on the beach. Thank goodness it was getting dark and no one was around. He withdrew from her body and pulled down her dress, fastening his trousers. She turned around to face him, her cheeks flushed from the vigour of their lovemaking, and she sat back on her knees. His hand came out to stroke her hair behind her ears, taming it.

He wondered at the hold she had over him. He'd felt it from the moment he'd seen her on the battlements in Ryestone, waving that ridiculous flag back and forth. He just wanted to be near her, closer to her—but he was fighting it with all the strength he could muster.

It had been just days since their wedding and she and Gytha had settled in well. They'd had no more trouble from the men in Nedergaard, but Knud had started talking about new raids, where they would travel to next, and he'd felt a strange sense of dread settle in his stomach. He hadn't been able to put his finger on it until he'd looked at her in the longhouse, over the fire. And then he'd realised—he didn't want to leave her. He wanted to be with her and Gytha, always.

He wanted to swim and ride, make her laugh and smile, like she made him. But it scared him, because the closer they got, the nearer she was getting to finding out about his past and he felt more and more guilty for deceiving her. He was worried what her reaction would be if she were to find out. Would she still want him?

He despised himself. Despite all the harsh treatment she'd suffered, she was still kind and pure-hearted. He knew she would do anything for him and Gytha, even Brita and Knud—possibly Erik, and he found himself forming fists with his hands about that. He'd been jealous of their easy conversation in the hall earlier, the way his friend had made her smile.

What had happened to him had hardened his heart, making him cold. How could he make her happy? Was it wrong of him to subject her to marrying someone like him? Had he made a terrible mistake that she would never forgive him for? There was no way he could allow her to tell their child he was her father, not yet, not without her knowing the truth about who— *what*—he really was.

He leaned over and cupped her chin in his hands. 'Are you all right?'

'Yes.'

And then he frowned. 'I'm sorry—for taking you from behind,' he said, suddenly realising he'd done exactly what she'd told him Atol used to do.

'Oh, please,' she said, furious with him all over again. 'I know you're nothing like *him*. You can take me however and whenever you want.'

Her words amused him, lightening his mood a little, and a smile played at his lips. 'Is that right?'

'Yes,' she said simply.

Sitting opposite her on the sand, after the intimacies they'd shared this past week, he knew he hadn't been fair. She had given him everything he could have ever wanted and he'd been holding back from her, taking her body with his over and over again, but withdrawing from her in other ways.

'I'm sorry I've been…difficult,' he said. 'I'm used to my own space, my own company.'

She nodded.

'And sometimes it's too much being around you. I want you—all of the time.'

It was her turn to smile then. '*All* of the time?'

'Yes.' He closed his eyes briefly. 'I want you to relinquish the control you have over my thoughts—my body.'

'Never,' she said fiercely and came towards him and wrapped her arms around his neck, holding him.

He swallowed. He didn't deserve her.

'Rædan, I don't want you to go on that raid,' she said. 'We don't need any riches... Surely you don't need to conquer any more lands? But Gytha and I—we do need you alive and well.'

He nodded. 'Where is she?'

'Still in the longhouse.'

'Let's go and find her and get you both home,' he said and took her palm in his, pulling her up. They walked back along the moonlit beach, hand in hand.

Up above them, the sky began flashing with beautiful orange and green lights. 'What the—?'

'They're the *norðrljós*, the Nordic Lights,' Rædan said.

They looked like huge flames of fire, blazing in the sky, initially sending a bolt of fear right through her. 'Are they a bad omen?'

'No.' He laughed. 'The story goes, it's the Bifrost, the bridge between Midgard, where we live, and Asgard, the world of our gods. Other people believe it's the reflections of the Valkyries' armour—the angels of death—as they lead fallen warriors to Odin in Valhalla.'

'Can it be true?' she said, staring up at them in wonder.

'Who knows?'

'It's magical. We should show Gytha. She so loves hearing your stories.' If only some of them were about himself, she thought.

As they approached the hut, they saw a figure sat outside and Rebekah realised it was Erik. 'There you are!' he said, sounding relieved. 'We all wondered where you'd got to.'

'Everything all right?' Rædan asked.

'Yes, I brought the little *pika* back as she was getting worried about you. She's inside looking after the dog.'

'Thanks, Erik. Want to stay for a drink?'

'No, I'd better be heading back.'

'Thank you for looking after her,' Rebekah said. 'That was very kind.'

They watched him go and she turned to Rædan and whispered that she liked Erik. 'He's a good man.'

Rædan nodded and pushed open the door. His whole body tensed, he went stock-still. 'What do you think you're doing? Put that back!' His voice was lethal, causing Gytha to drop the plank of wood in her hand and shrink away from him.

It was the first time Rebekah had heard him raise his voice at their daughter and she was shocked.

'Rædan!' she said, stepping forward, putting a hand on his arm.

'That's not to be touched.'

'I'm sorry,' Gytha said quickly. 'I saw something shiny beneath the floorboards. And then I realised the board moved, so I lifted it up and…'

'Put it back! Now.'

His grey eyes had darkened, turned cold, and it made Rebekah shiver. 'Rædan…' she said, interjecting again. 'Whatever it is, she didn't mean to touch it. She didn't know.'

His face taut, he raked a hand through his hair. 'Just leave it,' he said. 'Go to bed.'

The girl dropped the floorboard, leaving the hole underneath uncovered and ran behind the curtain, sobbing. Rebekah heard the soft thud as the child threw herself on to the bed.

'Was that really necessary?' she asked, turning on him. 'What is it that's so important? What do you have down there?'

'Nothing,' he said, trying to kick the wood back into place with a violent curse.

She could feel the tension rolling off him. She frowned. 'Well, you got pretty upset over nothing... Oh, my God, is that a hoard of stolen goods down there?'

'What?' he asked. He sounded—and looked—dangerous. 'No!'

'Then what is it? What's in there?'

'Nothing that concerns you.'

Her brow furrowed. 'Is that really what you're going to say to me, after tonight? That you don't think anything about you concerns me?' she said, hurt all over again, that chasm between them reopening. 'It must be something important for you to shout at Gytha like that.'

'This is my home and perhaps I don't want everything being meddled with.'

'You should have thought about that before you brought us here. You should have considered it before you insisted on me becoming your wife!' She stepped closer, looking down into the floorboards. 'Oh, my God. Is that—are they—shackles? Were they meant for me?'

'No!' he roared again.

He slammed the board back into place with a final stomp of his foot. 'I'm going back out. I'll be gone a while. Don't wait up.'

And she watched the door slam behind him, leaving her wondering what the hell had just happened.

After she'd dried Gytha's tears, Rebekah ushered her daughter back along the beach and into the longhouse. It was strange how in a matter of days the place had started to feel familiar. Now, when she walked in, there wasn't that lull of noise and no one turned to stare. Since marrying Rædan, the people had accepted her.

She had convinced her daughter her new friends would still be up and would be able to cheer her up, and she'd been right—as soon as they arrived, Gytha was whisked away to play and Rebekah focused on the reason for her visit—she needed answers. She had to track down Knud and Brita.

She found the Jarl mid-conversation with some of the men and bravely tapped him on the shoulder to get his attention. He turned towards her and she motioned apologetically for him to step aside.

'Is everything all right? Where's Halfdan?' he asked, looking around for his friend.

'Could we talk somewhere, alone?' she asked, gripping hold of the sack with the heavy metal of the shackles inside.

He looked puzzled, and gestured for Brita to come with them. They stepped away from the throng of people in the cloying hall, into one of the back areas.

'What is it, Rebekah?'

'I'm sorry to interrupt,' she said. 'It's just, well, Gytha found these.' She turned the sack upside down and shook out the worn metal bonds. They clattered on to the table.

Knud's gaze snapped to Brita's and Rebekah's heart began to pound. She felt sure they'd both seen them before.

'Do you know what they are?' she asked.

'They look like shackles,' Knud said, after a long moment.

'Yes, I can see that,' Rebekah said. 'But why does Rædan have them underneath his floorboards?'

Brita threw another glance at her brother before saying, 'Perhaps that's a question for him.'

'I tried, but he wouldn't explain. In fact, he got so angry, he stormed out. I'm not sure where he's gone. I'm worried about him.' It was as if he was withdrawing from her, from everyone, wanting to be alone. Why did he keep doing it? She couldn't help him, like he'd helped her, if she didn't know.

'He does this. He likes to be on his own. I'm sure he'll be back. Then you can ask him again,' Knud said, turning to leave, clearly not wanting to betray his right-hand man.

'Why can't you tell me?' Rebekah said, a pit emptying in her stomach, as if they were keeping something truly terrible from her. From the looks on their faces, it certainly couldn't be anything good. 'Did Rædan keep slaves before he brought me here?' Surely it couldn't be possible? He'd always seemed so against it. But what other explanation could there be?

Part of her felt guilty for going behind Rædan's back, for talking about him with his friends. But she needed some answers. 'He won't open up to me—he just keeps shutting me out and I desperately want to understand so I can help him,' she said, wringing her hands.

Knud looked towards Brita and a silent understanding seemed to pass between them. She nodded. 'Has he told you he uses the treasure he wins to buy slaves at market?'

'No,' she gasped. She couldn't believe he actively traded people's lives…

'He buys them, uses every piece of silver he has, in order to release them from their bonds.'

'What?' The room spun. 'Why?' It was an incredibly noble thing to do. She had no idea. 'So, these shackles belonged to one of them?'

'No, Rebekah. They're Rædan's shackles,' Knud said gently. 'You see, a few years ago, *I* bought *him*.'

Chapter Eleven

'*Bought* him?'

Rebekah thought her heart had stopped beating.

'Yes. At a market. He'd come off a ship and, among others, he was for sale. But he was no use to anyone. He was at death's door. I looked into his eyes and saw something—let's call it a meeting of minds. I'd never seen a man, or an animal, so mistreated, but there was something about him that drew me.'

'Rædan was a slave?' Pain bolted through her. This couldn't be true.

'Yes.'

'The night he left you, your Saxon Lord burst into his home, beat him, stripped him and handed him over to a slave trader.'

'No!'

'He'd spent six years on that ship when Brita

and I found him. We traded a few silver ingots for him and brought him back here. We weren't sure if he was going to make it—he'd lost the desire to live.'

Rebekah sank down on to the bench behind her. Her heart lurched for that eighteen-year-old boy she had known, with laughter in his eyes, his whole life ahead of him. Images came into her mind of him being shackled and chained, all alone. And it was all because of her. If he'd never met her, that would never have happened. How did he not despise her?

She had hated Atol before, but now she wanted him dead. How could he be so cruel?

'He had a lot of untreated injuries. We did our best, but he didn't think he deserved anything we did for him. He wanted to shut himself off from the world—I think it was the only way he could cope. He still does that now, sometimes. He retreats to a dark place.'

Just like he'd done tonight.

'Why didn't he tell me?' she said, shaking her head.

'He's ashamed, Rebekah. Wouldn't you be, if you had been sold away from your family, and spent all those years obeying orders, sleeping on faeces-covered floors like a dog, kept alive on scraps? And we probably still don't know the half of it. I don't know how you recover from an experience like that, but amazingly, he has. That's why we call him the Reborn. He died as a boy and came back to life as a man. And look at what he's achieved—look at the legacy he'll leave.'

Rebekah knew Knud was talking about conquering faraway lands and raiding, but her mind instantly went to Gytha—his child. His love for her and the values he taught her would live on through her, and so far, he'd been nothing short of wonderful. Apart from tonight. Although now she knew why he'd reacted the way he did...

Seeing his child holding those shackles must have been a terrible shock, bringing it all sweeping back. But why had he kept them? And then a thought hit her—was this why he was holding back from telling Gytha he was her father? Because he was ashamed?

She thought back to all the times she had suffered at the hands of Atol over the years, but Rædan had had to endure far worse treatment. He'd listened to her speak of her pain, even helped her to heal, yet he hadn't shared the torment of his horrific past with her. He'd just bottled it all up, kept it inside. But now she understood why he might struggle to trust her, or anyone.

'*He wanted to shut himself off from the world,*' Knud had said.

And she could see that in the way his face had darkened earlier, the way he'd stormed out, walking away from her, not wanting to talk or explain. Well, no more.

She thanked Knud and Brita for being honest with her and Knud insisted Erik walk her and Gytha back to the beach. Again. Erik rolled his eyes, but she was grateful for his unwavering kindness. She realised Rædan had been right— most of the people here were good, honest folk. She thought she and Gytha could be happy here, if he could just let her into his heart.

She put Gytha to bed and sat at the table, stitching some of the fabric he had given her, waiting for him to return. It was getting late and she was beginning to worry about him.

Her head resting on her arms on the table, she kept drifting off into a dream-like sleep. But every time she closed her eyes she was haunted by wispy images of a boy, jumping over the side of a boat into deep blue water, drowning, and no matter how hard she tried, she couldn't reach him. Not like he'd saved her.

* * *

Finally, she heard his familiar heavy footsteps, startling her awake. Loyal Runa tried to get up to hobble to the door to see him, but she didn't quite make it.

He ducked his head as he came through the door, stooping in the small space, and he looked so male and virile, so formidable, she wondered how she was going to do this. How she was going to reach him.

He seemed startled to see her awake, waiting up for him.

'What are you still doing up?' he asked gruffly.

'I was worried about you. Where have you been?'

His fists bunched by his sides. 'No more questions. It's late, I'm going to bed.'

'Wait,' she said, gripping his arm, and he stilled. Her hand drifted down his tunic, pushing up his sleeves to smooth over his wrist. She brought his forearm up in front of her, to study the thick, dark swirling patterns of ink, and peering closer, she saw the scars. The trauma to his skin where she now knew he'd worn shackles. For six long years?

She'd felt the marks the other day, when they'd been making love in the steam bath, but she hadn't realised what they were. But she'd seen the flash of panic, maybe dread, in his eyes as her fingers had drifted over the ridges. Her palm swept over them again now, but he fiercely yanked his arm away.

He stared down at her, dismayed, and wary apprehension ebbed through her. 'Rædan, why didn't you tell me?' she whispered.

It was a long time before he spoke, and even then, his voice sounded strange—distant. 'You *know*?'

'Yes.'

'What—that I was beaten, shackled and sold to a slave trader by your ex-lover?'

She took a step towards him, shaking her head, desperate to lose this awful distance between them. But he'd shut down, she could see it in his eyes, and in the way he drew his arms across his body as a barrier. She instinctively knew he wouldn't want her pity—it would just make it worse. Instead, she tried to keep her voice level and controlled. 'Yes, I made Knud and Brita tell me…but I want, need, to hear it from you. Will you tell me about it now? Please?'

Rædan didn't want to burden her with abominable stories from his past. He didn't want to tell her what had happened to him, because he didn't want anyone to know the humiliation he'd suffered.

Especially her.

It had been a week since their wedding, and apart from the dark moments of today, they'd been getting on well, especially during the long nights. He didn't want the past, the truth, to change how she felt about him, because how could it not? This was about his honour and how Atol had it taken from him.

His ruined pride.

He didn't want to see his shame reflected in her eyes. He thought she'd started to care for him again, he had felt hope for the first time in years. But if he told her, she would think differently of him, think him weak... And that would be the end of him.

But staring down at her, he realised she already knew—and she wasn't going to let this lie. She would keep probing, continuing to ask him until he told her. He couldn't carry on keeping her at bay with his words, feeding her scraps of information when he felt like it, while wanting to get closer all the time with his body.

No, his pride had ruled him for too long. It was time to get this over with.

'I was a captive on a slave ship for six winters. I went from having everything I'd ever wanted, to my world being shattered in an instant.' He tried to stick to the facts, his voice sounding remote, flat. 'When you left my bed that night, I was just drifting off to sleep, when Atol's men stormed my room, dragging me out of the house. They beat me, blindfolded me and deprived me of my clothes. I was so disorientated. I didn't know what was going on. I thought it was my punishment for sleeping with you. It was only when they put the iron collar around my neck, the metal cuffs on my wrists, that I realised things were worse than I thought. That this was serious. But no one heard my cries for help.

'Every day was a struggle—there was barely any food or drink, and hardly any chance to sleep. I was closely guarded, forced to carry out work, with no interaction apart from being yelled at or savage beatings. The violence was extreme,' he said, motioning to his scar through his eyebrow. 'Most nights, I slept on the ship, wherever there was space, with no blankets, just my chains. Sometimes I didn't sleep at all. When we weren't out at sea, I was thrown into a grub hut with others like me.'

She sank down on to the bench and took his hand, bringing him down with her. Her fingers entwined with his and her touch encouraged him to carry on.

'At first, I dreamed of escaping and even tried a few times, desperate to return to you and my father, worried about you both and what they'd told you had happened. But then the ship returned to Ryestone for supplies and I saw you and Atol announce your engagement and I lost all hope…'

'I had to stop caring. I had to shut off my emotions to survive.'

'After six years, I was ready to die when Knud found me at the market. And when he paid for my freedom, it was overwhelming. He released me from my slavery bonds, removed the iron collar from around my neck and the chains from my wrists. He welcomed me into his own home and showed me kindness. He fed me, washed me, cut my hair… I'd worn the same clothes for years, day after day, and I was so ill, I could barely speak.'

He laughed then, bitterly. 'But even after his help, I still didn't trust him. Every day I'd wake up and wonder what he would do to me—if it had been some trick. Or what if he gave me back? My life didn't feel like my own.'

He glanced up and realised tears were streaming down Bekah's face, but he didn't stop. She had wanted to hear this. He didn't think he could bear it if he told her and she rejected him, but he also knew that if they were to have a chance at making this marriage between them real, he had to tell her everything.

'Slowly, Knud helped me rebuild my life. He gave me this place and it was my refuge— where I felt comfortable.' He tried to smile, but it crumpled. 'You asked me how I became a Dane? A Danish family bought me, like cattle at a market, but they chose to set me free.' he shrugged. 'And I decided to stay. Knud introduced me to the people as his friend, never telling them the truth of my origins. I don't know why he was so good to me.'

'You've more than made up for it. You're his most distinguished raider, his best fighter and his best friend. Rædan, why didn't you tell me?' she said, her voice sounding hoarse with emotion. 'I had no idea.'

'Why would you? I haven't exactly been forthcoming.'

'That's an understatement,' she said gently, squeezing his hand.

'I was ashamed,' he admitted simply, looking into her eyes. 'I don't think my pride has ever recovered. I'm not sure it ever will. Hell, Bekah, I didn't think I was good enough for you back then. I often thought, in the years we were apart, that perhaps you didn't want to be with me because I had nothing to my name…' he ventured.

Shock at his confession made her gasp. 'What? But I did want to be with you. I would have married you in a heartbeat.'

'Well, I thought being a slave pretty much ruined my chances with you. I had a lot of time to think about everything when I was on that ship. And as I recovered, I thought more and more about what Atol had done—and I wasn't sure if you'd been a part of it.'

She shook her head, vehemently. 'I wasn't.'

'I know that now,' he said, stroking a finger down her cheek. 'I let the violence, the sense of abandonment, the feelings of worthlessness rule me for so long, I had to do something to take back control—so I took to navigating the seas, conquering lands. It was ironic, given that I'd been chained to a ship I couldn't leave for so long that I felt at home on the waves. But it was what I knew.

'And I began to think about revenge, wondering if it would make me feel better. I learned how to fight, deciding no one would overpower me ever again, and I proved myself useful to Knud in combat and in seafaring. It gave me a focus. I started making a name for myself on our raids and then Knud suggested we head inland, to Ryestone…

'I wanted vengeance. I came to Ryestone fully intending to kill Atol. I wanted to punish you…and I'm ashamed of that now. When I saw you again, I behaved just like those men who had taken me captive because I wanted you so much. I tried to steal you away and I'm sorry, Bekah.'

'You're nothing like those men, Rædan. And I wanted to come. It was my choice, remember?'

'I know I'm far from perfect and difficult to live alongside. There are many things I struggle with… Have you seen caged chickens pick out their own feathers in stress? That's like me. I can sometimes go a bit stir-crazy in a small space, cooped up with others. I need room to breathe, I can't be confined… I struggle to trust people, which is why I'm always on guard. And the thought of having my freedom taken away from me again...'

'I understand,' she said, nodding, letting all the things he was telling her sink in. 'Was that one of the reasons you didn't want to marry anyone? You thought you'd be giving up your freedom? I saw your face during the handfasting ceremony...'

'Yes,' he said simply. 'I swore I'd never belong to anyone else, ever again—like you. I think when you've been under someone else's control for so long, you forget how to live. And those cords around my wrist were pretty symbolic,' he said, managing a smile. 'But I don't regret it. Yours and Gytha's safety means more to me than anything. I'm just sorry I made you do it.'

'I haven't done anything with you I didn't want to do, Rædan. And I want to be there for you, to help you to recover from this ordeal—like you did me. That is, if you want me to.'

His heart lifted. Did she mean it? He gripped her fingers tighter. 'I know I've hurt you, Bekah. I guess I was trying to isolate myself as a means of protecting you. I'd spent so long feeling demeaned, worried you'd feel ashamed to be with me...'

He reached out and tucked a strand of her hair behind her ear, saw the sadness shimmering in her eyes.

'I would understand if you don't want to tell Gytha I'm her father. I don't want her to find out about my past and be humiliated, to have that stain on her reputation as she grows older. I'm sorry I shouted at her earlier—was she all right?'

'It will all be forgotten by the morning.'

The child had shrunk away from him, her eyes filled with confusion, hurt—and he hated himself for that. 'I promise I shall make amends to her.'

Rebekah nodded. 'Why did you keep them? The bonds?' she said gently.

His brow formed a line. 'I don't know. I couldn't bring myself to get rid of them. They were a part of me, somehow. A reminder of where I've come from—what I've overcome. Perhaps a reminder that nothing could ever be as bad as that again. But I can get rid of them in the morning, I don't want them here any more, poisoning our life. And now, let's go to bed,' he said, kissing her hand and rising to his feet.

It was a relief to have told her about his past. He wasn't sure if she still wanted Gytha to know who he was to her—he imagined it would take a while for her to decide how she felt about it, but it was good to finally have her know the truth. He didn't want there to be any secrets between them, even if it meant she no longer wanted to share his bed. He hovered, waiting for her to utter her goodnight, to leave him and retreat to the back room, behind the curtain.

But she surprised him by opening the door to the little cupboard room and making her way inside.

They crawled under the covers and he pulled Bekah into his chest. She lifted her face up to his, placing her palm on his cheek and kissed him, softly, reverently. The way she smiled at him, looked up at him, it made him feel like he could be a better person, someone worthy of her and Gytha. Was it possible this woman could help him rebuild his shattered pride?

'You asked me what I did with the treasure I take from the raids…' he said, stroking his fingers up and down her back. 'I trade anything I take for silver and with the silver I buy other slaves at market and release them from their bonds… I don't need or want the treasure for myself. I don't need anything—or didn't until you and Gytha came along. If you need a better place to live—'

'I don't,' she said, adamant, shaking her head. 'I have everything I need right here.'

Her hand on his heart, he wanted to bask in her warm affection for ever and, for once, he managed to fall into a deep, peaceful sleep.

Chapter Twelve

Rædan woke to the noise of impending doom. The howling sound of the warning horn was ringing out across the bay and it sent his hackles rising. Launching himself out of bed, he picked up his sword and raced out of the door in just his trousers, Runa at his heels.

The sight outside the hut took his breath away, sending his adrenalin soaring. Surrounding the farm was a wall of Saxon soldiers, Atol at the helm and Ogden by his side. The traitor! Had he left this place and sought a reward from the Saxon Lord for showing him the way here? Every muscle in his body tensed and his blood chilled.

And behind them, on the shores of his beloved fjord, was a fleet of six Saxon ships. He cursed. This was not good. He'd let down his guard and look what had happened. He had brought this danger to their door.

'Light up the village,' he heard Atol say, as the man shook down his chainmail tunic, as if he hadn't just given an order to kill people. One of his men signalled to the ships and within moments, Rædan heard the sound of arrows piercing the air, the flames lighting up the morning sky, whipping towards the farmsteads of Nedergaard. Rage burned in his stomach. This man was evil to the core. He needed to be stopped, once and for all.

He hoped Rebekah and Gytha would have the sense to stay inside, hide away. He didn't want them anywhere near these brutes. But then he heard the creak of wood, footsteps, and Rebekah gasp, and he clenched his jaw, the grip tightening on his sword.

'Stay back,' he ordered.

'Ah, there she is. My bride, my beauty,' Atol said, pulling up the chainmail on his arms.

'She's not your anything,' Rædan bit out.

'You know, when you left my shores, Heathen, taking my woman and my child with you, I knew I couldn't let a poor stable boy from years ago, who couldn't even afford the *morgengifu* to marry the girl he loved, ruin my life.

This is the man,' he said, turning to his Saxon soldiers, 'who had no land, wealth or title, so he decided to steal my father's silver.'

'You know I never took anything from your family.'

'You deny taking my woman? But she is standing right there, beside you. All these men are my witnesses. It is a crime that carries the penalty of death.'

'Actually, I'm his wife now,' Bekah said, coming from behind him, her chin tilted up in that defiant way Rædan had come to know and love, and, despite his fear for her safety, his heart swelled with pride that she was sticking up for him, wanting to be seen at his side. It was all he had ever wanted.

'As you never had the good sense to marry her, I did,' Rædan added, backing up her claims.

A cruel sneer carved across the man's face. 'Just as well I didn't come for you then, isn't it?' he said. 'Surely you didn't think you were worth the trip across the ocean, Rebekah? No. It's the child I need. So where is she?'

With dread chasing through his blood, Rædan heard the door to the hut swing open behind them.

'No, Gytha, stay back. Get inside,' Rebekah cried.

But it was too late. All the men had turned to see the little girl standing there, in her nightgown, her bottom lip wobbling, and Rædan's heart shattered. It was his duty to protect her and he would do everything he could to keep her safe.

'Men, seize them,' Atol said, as he began to back away, allowing his soldiers to move in on Rebekah and the child. Rædan readied his weapon and planted his feet in the path of the men. The odds weren't exactly in his favour, but when had they ever been? This man had sent him to hell, but he'd made it back and he realised now he'd go through it all again, willingly, if he knew it would lead him to this week with Bekah and Gytha, a family at last.

As the tips of their blades met, adrenalin soared through his blood. But then Rebekah lunged forward, moving her body between them, intervening. And her hand came down to rest on their swords, stilling their weapons.

'Stop this!' she said, looking between them all, taking the chance that her Saxon soldiers were still loyal to her.

'Gytha and I will go with you,' she said, her

defiant eyes focusing on Atol. 'If you promise to leave this place, and this man, alone.'

'Bekah—no.' Rædan jerked forward. She didn't know what she was saying.

Atol seemed to be weighing up the situation, her words. He raked his eyes over Rebekah's body, licking his lips, and Rædan's stomach churned.

'Very well,' the Saxon Lord said. 'You have your uses, after all.'

'Promise me that you will leave him alone. For good.'

'I promise,' Atol sneered, seemingly satisfied, putting his sword away, his men crowding them.

And Rædan felt his world begin to shatter around him, his heart beginning to break.

'You can't win this, Rædan. And I can't keep letting you put yourself in harm's way for me. You're far too important. I love you so much and it will be enough to live, knowing you are alive,' she whispered, placing the softest kiss on his lips, a tear running down her face. She picked up Gytha, whose face was distraught, her arms reaching out for him.

'Come then, my little whore. Shall we?' Atol said.

And with an inner strength that surprised

Rædan, Rebekah allowed herself to be taken,
the man's hands on her skin, pulling her away.
They were retreating, leaving him on the sand,
at a loss, his despair spiralling through him.
He was watching her go and he couldn't believe she was giving herself up for him. She had
stopped the fight, knowing he couldn't win, to
save his life. And she had negotiated to get the
men away from here, to protect the people of
Nedergaard. He couldn't believe she was putting him before herself. That she thought he
was worth it.

But she must also know he would come after
her. That he would never let her go. She had
to, although he had never told her how he felt.
His thoughts returned to last night and the way
she'd held him in her arms, letting him know
she was there for him. She had told him she
had everything she needed, but he hadn't said
the same in return.

But she was, she was his everything. He determined if he ever held her in his arms again,
he would tell her he loved her. And he wouldn't
stop telling her for the rest of their lives.

He hoped she was doing all right. There was
no telling what the thought of being back at
Atol's mercy would do to her. He imagined it

would be like being put back in shackles for him. But he would give himself up for her if he had to. Only now, if it happened again, he didn't think it would break him. Because he'd have the strength to fight, knowing there was hope, that Rebekah cared for him.

It bolstered his resolve. He picked up his sword and ran as fast as he could along the beach to the longhouse, his chest pounding, his anger simmering over. Farmsteads were burning, people and animals darting all over the place, and he had to fight against the tide of villagers fleeing their homes. The guilt hit him— he knew this was his fault, for he'd brought this upon them. But there was no way he could give up now.

He loved her.

He'd been a damn fool not to tell her that before. But now he wanted to. And he would tell Gytha he was her father. He wanted to scream it from the flaming rooftops. He wanted everyone to know.

He had to get them back, so he could show them how much he cared.

With cool dread flowing through him, he realised he hadn't been able to protect Rebekah from Atol before and, because he hadn't killed him, because he'd shown mercy, the brute was back, still hurting her, still coming between them. Well, enough was enough.

He found Knud inside the longhouse and they shared a knowing look. 'What took you so long?' his friend asked. 'And where's your woman?'

'Where do you think?'

Fear chased his blood at the thought of Bekah on that boat, with him. This was her worst nightmare, so he had to stay focused, she was depending on him.

His friend cupped his shoulder, bringing him back to the moment. 'They attack one of us, they attack all of us. I presume this is the Saxon Lord, come to retrieve his woman?'

'She was never his woman,' he ground out.

'Why didn't you just kill the man when you had the chance?' Knud asked.

'Good question.'

'I know why. It's because you're a better man than the rest of us, Halfdan.'

He wondered at how Knud, and Bekah, always saw the best in him. Wasn't it time he started to see those things for himself?

'How did he find us?'

'Ogden. He must have led him here for a reward.'

'Damn him,' Knud cursed.

'Why didn't we just kill *him* when we had the chance?' Rædan said, repeating his question.

They walked outside to find the men of Nedergaard lining up on the sand, creating a shield wall, the earth rumbling beneath their feet. And Erik nodded to him, as if to say, *We're with you*.

'What do you need?' Knud asked.

The idea of turning this place into a battleground tore at his heart. Was this what he deserved for bringing conflict to others' shores? And right there and then, he determined, if they survived this, he would never go raiding again. He realised now his life in captivity had changed his perception of the world. It had hardened him and he'd been striving to make a name for himself, to restore his self-worth ever since. But no more.

He didn't need any of those things Atol had mentioned—land, a title, treasure. He had known that when he was eighteen and he knew it now. He realised Bekah had given everything up to be with him. If they were to make it through this, all he needed was his family. His people. Nothing more.

'The most important thing is their safety.'

Knud nodded in silent understanding.

'Well, whatever we're going to do, we'd better do it fast—the Saxons are leaving.'

'Half of you, to the boats,' Rædan roared. 'The rest of you, don't let them out of the fjord.'

He jumped into one of the longships and they cast off from the jetty, and he willed Thor to steer the tides in their favour. From the shore, he saw the men lighting up the spears and they released them over the top of the Saxon ships, blocking their path to the ocean, halting their journey, giving his men time to catch up with their foes. He hoped to the gods the fire arrows wouldn't scare Rebekah too much. If she could just hang on until he got there…

Their ships coming up alongside the enemy, there was no hesitation. The Danes jumped into the Saxons' boats, launching the attack, and instantly, all around him, the men were tussling, facing off with their adversaries. Swords clashed, fists were flying, and the boats toppled under the frenzy of the action. It was brutal, bloody, and as Rædan struck down each opponent, he glanced around, trying to find Rebekah and Gytha, his heart beating so loud it was like a drum roll echoing round the bay. Which ship were they on?

The water of the fjord was turning red, as he and Knud cut down more men and bodies were cast into the icy depths. And then, in a heart-stopping moment of elation and fear, he caught a glimpse of Rebekah's fiery locks two ships ahead. Fires were breaking out on the boats from the arrows, thick smoke curling around the men. He saw Rebekah standing up to Atol with a strength he had never seen her possess and he just wanted to take a moment to admire her, to breathe her in. His beautiful wife. There was no way he was going to let that man take her from him.

With ruthless determination, he gritted his teeth and pushed through the sparring men, shoving a few out of the way with the hilt of his sword and running up to the prow. He leapt off the end and into the hull of the next boat, and then he did it again, charging over the benches, reaching the prow and throwing himself over. He turned back to see Knud grinning at him, before his Jarl reared over Ogden, knocking the traitor to the floor, before hoisting him up and toppling him overboard, into the blazing debris of one of the boats floating on the fjord.

Rædan landed at Rebekah's feet and quickly uncurled his big body, righting himself. His hair around his shoulders, his chest bare with his warrior ink on show for all to see, he knew everything he had been through had prepared him for this moment, to fight this man. He pointed his sword at the brute who held her hostage. 'Did you really think I'd let you separate me from her again?' he said.

Quick as a flash, Atol grabbed hold of Gytha, bundling her backwards, pulling her against his chest, holding her in place with his sword.

'No!' Rebekah cried.

'You want to kill me, Heathen? You'll have to kill us both,' he said. And Rædan saw the fear in Gytha's eyes at being used as a human shield. 'Drop your weapon and I'll consider not harming the girl.'

Rædan followed them closely, as they staggered back across the deck, his sword trained on the man, not sure what Atol's next move would be.

He glanced back at Gytha, her bottom lip wobbling, and over at Rebekah. He didn't want his daughter to find out this way, but he couldn't keep it quiet any longer. The truth might just save her.

'Atol, the child is mine. Did you not notice the resemblance all these years?'

Gytha stared up at him, shocked. Then she and Atol looked to Rebekah, to confirm or deny the claim, and she nodded, upholding what Rædan had said. 'It's true. I was with child before we were together,' she said to Atol. 'Your blood doesn't flow through her veins. She means nothing to you. Can be no use to you. Please...let her go.'

A hushed awe rippled around the Saxon men on the ship and pure anger clouded Atol's features. He took in the child's features and, despite Gytha possessing her mother's hair and eyes, Rædan knew the man was seeing the resemblance to her father for the first time, the truth finally dawning.

'So you see, the child cannot win you any lands or power. Release her.'

'Well, well, my little whore. Perhaps that's why I never thought you were good enough to marry,' Atol said, lifting his sword so it lay across the child's throat, a rage all-consuming making him tremble.

The far end of the boat was like a raging inferno, devouring the wood of the ship, creeping its way closer towards them. Rædan didn't think the Saxon soldiers would make it home, not in these vessels. But would Bekah and Gytha—and his men? Or would all their lives end together at the bottom of the fjord?

In his red mist of rage, the tip of Atol's sword inched into the little girl's neck and she cried out.

'Stop this!' Rædan said, reaching out to grip the blade, the sharp edge slicing into his skin, drawing blood. His other hand came up to grip the Saxon's neck, choking him. 'It's me you want to punish, not them. They are no use to you any more. But I can be…'

He would give his life for his child. He would trade his life for hers in an instant. He would prove to her, and Rebekah, that he was worthy of being her father.

The man stilled. 'I'm listening,' he said, struggling to breathe.

'I offer you this deal… Tell your men to stand down, to stop the attack, and my men will do the same. Tell them it's me you want to capture. Leave this place and Rebekah and the child alone, and I will come. Willingly.' His defiant eyes focused on Atol.

'And if I don't?'

'Then know that if you don't die here today, I will come after you. Hunt you down…'

Atol's vein started to throb in his forehead, his face turning red.

'All right. A trade. An eye for an eye. I shall take you in the girl's place. The Heathens' greatest warrior. Now drop your sword.'

Rædan inclined his head in agreement and in an act of defeat, going against his every instinct to fight, he let his sword clatter to the ground, and sounded to his men to stop their attack. Atol pushed the girl away and seized Rædan.

'Cage the beast,' he instructed his men and once more Rædan felt the cold hardness of metal encasing his skin, chains pulling him away.

'No!' Rebekah cried, struggling against the rope that was binding her. But the Saxon men all began to bundle into the two ships untouched by the flames, dragging Rædan with them, leaving the Danes in the middle of the water, amid the carcasses of the burning vessels.

Knud landed in Rebekah's boat and dropped to his knees, untying her bonds, and when she was free of her restraints, she and Gytha embraced, tears falling down their cheeks.

'"No one has greater love than to give up one's life for one's friends", is that not what your God, your Bible, says? Halfdan must really love you if he's willing to be caged again to save you,' Knud said.

She looked across the water at the departing Saxon ships and, with horror in her heart, she realised the crumbling boat she and the Northmen were on was drifting further away from the Saxon vessels. Knud and his men were attempting to put out the flames in the hull, dousing them with water, but Rebekah was only able to focus on the man she loved. He was in trouble and the distance between them was growing wider by the moment.

She gripped Knud's arm. 'We have to do something. We have to go back. I have to save him.'

And yet, even while they were talking, she saw Atol and his men lower Rædan into one of the battered ships, chaining him down, laughing. And then, they all watched aghast as the Saxon Lord began to set fire to the vessel, as if lighting a funeral pyre, grinning in satisfaction. He always had to have his way...

'No!' she screamed. 'Get me over there!' she begged Knud, yet she knew as well as he that the boat they were on was slowly sinking and needed to get back to shore.

But she would never give up on him. She had determined to do whatever it took to show him that he could trust her, that she wouldn't let him down, and without thinking, she asked Knud to get her child to safety and threw herself into the water, just as she had done that day back in Ryestone. Only this time, she knew how to swim, for it was one of many things Rædan had taught her, including how to love so deeply, you would be willing to die for that person, to face your worst fears.

Thrashing through the water, she reached the burning ship that was an inferno of wood and sail. Heaving herself over the side, she coughed and spluttered her way through the smoke and flames to where Rædan lay in the middle of the hull, strapped to the deck. She was absolutely petrified of the fire, of losing him…

'What are you doing?' Rædan roared when he saw her. 'Don't be a fool, Bekah. Get away from here. Leave me.'

'No, I can't. I won't,' she said, kissing him hard on the lips, before assessing the iron collar around his neck, the metal encircling his wrists.

'How do I get these off? Rædan, what do I do?'

'You can't! Bekah, you have to go. This ship is going to burn.'

She shook her head. 'I'm not leaving.' And then she was up on her feet again, looking around in wild desperation, searching for an answer, a way out of this. Glancing up, she saw Atol staring at her across the water, through the waves of heat, in total disbelief that she would risk her life for this man. It spurred her on.

Finding an axe, she brought it back over to Rædan, holding it up. And then with a new determination, she heaved it above her head before bringing it down on to the wood, chopping the deck up over and over again, until finally, although his bonds were still attached to the wood, Rædan was free from the ship and she pulled him up. She threw her arms around him, kissing him fiercely.

'You're crazy!' he said, shaking his head.

'Yes, about you. Are you all right? I saw him put the chains on and…'

'I'm fine. I can cope with any torment, knowing you care…'

A deafening crack came from above, as the

mast of the ship broke in two and came crashing down beside them.

'This ship isn't going to make it back to shore,' Rædan said. 'We're going to have to jump. Are you ready?'

'Yes.' She nodded, then, taking his hand, they dived through the ferocious flames, singeing their clothes, their hair, before plunging deep into the cool water of the fjord.

When they reached the surface, Rædan steered them over to a large, floating piece of wood, tugging her on to it. Wet and exhausted, parts of their skin blistering from the fire, Rædan lifted his chains over her head, so that he could pull her into his arms, holding her tight to his body.

'Are you hurt?' he asked, checking her over. 'Are you all right?'

She nodded. 'Yes… No,' she said, shaking her head, the tears welling in her eyes, and he kissed her gently.

'You were very brave, Bekah, facing the flames like that, facing your fear. Thank you for coming after me…'

'I didn't care about the fire. I was only worried about losing you. It would destroy me if I lost you again.'

'I've been holding back from telling you how I really feel, Bekah, because I've been so worried about losing *you*. My damn pride just wouldn't let me. Then the worst happened. And now I know I can't deny us love and joy just because I'm scared of losing it. I want this to be a proper marriage. I know what it's like to have nothing. To be nothing and—'

'Rædan, when will you see you've always been my everything?' she interrupted, holding his face in her hands, as she trod water.

His eyes shone down at her. 'I love you, Bekah. I always have.'

'And I love you, too.'

He kissed her again then, as if he was kissing goodbye to who they were in the past and welcoming them both into the future. And when they finally pulled apart, the ship was beginning to crumble around them, the smoke billowing up into the sky, like a flare, signalling to the gods up above that they'd made it.

'It's a bit like Ragnarok,' he said.

'What's that?'

'A huge battle between the gods and their enemies, when the world is engulfed in flames, before it's reborn.' He turned to Rebekah. 'And then, they say, two humans will repopulate the world.' He grinned as he began to kick his legs, pushing the wooden panel and his wife to the shore.

'Is that so? Perhaps you won't want me any more now my hair's all singed,' she said, patting her scorched locks.

'It will grow again. Just like my love for you.'

When they finally reached the shore, the other soaking wet Northmen and the villagers were waiting for them, cheering. Gytha bounded over to them and they pulled her into their arms as they huddled on the sand.

'You were so brave,' Rædan told her. 'Just like your mother.'

'And my father.' She grinned.

He swallowed.

'I'm sorry I told a lie when I said that Atol was your father when you were little, Gytha,' Rebekah said. 'The truth is, Rædan is your real father. I've been wanting to tell you for a while now.'

'Is that why we came here? You wanted us all to live together?'

'Exactly.'

'I'm so glad we did,' the girl said.

Rebekah smiled. 'I confess I only recently told Rædan…'

'And when I found out, I thought it was the best news I've ever had,' he said.

Gytha grinned then. 'Me, too,' she said, wrapping her arms around his neck. 'So…can I call you Father from now on, because you are—my father?'

Rædan smiled and he wiped the tears from his eyes. He took her chin between his fingers. 'I'd really like that.'

A cough interrupted their reunion and Rædan looked up to see Knud staring down at him. 'Do you want us to get the boats and go after them?' the Jarl asked. 'We could still catch up to them.'

'No,' Rædan said. 'If I'd lost what Atol lost today it would be my whole world,' he said, embracing his family. 'And I don't want to take any more lives, I want to create them,' he said, looking at Rebekah. 'With you.'

Epilogue

Sitting on the bed, with his wife lying back against the furs, Gytha and Runa watching, Rædan was holding her foot as he dipped the tip of the raven feather into the dye and placed it to her skin. She kept giggling at the tickling sensations he was creating.

'Keep still,' he said, berating her, his striking grey gaze twinkling at the beautiful women in his life. 'You know, they say a raven feather can unlock a woman's heart?' He grinned.

'Really?' Gytha said, leaning forward, her chin in her hands.

His girls had told him they loved hearing his stories about Nedergaard and about his Norse gods, but especially the tales that featured him. And he was slowly getting better at sharing them.

'There, I'm all done,' he said and released

Rebekah's foot from his grasp so that she could take a look at the ink he'd drawn on her skin. The little symbol he'd created had nine staves, containing all the runes.

'What is it?' Rebekah asked.

'The Web of Wyrd. It represents all the possibilities of the past, present and future. It's a thank you, for shaping my destiny,' he said, kissing the sensitive skin again, and then he bent over to kiss the huge swell of her belly through the material of her dress.

He was delighting in seeing her body grow and change, knowing she was carrying his second child inside her. He constantly wanted to have his hands on her stomach or press his ear up to her skin, listening for the heartbeat.

'Do you think it'll be a boy or a girl?' Gytha asked.

'I don't mind, as long as they look like you two,' he said.

'And I don't mind, as long as they carry on the legacy of the most wonderful man I've ever known,' Bekah said, her eyes glowing up at him.

And he felt like the luckiest man alive.

That night, as Gytha lay asleep in the other room, Rædan curled up in bed beside his wife, his arousal pressing into her bottom, and he drew her beautiful red hair back away from her ear. It had grown back to its former glory and he thought it looked even more radiant than before.

'You know, I never wanted to belong to anyone again. But you, Bekah, own my heart and my body. You have helped me to love and respect myself again and because of that I will be a slave to you for the rest of my days. Now tell me what I can do for you…'

Rebekah giggled, and he thought he'd never tire of that sound. 'I want you inside me, making love to me,' she said, wriggling back against his arousal, and he groaned. Her hand came up over her shoulder to hold his jaw. 'I can't believe how far we've come from when I agreed to spend the night with you, the Northman, back in Ryestone.'

'Me either. But I never wanted just one night with you, Bekah. I always wanted you for ever.'

'And I you,' she said.

And as he thrust inside her, slowly, deeply, intimately, he knew that he would live out his days a happy man, for he had everything he ever wanted and more.

* * * * *

COMING SOON!

We really hope you enjoyed reading this book.
If you're looking for more romance, be sure to
head to the shops when new books are
available on

Thursday 19th January

MILLS & BOON®

Coming next month

A SEASON OF FLIRTATION
Julia Justiss

Maggie gave her a shrewd look. 'What do you think of him? You've met, I trust?'

'He's an impressive young man,' Laura said carefully, trying to keep her tone neutral.

"Is he handsome?" Eliza prodded with a grin.

"Quite." Laura laughed. "Also quite dismissive of Society ladies. He thinks we are all empty-headed and frivolous."

"You'd be the lady to convince him otherwise," Maggie said. "Laura the mathematician. Not that you need to win his favor, of course. A banker's rich daughter may find an aristocratic husband, but a banker's son would be entirely ineligible as a match for you."

"How fortunate I am not angling for a husband," Laura retorted. No matter how appealing she might find the admittedly unsuitable Mr. Rochdale.

Continue reading
A SEASON OF FLIRTATION
Julia Justiss

Available next month
www.millsandboon.co.uk